HER HEART IS AS V
AND HE WILL STOP AT N

PETOSKEY STONE SERIES

DANIELLE BAKER

ISBN # 979-8-9880456-2-5

Also by Danielle Baker

Petoskey Stone Series

Love Unbound
Best Kept Secrets

Upcoming Novels in the Petoskey Stone Series!

When Hearts Collide
Stay With Me
Hard To Love
That One Night

New Series Coming in 2024/2025!

The Bliss Garden Girls
Once Upon A Kiss
Protecting Her Heart
Broken Promises
Forget Me Not

New Prequel Novella Trilogy Coming 2024/2025!

STORM! Novella Trilogy
STORM! Serenity
STORM! Spencer
STORM! Summer

Dedication

This is for all the good girls
that are emotionally attached
to fictional characters.
You’re welcome.

ONE

She looked up, her eyes meeting the intense gray-blue gaze the same color as storm clouds from across the lavishly decorated event tent. The man was quite possibly the most handsome man she'd ever seen in her life. The candles lit throughout the space and on all the white linen covered tables cast flickering shadows that danced everywhere, picking up highlights in his dark-blonde hair and casting half of his impossibly handsome face in shadow.

His suit was fit snugly to his body, gray dress slacks that delineated his long legs and left little to the imagination at the apex of his thighs. A matching gray, slim cut suit vest was buttoned closed over a black dress shirt, showing off his impressive upper body even though he was covered up to his neck. The material of the black dress shirt stretched across his shoulders and over his bicep as his arm relaxed, lowering it from taking a swallow of his drink. The forest green necktie that all the other members of the groom's party wore had been loosened at his neck, and the top button of the black dress shirt had been unbuttoned. The sleeves of the shirt had been rolled to his forearms, and the candlelight shone on sun-bleached arm hair that dusted deeply tanned skin. His fingers were long, nearly wrapping around the highball glass in his hand.

She swallowed hard, her entire body completely still as he raised the glass of amber liquid in silent salutation before bringing it to his lips. All the while, those storm-cloud, gray-blue eyes never left hers.

And she felt it all the way to her toes. Among other places.

Which just pissed her off, honestly. Who the hell was this guy?

Hardening her gaze, she stared at the obnoxiously handsome stranger across the room until he dropped his eyes, though she knew the second he raised them back to her, her entire body going hot. She refused to look over in his direction again. She wouldn't give him the satisfaction of seeing how his attention affected her.

Not *that she was affected by that tall, brooding, insanely attractive specimen of man…*

Her body disagreed otherwise; her heart hammered in her chest, making her breathing much more labored than walking across a room would entail, and her nipples were damn near begging for him to look at them, the way they were peaked beneath the corseted bodice of her dress. Hopefully he couldn't see…

Her sister found her then, and she leaned down and hissed, "Who is that?"

Her sister just smiled knowingly and leaned closer to whisper, "That *is Free's cousin, Kasey."*

"He seems like an ass."

Her sister admonished her, but she wasn't listening. She made a disgruntled sound in the back of her throat. "He's cocky and it's damned irritating, the way he keeps looking at me."

"Then maybe you shouldn't have worn that dress," her sister teased, winking.

She rolled her eyes and brushed her long hair over her shoulder, taking a deep sip of her champagne. The dress she'd worn was perhaps a little over-the-top sexy, but how often did a girl get to dress up and make jaws drop? Could she really be upset with the poor sucker for being pulled into her like a personified version of a Venus Fly Trap?

Tommy would be there soon anyway, so the poor guy would get the hint soon enough, if he hadn't already.

But as the evening wore on, he clearly wasn't getting the hint. Those thundercloud gray-blue eyes followed her wherever she went. As she stepped to the bar to get another glass of champagne, she knew how good the backs of her legs looked as she walked in her sky-high heels. Feeling devious, she put an extra little sway in her hips as she moved across the floor. When she glanced through her lashes at him, she was perversely delighted that it hadn't gone unnoticed. Ha. Poor sucker. Eat your heart out.

She was approached by a young blonde who asked her to dance, which she accepted with a grin. He was boyishly cute, though she admitted to herself he reminded her too much of her own little brother for her to consider him attractive in that sense. He was stiff as he stood with his arms around her lightly, and she wanted to laugh. It reminded her of those awkward middle school dances.

The blonde kid's eyes went up when something caught his attention over her shoulder, and then the sexiest, smoothest southern drawl she'd ever heard hit her full in the belly, making her knees wobble slightly. The younger kid dropped his arms from around her waist, stepping back as the owner of that voice came into view, and she stiffened immediately when she realized it was Mr. Storm-Cloud-Eyes from across the room. He held out one of those outrageously sexy hands and murmured low, "I believe this dance belongs to me."

She couldn't say no without creating a scene, and not wanting to do that to the bride and groom, she had no other choice but to accept. Setting her hand—dammit why was she shaking—*in his, she sucked in her breath at the electricity that arched between them at the contact.*

Her eyes flushed up—way up, Christ was he tall—*to connect with his just as his other hand slid around her waist, pulling her close against the hardness of his body. His hard thighs brushed against her bare ones, his hips aligned with hers, and he brought her in close enough for her breasts to come to a rest against his broad chest. If her nipples weren't trying to get his attention before, well, they sure as hell were now.*

And dammit if he wasn't the single most attractive man she'd ever laid eyes on, especially up close.

Mr. Tall-Blonde-and-Sexy moved them across the dancefloor, swaying effortlessly while keeping her effectively trapped inside the circle of his arms. Every time they moved, his thigh would press between hers and her breath would catch. What was wrong with her?!

Pump the brakes, woman!

"I have a Tommy," she blurted out, then could have kicked herself, turning a vicious shade of red in embarrassment. "I mean, I have a boyfriend. Tommy."

Her teeth gnashed together when she heard it—no, she felt *it as it rumbled against her breasts that were pressed so close to his chest—as he laughed at her. The fucker was laughing at her!*

"Mmmm," he murmured low, so low that it too, vibrated into her chest, making her nipples tingle. This was not going well. "Is that why you won't look at me? Because you have a 'Tommy'?"

Annoyance flashed through her, and she stiffened her body slightly against his. "I've barely noticed you."

He leaned closer then, dropping his head so that his mouth was just breaths away from her ear, and he murmured in that slow, sexy drawl, "That's not what your body is sayin', darlin'."

She spluttered in indignation and made to pull away, but his arm tightened just the slightest around her waist, his hand capturing hers more fully, and at the way his fingers spread wide across the lower portion of her back, she was struggling to remember why *she was pulling away. Shit, she was struggling to*

.*remember how to* breathe.

"And if your 'Tommy' were doing his job properly, your body wouldn't be so hungry for mine right now," he continued, his voice barely above a whisper. At the same time his words registered, his palm pressed against her lower back, bringing her firmly against his hips, and she felt his hard length press into her middle. She gasped in shock, at his words, at his boldness, at the feel of him hard against her. His nose nudged her temple, his lips moving against her high cheekbone, directly next to her ear, and it made goosebumps flash across her entire body. "I'd love to get my mouth on those pierced nipples you think you're hiding beneath that dress. I'll bet he doesn't even play with them. Hmm? Does he make you come? Or do you fake it to make him feel better about himself? I guarantee you wouldn't have to fake it for me, darlin'. Your body knows it, too."

This time the gasp that escaped her was a confusing mix of arousal and outrage, and she pushed against his chest hard enough to force him to let her go or cause a scene. Her eyes went wide when she caught sight of a sandy brown head across the room, his brown eyes fixed on her and the man that had been holding her entirely too close. And what was worse, this jackass had probably known all along Tommy was standing there watching. And for how long? What had he seen?

"Fuck you," she snapped heatedly, risking one last look up into those eyes before she turned on her high heels and walked off the

dance floor, leaving him standing there in the middle of the room.

Striding toward Tommy, she slid her arms around his shoulders and leaned into him for a deep kiss, sinking her tongue into his mouth. He kissed her back, wrapping his arms around her waist possessively. This kiss was so different from all their other kisses. This was heady, primal, and she felt it all the way down into her belly. An approving growl rumbled through his chest into hers as he curved his tall frame around her, pulling her even deeper into the kiss. His hips pressed into hers, and a gasp tore through her at how hard he was against her. Her body was on fire.

Pulling away to breathe, she raised her eyes to his. But they weren't the soft, honey brown she was expecting. Instead, she was caught in that storm-cloud, gray-blue gaze that could only belong to one man… Mr. Steal-Your-Girl Kasey.

Shauntelle Kendall woke with a start, her body jerking like she'd been about to fall in her sleep. Her eyes adjusted slowly to the inky darkness of the room while her heart hammered out a heavy cadence in her chest. Her body was flushed, tingling all over, her lower body aching with a need that would not be soothed.

Sitting up, she scrubbed her hands over her face, pushing the long braid she kept her hair in at night over her shoulder. The sheet was a tangled mess around her long legs, and she struggled in the dark to extricate herself from them. Swinging her legs over the edge of the bed, she stood, crossing the room to the door, unmindful that she was in nothing but a pair of skimpy boy-short underwear and a loose fitted men's t-shirt.

Padding down the short hallway to the bathroom, she stepped inside and flipped the light on, staring at her reflection in the sudden brightness of the room. Steve, the tortie cat she'd adopted from the shelter several months ago, weaved around her ankles, meowing, demanding her breakfast.

It was the same dream. Over and over again. For months. She grunted at her reflection as she splashed cold water on her face and corrected herself; a year. It had been a year of this stupid dream.

And it was always Kasey that she was kissing, not Tommy. Tommy, *her boyfriend. Her fiancé.*

Then, hanging her head sadly, she sighed and corrected herself again; *no, her ex-fiancé.*

Grabbing the hand towel hanging next to the sink, she blew out a heavy breath, forcing the thoughts away. She couldn't think about that right now. It had been seven months since they'd split, but the pain still lanced through her from time to time.

Leaving the bathroom, she made her way into the tiny kitchen, prepping a large pot of coffee to percolate. She added an extra scoop of grounds just for a little extra kick, then switched the toggle to turn it on. When the little red light didn't come on and the usual gurgling sound of the water beginning to run didn't sound off, she swore under her breath and checked to make sure it was plugged in and that the breaker hadn't been flipped. She unplugged it and plugged it into a different outlet, but nothing happened.

"Dammit," Shaun muttered sourly, letting her shoulders drop in defeat. She had made the mistake of choosing the least expensive coffee maker she could find at the time, and it was living up to its cheap ticket price. Her sister Jodi had told her to splurge on a better quality one, but Shaun was stubborn.

She could just hear Jodi saying "I told you so" and grimaced.

It was going to be a rough morning if there was no coffee.

Murder seemed highly probable.

Making her way back to her bedroom, she dressed quickly, shoving her legs into the same tight jeans she'd worn the day before that were still in a heap on the floor. Pulling the loose t-shirt over her head, she tossed it into the laundry basket in the corner of the room. She rummaged through the dresser until she found a sports bra and squeezed into it, adjusting her breasts in the tight confines of the material. Tugging on a lightweight, long-sleeved hoodie, she grabbed up a Detroit Tigers baseball cap and put it on her head to contain the flyway's that had escaped her braid throughout the night.

As she drove, the sky began to lighten on the horizon,

painting the sky with golden light, which highlighted the leaves that were in full autumn color. Everything was bathed in deep reds, bright oranges, and golden yellows of mid-October in northern Michigan.

A new coffee maker was on her list to buy today—the only item on her list—but this was an emergency situation, so gas station coffee would have to do for now.

Pulling into her favorite gas station convenience store, she climbed out of the truck and headed inside. As the door shut, she heard a car horn blast from the road.

"Hiya, Frank," she called, and he grumbled a curt hello back. She grinned; Frank was a grumpy old coot and had been the night cashier here for ages.

Pursing her lips, she eeny-meeny-miney-moe'd which basic convenience store coffee blend to choose, settling on a dark roast that looked like it had been left to sit for a while, which meant it would be a little burnt and strong as hell. She poured a large cup full and brought it to her lips, her entire body wiggling with anticipation at the first sip. It burned her tongue, and she hissed in pain before taking another hedonistic sip.

Shaun reached for a lid and capped it carefully, cautious not to let any of the precious liquid slosh over the edge of the cup, then turned to head toward the cashier counter.

She was brought up short when she ran headlong into a

tall, unyielding body, and she watched in dismay as her coffee fell from her fingers, the Styrofoam cracking down the side of the cup as it crashed to floor. The lid flew off, sending hot coffee splashing all over the tiled floor and soaking her shoes and the bottom of her jeans, as well as sloshing over a pair of well-worn work boots that were standing *far* too close.

"Oh you have got to be shitting me—" she snapped in annoyance, the scathing retort falling off her lips before she could stop it, because honestly, *who stands that close to someone else?!* Planting her hands on her hips and raising her eyes to the face of the man she'd run into, her eyes went wide, and she shook her head in disbelief.

She had rotten luck this morning, but *this?* The universe was clearly *not* playing fair.

"No. Nope," she muttered darkly, backing away as she growled in exasperation. "*You.*"

TWO

"Me," he said, and that smooth, sexy drawl met her ears, just like it had done in her dream. His mouth tugged up at one corner into a smirk. Her lips pulled back over her teeth in a snarl at that stupid, cocky grin. She wanted to slap it right off his smug face.

"What are you doing here? Dammit, you owe me a cup of coffee!" she fumed, her hands still planted firmly on her hips.

"Hi, darlin', it's nice to see you, too," Kasey Corcoran murmured in that drawl that always made her belly do somersaults, ignoring her exclamation. "You're kinda cranky in the morning, aren't you?"

Shaun seethed, clenching her teeth together so tightly her jaw ached. "You spilled my coffee. What are you doing here?"

Reaching around her, she watched as he plucked a fresh cup from the stack and set it down on the rail before filling to the brim, then snapped a lid onto it. Picking it up, he held it out to her. "Better?"

"No!" Shaun snapped, though her fingers closed around the cup, her fingers grazing his. She dropped her gaze to the floor, where the mess of her first cup still covered the tile. "I should clean this up."

"It was my fault," Kasey murmured, finally stepping back from her. She sucked in a much-needed lungful of air as he retreated from her bubble.

"You still haven't explained why you're here," Shaun mumbled, though she did take perverse pleasure in watching him sop up the coffee mess with a handful of napkins. Frank was unaware of what had happened as he grumbled to himself from behind the cashier counter.

"I was going to get some coffee," he said as he straightened, tossing the wet napkins into the trash receptacle beside them. He grabbed a sanitizer cloth and wiped his hands on it before tossing it into the trash as well. He was dressed in well-worn jeans and a faded grey Henley shirt with the sleeves pushed to his forearms. The small V created by the two buttons undone at his throat gave her just a peek at his chest below his sternum. A white, Texas Longhorn ball cap was on his head, and the lower portion of his face was shadowed with several days' worth of dark blonde facial hair growth. When her eyes continued their upward trajectory, landing on his, she glared at him when she realized his eyes were following her perusal of him, his lips upturned at one corner.

"I meant *in Petoskey*. In northern Michigan. What are you doing here?" she repeated on an annoyed huff.

He shrugged those impossibly broad shoulders, making the muscles beneath his shirt bunch and move. He proceeded to pour himself a cup of coffee, a light roast, then lidded it before turning back to her. Leaning close, he whispered conspiratorially, "I came here just to annoy you, darlin'."

Shaun rolled her eyes and stepped around him, heading toward the cashier counter where Frank waited. Setting the coffee on the counter with more vitriol than necessary, she zippered open her wallet to fetch several dollar bills out of it.

"I'll get both coffees," Kasey said from over her shoulder, speaking to Frank, who answered with a grunt before accepting the cash that Kasey extended.

"I don't need you to pay for my coffee—"

Her words stopped on a gasp when his fingers gripped her chin, hard enough to bite a little, tilting her face up so she was looking at him.

"Do you have to argue about everything?" he asked roughly, and her damn traitorous heart clip-clopped in her chest at the feel of his fingers on her skin. His eyes searched hers, and then he murmured, "You can say thank you. It won't kill you."

Wrestling her chin out of the grip of his fingers, she glared up at him. "*Thank you*," she gritted out through clenched teeth, barely above a whisper.

His eyes lightened in amusement, but before he could

respond, Shaun heard a loud gasp from their left and then a squeal of "OhmygodOhmygodOhmygod" as a blonde head came into view. "No. Freaking. *Way!* You're K.C.! Number 33!"

Shaun rolled her eyes and let out a derisive snort as the blonde woman rushed over to stand in front of Kasey, essentially shoving Shaun out of the way. Shaun made a face at Kasey over the woman's head and Kasey's eyes narrowed just the slightest, and then Shaun slid out the door before he could disengage from the overzealous Nascar fan.

She had just climbed into the truck and closed the door when he hurried out of the gas station doors, his eyes scanning the vehicles until he found her. He came toward her driver's side door as she started the engine, and he rapped his knuckles on the window.

She stared straight ahead out the windshield, chewing on her lip as she contemplated whether to roll the window down or not. Glaring at him from the corner of her eye, she sighed heavily and pushed the button to slide the window down.

"Did your fan ask for a picture?" she asked, her tone acidic.

"You're prickly this mornin'," he murmured in that belly melting drawl as he folded his arms across the windowsill so he could lean in close, ignoring her question. He balanced his coffee on the edge of her window, fingers wrapped around it.

"Kasey, it's barely six am. I didn't sleep well last night, my coffee maker took a shit this morning, and you spilled my replacement cup. Sorry I'm not feeling particularly loquacious."

"Hey, I bought you a fresh cup to make up for it," he said, grinning winningly at her, which just made her gnash her teeth together harder.

"And you never answered my question."

"Yes, she asked for a photo. Yes, I took the time to let her take a selfie. Hazard of the trade." His grin widened and she rolled her eyes. Lord, they were getting a workout today.

"That's not the question I was referring to," she snapped.

"And which question *are* you referrin' to?" he asked, shifting his weight from one foot to the other, still leaning on his forearms on her windowsill.

"What are you doing here? Why are you in Petoskey? Isn't this a little outside of your usual route?"

"I'll have you know that I have very important groomsmen duties that require my attention," he murmured, grinning again. He bobbed his eyebrows once. "Don't tell me you didn't get the invite to the engagement party."

Shaun could feel a muscle in her jaw twitch with how hard she was grinding her teeth together. His arrogant teasing this early in the morning was grating on her nerves. "I'm the maid of honor; of course I was invited. My parents are hosting. I just didn't think you could carve time out of your busy, high falutin' celebrity schedule to make it."

"You wound me," Kasey said, placing one hand, palm flat on his chest, in feigned pain.

Shaun rolled her eyes. "I doubt anything could puncture that giant ego of yours. I don't need to stroke it."

She stumbled over the last two words, the unintentionally provocative statement making little fireworks go off in her belly when his eyes darkened at her words. She held her breath as he leaned in closer again.

"You can stroke anythin' you like, darlin'."

That viciously delectable memory of a hard ridge pressed against her abdomen while they were dancing flashed, unbidden, into her mind, making her flush hot all over. For just a heartbeat, she imagined finally getting her hands on him, on everything… and in the next second she straightened her spine, sitting up straighter in her seat as she hissed, "You're disgusting. Does that line ever work for you?"

"Why don't you tell me?" he drawled, winking at her. She put the truck in reverse, glaring stonily at him until he chuckled and leaned away, taking a step back from the side of the vehicle. "I'll see you, Shaun."

Hitting the accelerator with a little more gusto than intended, she peeled backward out of her parking spot before slamming on the brakes. Shifting into drive, she pulled away, leaving Kasey standing in the middle of the parking lot behind her.

THREE

Ten minutes later, Shaun pulled into her older sisters' driveway. Shaun knocked and waited, and then a bleary-eyed Jodi opened the front door, her long, curly dark brown hair a sleep-tousled mess as it tumbled over her shoulders. She was still tugging one arm into the armhole of one of her fiancés t-shirts, which made Shaun smirk.

"Shaun?" Jodi mumbled, blinking several times. "What are you doing here? What time is it?"

"Early. Sorry. Got any coffee?" Shaun asked sheepishly.

Jodi groaned but opened the door wider to let her in. "Let me go put on some pants."

Shaun walked into the kitchen as Jodi disappeared down the hallway, flipping the toggle on the coffee maker that sat on the counter, knowing her sister already had it prepped and ready to go. She heard Free's deep voice from the bedroom, then a startled squeak and a giggle as the bed springs creaked. Shaun smiled. She was innately happy that her sister had finally found her happily ever after. She deserved it after leaving her abusive, douchebag ex-husband.

Several minutes later, Jodi reappeared just as Shaun was pouring a cup of steaming hot coffee into a mug, coming around the corner into the kitchen. Her hair was slightly more tousled than it had been before, and her cheeks were flushed. Shaun wiggled her eyebrows, and she laughed when Jodi blushed a deep crimson, hugging the folds of her long-sleeved cardigan over her middle.

Jodi reached into the cupboard and plucked a coffee mug off the shelf, then poured herself a cup before lightening it with a dash of French vanilla creamer. Turning, she settled her back against the counter and held the mug between both of her hands. Shaun sat at the little peninsula on a barstool, leaning on her elbows on the counter.

"What brings you out so early?" Jodi asked, and Shaun shrugged.

"Couldn't sleep and then my coffee maker took a shit this morning," she said, nodding in hello as Freeman walked around the corner, dressed in jeans and a t-shirt that fit snug across his chest and shoulders. He'd already tugged on well-worn, black cowboy boots, ready for his workday to begin at Blue Haven, Shaun and Jodi's parent's ranch. His dark hair was worn slightly longer, and the lower portion of his face was covered in a well-trimmed beard. Shaun had to admit that Freeman was *Fine*, with a capital F. And if what Jodi had let slip was true, their love life was far from lacking.

"Morning," he murmured, crossing to the coffee maker and pouring himself a cup before leaning his hips against the counter next to Jodi, their shoulders nearly touching.

"That dream again?" Jodi guessed, and Shaun nodded, her eyes slicing over to Free before dropping back to her coffee. She would *die* if Jodi had told Free about her recurring dream, or that it centered around his arrogant, pain-in-the-ass cousin.

"Jodi has this recurring zombie nightmare," Free murmured, bumping his shoulder into hers, and then grinned down at her when she glared at him out of the corner of her eye. Shaun laughed out loud.

"You've been having that nightmare since we were in high school!" Shaun cackled as she remembered the night she'd conned Jodi into watching World War Z.

"Well, why did they have to make them *so fast*?" she exclaimed, laughing too, then shuddered. "Urgh. Zombies are supposed to be *slow!* Those ones are *terrifying!*"

Shaun laughed as Free leaned down to press a smacking kiss to Jodi's lips before pushing his hips away from the counter. "I've gotta go. You girls behave. No margaritas this early in the morning."

"No promises," Shaun called as he left the kitchen, and she heard him chuckle. A moment later, the front door opened and closed, and Jodi hopped up into the barstool next to Shaun. "You haven't told him about the dreams, right?"

"Of course not," Jodi said and waved her hand dismissively. "He might be my fiancé, but I don't share *everything* with him. Your secret is safe with me."

"I didn't realize he was coming to the engagement party this weekend," she said, taking a drink of her coffee.

"Free said he was trying to make it," Jodi said and nodded around another sip of her own coffee. "I hadn't heard if he was able to."

"Oh, he definitely did," Shaun muttered darkly. Jodi's dark brows pulled together in confusion and Shaun sighed. "I had the unfortunate displeasure of running into our favorite arrogant Nascar driver already this morning."

Jodi's jaw dropped open. "What? Really? Where?"

"Well, after I realized my coffee maker kicked the bucket this morning, I needed coffee, so I went down to Ted's. And who should I run into—*literally ran into*—but Kasey fucking Corcoran. Arrogant bastard." Jodi cackled over her coffee cup and Shaun glared at her. "*It's not funny!* He spilled my coffee because he was standing so damn close!"

"I've never met two people that antagonize each other the way you two do," Jodi said, still chuckling as she shook her head. "Even from two thousand miles away, he still ruffles your feathers."

"If he ever *stayed* two thousand miles away, I'd be fine," Shaun muttered sourly, then stood to cross to the coffee pot, filling her cup and then held it up in silent inquiry. Her sister shook her head, and she slid it back onto the hot plate before returning to her seat. Pushing her cup out of the way, she folded her arms on the counter and buried her face in them, rolling her forehead back and forth as she let out a long, frustrated groan. Speaking into her arms, her voice was muffled as she grumbled, "Urghhh. He just drives me *insane*, Jodi! And this dream! Ugh!"

Twisting her head so that her cheek lay on her folded arms, she looked up at her sister, who just smiled knowingly, her sapphire blue eyes mischievous as she took a sip of her coffee. "Is it always the same?"

"For the most part, yes. It replays that night at Shane and Cassie's wedding. I remember seeing him across the room for the first time, and then dancing with him." She heaved a deep breath and squeezed her eyes shut. "The way he held me against him while we were dancing, like he wanted to imprint his body on mine, or maybe vice versa… and then Tommy shows up and sees us—" Shaun's voice cracked slightly as she stumbled over his name, and she swallowed past the lump of emotion in her throat before continuing, "—and I remember walking over to him and kissing him so Kasey would see it and leave me alone. But in the dream, when I pull away, it's not Tommy who I'm lip locked with. It's Kasey. Kasey, every single time. But the worst part is when I wake up, I hate that it ended. Like I wanted it to keep going… I can't stand him, Jodi. I don't get it and I don't understand why my brain keeps doing this to me."

"Maybe you just need to get laid," Jodi said and shrugged, though she smiled behind another sip of her coffee.

Shaun groaned, rolling her head so she could bury her face in her arms again. It *had* been a very long seven months. And a vibrator only did so much. She missed the *real thing*.

"I still remember the night he came up for a visit… shoot, was it New Years Eve?" Jodi asked out loud, but Shaun knew exactly what night she was referring to. "It had to be, because we were at the party out at the Mountain…"

She knew exactly when he walked in.

Shaun stood at the bar in the Snowflake Lounge at Boyne Mountain Resort a town over from Petoskey. The lounge was decorated in black and gold and silver everything, the lighting low and the music was just loud enough to make conversations difficult to hear, and the room was crowded with other New Years Eve celebrants.

But she knew the moment those gray-blue eyes landed on her from across the room.

She'd recognize him anywhere. Even if she hadn't seen him in four months, if they'd only spent a handful of minutes together. That incredibly tall, lean body. That sandy blonde hair that always looked like it was just a tad too long. Those dangerously sexy hands with those long fingers that looked like he knew exactly what to do with them, no matter what he was doing with them.

She knew exactly what that body felt like as they danced, pressed together from thighs to chest.

He was dressed in dark navy slacks and a light, dusty blue dress shirt. There was no tie around his neck, and the top three buttons of his shirt were left undone at his throat, revealing several inches of deeply tanned skin in the V formed there. The sleeves were rolled up to his forearms, and a watch was strapped around one wide wrist where his hand dangled at his side. The other hand was tucked into his pocket as he shifted his gaze away from her.

Leaning to the side, she hissed through her clenched teeth, "You failed to mention he *was going to be here!"*

"Huh?" Jodi asked, glancing around the room, her blue eyes widening when she spotted who Shaun was talking about. "Oh. Uhh, I didn't know either."

While the two women waited for the bourbon neat and vodka tonic that they'd ordered, Shaun brought the champagne flute in her hand to her lips and took a long swallow, finishing what was left in it before sliding it across the lacquered bar for the bartender to refill.

Kasey made his way across the crowded room, stopping at the table where Freeman sat with several other members of her family, including Tommy Chandler. Her fiancé.

His eyes drifted back to her more than once in the time he stood there speaking to the others at the table. From where she and Jodi stood at the bar, she couldn't hear what was being said. Tommy glared daggers up at him, though he seemed totally unaffected by it, paying the other man little to no attention.

When the bartender pushed the drinks across the bar, Jodi picked up the bourbon and her champagne, and Shaun collected her own glass of champagne and the double vodka tonic Tommy had requested before making their way back to the table. She was painfully aware of Kasey's eyes on her, and she felt her skin growing hot. She had chosen a long sleeved, black top with a deep cowl neck that left the tops of her breasts and an eyeful of cleavage on display, paired with a dangerously short, sparkly, sequined gold skirt that hit high on her thighs. However, it was the thigh high, black high heeled boots that encased her legs and left a swath of bare skin between the tops of the boots and the hem of her short skirt that seemed to catch his attention the most.

Shaun stared stonily at Kasey as they approached, then as she handed Tommy his drink, he tugged her wrist, bringing her down so he could capture her lips with his. He hadn't forgotten the way Kasey had been holding her at Shane and Cassie's wedding either, apparently.

Free had risen from his seat, and he motioned around the table as he said, "Kasey, you remember Jodi—" Shaun watched as Kasey tipped his head and grinned warmly at the tiny brunette standing beside her.

"Hiya, doll," he said, reaching out a hand toward Jodi, and Shaun's belly flip-flopped at hearing that drawl again. "I hear congratulations are in order."

Jodi laughed, holding out her left hand. He examined the glittering diamond on the third finger and whistled, making Jodi blush.

"If you ever get tired of this grumpy old man, you let me know, doll," he murmured and winked. Free elbowed Kasey in the side and they chuckled together. Tommy rose to his feet, standing close beside Shaun, sliding one hand low on her back. She leaned into him as Kasey's eyes sliced toward the two of them.

Free continued with introductions, motioning to them as he said, "Kase, you remember Jodi's sister, Shaun? You two met at Shane and Cassie's wedding several months ago." Shaun fought the urge to roll her eyes. Like any of them had forgotten they'd met before.

"Nice to see you again," he drawled, and one side of his mouth tugged upward just the slightest, making Shaun grind her teeth together as he extended his hand to her. She placed her hand in his for the briefest shake before pulling it back. He turned those gray-blue eyes to Tommy, extending his hand. Shaun held her breath as Tommy gripped the other man's hand, and she could see the muscles in both their forearms tensing with how tightly they were gripping.

"And this is Tommy, Shaun's fiancé," Free kept on, his deep voice neutral, but Shaun's stomach felt like it had dropped out of

her butt when Kasey's face hardened. He kept his eyes on Tommy's face as they dropped hands.

"I guess double the congratulations, then," he murmured, though it lacked the warmth or even the arrogant teasing from a moment ago. His words were edged with a bite. He let his eyes glance over her for the sparest moment before looking toward the bar, and then said, "Nice to meet you. Excuse me, I think I'll go grab a drink."

As Kasey sauntered toward the bar, Free and Jodi joined him, leaving Shaun and Tommy alone at the table.

"I don't like the way he looks at you," Tommy muttered, glaring stonily at Kasey's back.

"He's just a pompous asshole," Shaun said and shrugged, setting down her champagne flute on the black linen tablecloth. Looping her arms around Tommy's neck, she leaned in for a kiss. "Besides, you're the one that gets to kiss me at midnight."

Tommy grumbled something unintelligible over the loud music and planted his hands on either side of her waist.

After finishing her glass of champagne, Shaun wandered over to the bar and stood to Jodi's other side, as far away from Kasey as possible. Tommy headed outside and Shaun's face fell in annoyance. He had taken up smoking cigarettes again but was hiding it from her. She didn't care either way, but the sneaking and lying bothered her. If he couldn't be honest about smoking, what else could he keep from her?

The bartender came over and caught her attention, pointing to her empty glass, and she shook her head, leaning forward on her forearms on the smooth bar top. "Can I get a Paloma?"

The bartender nodded and turned away to mix it. Jodi leaned over and said, "Oooh, that sounds delicious. Maybe I'll get one of those next."

Shaun laughed when Free leaned over and murmured, "Do you remember the last time we had tequila? I ended up in jail."

Jodi laughed and said something about "Guess it's a good thing Josh isn't going to show up and provoke you into a fistfight this time" but Shaun wasn't paying attention. Her eyes met Kasey's over Jodi and Free's shoulders, and he raised his glass, which was filled with a dark amber liquor and took a sip. Her belly did that annoying little flutter when she watched his lips on the rim of the glass, his eyes never leaving hers.

The bartender came back with her tequila and grapefruit cocktail and Shaun thanked him, adding it to their tab. "I need to use the restroom, I'll be right back," she whispered to Jodi and then headed across the room.

Staring at herself in the mirror in the blessedly empty women's powder room, she pressed her palm to her stomach, between her ribs and belly button, the knot of anxiety and annoyance that she always felt around Kasey making her wish she'd either eaten more at dinner, or not consumed as much alcohol.

Washing her hands, she left the ladies room and made her way down a short, dimly lit hallway back toward the door that led to the main room. She stifled a startled yelp when a hand clamped on her wrist at the same time she heard a low, husky drawl from behind her, saying, "Shaun—"

She swung around, colling with his impossibly hard chest.

"Kasey!" she exclaimed, hating the breathlessness in her voice at the feel of his strong, warm fingers clasped securely around her wrist and the way his body was angled against hers from thigh to chest. "Let go."

But he shook his head, his fingers tightening on her wrist. "Since when are you engaged?"

"What?" Shaun gasped, stunned by the hard edge in his voice.

"Since when are you engaged to that buffoon?" he asked, his words coming out low and laced with animosity.

"Tommy *and I have been engaged since Labor Day weekend," she snapped, tugging at her wrist to no avail. His fingers were like a vice around her wrist. "Not that it's any of your business, Kasey!"*

"I don't like him," he muttered, his eyes narrowing.

A shocked, ugly snort of laughter escaped her, and then she hissed, "I don't care if you don't like him! I don't like you*!"*

Lowering his mouth to the shell of her ear, he whispered, "Your body tells a different story, darlin'."

Shaun couldn't stop the shiver that ran along her entire body when his breath fanned over her ear. But she steeled herself and hissed, "Fuck you. Believe it or not, but not every woman you meet is going to drop to their knees at your feet, you conceited jackass."

"Don't be makin' promises you can't keep, darlin'," he murmured, making her shiver again. Damn him. "I'd love to see you on your knees in front of me—"

White hot fury washed over her, and before she could even think of the consequences, her palm had cracked across the side of his face.

She'd never struck someone in her life! What was it about this man that brought out the absolute worst in her?!

She panted in the dim hallway and yanked her wrist out of his grasp. His jaw tightened and fear skittered over her as his eyes narrowed, but then his lips curved into a dangerously dark smirk, and he took a small step toward her so that his mouth was close to her own.

"I can't wait to unleash all that fire, Shaun. You're going to burn me alive, baby," he drawled, his voice a husky murmur. "You're fucking exquisite. And he can't handle you."

"And you think you can?" she sneered, but desire had curled low in her belly. Fucking traitorous libido.

"Wouldn't you like to find out?" he asked, his lips moving against the skin of her cheek.

"No," she whispered.

"Liar."

"I will slap you again," she warned through her teeth, but she

wasn't sure if she was speaking to him, or herself this time. "Fucking try me."

"When you kiss that limp noodle at midnight, I dare you not to think about me," he whispered and then chuckled when he caught her wrist in his hand as she raised it as if to strike him again. Bringing her palm to his mouth, he pressed a hot, open-mouthed kiss to the center of it, and she sucked in a shocked breath as heat spiraled through her.

"Fuck you," she grated out, though it didn't hold the same weight as earlier, her heart hammering so hard inside her chest it hurt.

"Is that an invitation?" he asked, then laughed when she snarled at him.

She tugged on her hand and stepped away from him, putting several feet between them. "You're despicable."

He slid his hands into the front pockets of his slacks and her eyes dropped to his lap involuntarily. He was hard behind the fly of his slacks, and the way his hands were shoved in the pockets pulled the fabric even tighter across the front. Damn if she didn't want to know just what he was working with under there… She snapped her eyes to his and he grinned wolfishly, sauntering closer to her, one step, then two. The fucker was practically prowling.

Without touching her, he leaned in just close enough and whispered, "Don't forget to think about me, darlin'."

And then he brushed past her and passed through the door

into the main room, leaving her alone in the dimly lit hallway, her breathing labored and her heart still hammering in her chest.

As the ball dropped on the tv screen, Shaun looped her arms around Tommy's neck and kissed him with everything she had.

But fuck if it wasn't Kasey's mouth she imagined slanting over hers as the clock struck midnight.

FOUR

Kasey Corcoran shoved his fingers through his dark blonde hair before replacing the white ball cap on his head, pulling the brim down low over his eyes. He huffed an annoyed sigh into the phone perched between his shoulder and ear. “Look, Charlie, I told you I was going to be gone this weekend. Bentley is set to qualify tomorrow and Saturday, and then race on Sunday. I’m in Michigan for the weekend. I’ll be back Tuesday at the latest. He’ll do fine.”

Charlie Hoffman, his manager, grumbled on the other end of the line. “Your sponsors want you in the race on Sunday, not Bentley.”

“I’m allowed to have a life outside of that fucking car,” Kasey snapped, stretching his long legs out in front of him under the booth table of the breakfast diner he sat in, waiting for Freeman to arrive.

“They pay you for your time,” Charlie reminded him gruffly.

“And I make them a lot of damn money,” he muttered back, then took a sip of coffee from the tiny banana yellow mug the waitress had brought him. "I'm taking one weekend off, Charlie. That's it. I think you'll survive without me for one weekend."

"You better be in Talladega by Wednesday, K.C.," he mumbled sourly.

"You'll see my ugly mug by Tuesday," Kasey reminded him. "Give Suzie a kiss for me."

"I am not giving my wife a kiss from you; she'd have a damn heart attack and then leave my sorry ass for you."

Kasey laughed. "You're probably right."

"Fuck off, Corcoran," Charlie grumbled, but Kasey could hear the amusement in his voice. "You can get any damn woman you want. You can't have mine."

Kasey scratched at his stomach idly, his thoughts immediately drifting to the fiery bombshell he'd had the pleasure of running into already that morning. He'd been in town for less than an hour, his red-eye flight into Pellston—which was the tiniest airport he'd ever flown into—had arrived half an hour ahead of schedule. He'd been driving through the small lakeside city of Petoskey, his GPS speaking to him through the speakers of his rental truck when he'd damn near crashed into the car in front of him when he'd seen Shaun climb out of a truck parked in front of a gas station he was passing. He'd swerved into the parking lot, making a passing motorist honk their horn in indignation. Forcing himself to move slower than his legs wanted him to, he entered the gas station convenience store, his eyes sweeping until they landed on her, where she stood over at the coffee station.

Her back was to him, and he watched her as he walked toward her, admiring her figure outlined in the tight jeans and the hooded sweatshirt she wore, though the fabric was more like t-shirt material as it clung to her waist and hips. Her hair was secured in a long braid that fell over one shoulder and a ball cap was on her head. She did a little wiggle after sniffing the coffee she'd just poured, and he couldn't help the grin that lifted one corner of his mouth or the stiffening of his cock behind the fly of his jeans.

Stepping forward, he caught that hint of Japanese cherry blossom that always seemed to cling to her, and he made to touch her shoulder at the same time that she whirled around, colliding solidly with him. Her coffee fell from her fingers, sloshing all over the floor at their feet.

And that wickedly sharp tongue made its appearance and he'd nearly laughed. *Christ was she feisty. All. The. Time.*

He fucking loved it.

"Earth to K.C.," he heard Charlie's voice and refocused on the call. "Did you hear me or are you having a stroke?"

"I'm not flatlining," Kasey mumbled, glancing around the bustling diner. He saw Free climb out of his blue F-150 out in the parking lot through the window and sat up straighter, leaning forward to clasp the tiny yellow mug in his large hand and bring it to his lips. "I'll be there Tuesday. I gotta go, Charlie. Talk to you later."

He hung up just as Free walked through the double glass doors at the front of the diner. Kasey waved a hand over the heads of the other patrons to get his attention, and a moment later his cousin was sliding into the booth seat opposite him. The waitress materialized out of nowhere, flipping the coffee cup that sat on the paper placemat in front of him over and filling it with coffee. She set the carafe on the table and asked if they were ready to order, and they nodded.

"The usual, Free?" she asked.

"Yes, please," Free said, smiling gratefully.

She turned toward Kasey, inclining her head just the slightest. Her gaze swept over his face, as if trying to place where she recognized him. He shifted in his seat, dropping his eyes to the menu. He didn't want breakfast to turn into an autograph fest. He placed his order of a skillet breakfast and extra slices of whole wheat toast without raising his eyes to the waitress again, thanking her as she sidled away.

"How was your flight?" Free asked and leaned back against the padded booth seat. He draped one arm along the back of the booth, his other hand wrapped around the small, tangerine orange mug.

"Crowded. That plane was tiny," Kasey grumbled.

"Don't you fly first class?" Free asked, teasing.

"Ha," Kasey muttered sardonically. "If it's a sponsored flight, sure. On my own dime, economy is just fine. Even if my legs do get cramped."

Free motioned to the ball cap still on his head. "Do you get recognized more often now?"

"Eh, sometimes. When I travel, I try to dress down; wear ball caps, sunglasses, and grow out my scruff. That sort of thing," he said and shrugged. "Though it didn't help much at the gas station this morning. I still got recognized by a fan. Had to take a selfie. Hazard of the trade, I suppose."

Free laughed out loud. "I didn't see Shaun as the type to ask for a selfie. Maybe to throw darts at."

Kasey's eyebrows jumped in surprise. "How'd you know about that?"

Free chuckled again, pouring himself another cup of coffee from the carafe the waitress had left for them. "She was already at the house this morning, all in a huff. You spilled her coffee, you know."

Kasey grinned. "Oh yes. She let me know."

"You enjoy pissing her off, don't you?"

Kasey shrugged again, though he grinned behind another drink of his coffee. "It's entertaining, for sure." That buffoon fiancé of hers came to his mind and his lips drew into a thin line. He couldn't remember if he'd seen a ring on her finger. He made a mental note to double check when he saw her again. Not that he expected a change in her relationship status. If that idiot had any kind of smarts, he'd never let her go.

He knew he wouldn't, if he ever got the chance.

There was a hideous green monster that seemed to crawl under his skin whenever he thought about that jackass. Touching her. Kissing her. He'd give his left leg to have those long legs of hers wrapped around his head, his face buried in her—

The waitress was back just then with their platters of food, and he shifted in his seat, adjusting the stiffening of his cock in his jeans. Freeman had warned him once about the Kendall women. And he hadn't listened. Nope. He'd gone ahead and tumbled right off the deep end. She was too beautiful. Too spicy. Too fucking *everything* to resist.

He noticed the waitress staring at him again, as if still trying to place him. He smiled, but again angled his face away as he thanked her. She walked away, but glanced over her shoulder once more as they dug into their food.

"Are you guys going to get along this weekend?" Free asked as he took a bite of toast.

"Probably not," Kasey replied honestly.

"Can you try? For Jodi, please?" Free asked, stabbing his fork into a sausage link. "I want this weekend to go well for her. She deserves it after not getting a wedding when she married that douchebag ex of hers."

"I'll behave," Kasey muttered sourly as he shoveled a forkful of hashbrowns into his mouth after smothering them with ketchup. Then he amended, "For the most part, anyway. She just makes it too easy to rile her up."

"You're a menace," Free chuckled and took another bite of egg. "I have to work today, but my evening is open. Roxy will be in later today, too. Actually, Jodi said she's kicking the three of us out for the evening so we can catch up."

"She does know the trouble the three of us can get into together unsupervised, right?" he asked, laughing. He pushed his plate away and leaned back in the booth.

Free laughed, nodding. "I think she knows if we're out together getting into trouble, you won't be able to bother Shaun."

Kasey rolled his eyes but grinned. "She may know me too well already."

"What will you do today?" his cousin asked then, mopping up the last of his egg yolk with his toast.

Kasey shrugged, crossing his arms over his chest as he fought a yawn. The waitress was back with their check. "I didn't sleep much on the plane; would it be alright if I head to your place and crash for a few hours? The hotel won't let me check in until after three."

"Sure, not a problem. Jodi will be there for a bit, she

doesn't go into the bookstore for a couple more hours," Freeman said as he pulled out his wallet, but Kasey handed the waitress his credit card, waving his cousin off.

"I invited you out for breakfast," he said as the waitress walked away, looking at his credit card. *Dammit.* Over at the counter, she whispered something to the middle-aged woman at the register, their faces lighting up. "And I've got about thirty seconds before this place explodes."

As the waitress returned with his credit card, she handed it back to him along with the credit card slip and a pen. He scrawled his name and a tip, then handed it back to her with a resigned smile when he noticed the cell phone clutched in her other hand. The middle-aged woman from the register stood behind her, and a moment later a tall, skinny guy with a white apron approached from the kitchen, peering over their shoulders at him.

"I *knew* I recognized you! Can I get a picture with you, K.C.? And an autograph?"

Free chuckled, but Kasey smiled with a nod and exaggerated his Texas drawl as he said, "Sure can. What's your name, darlin'?"

FIVE

Half an hour, and several dozen selfies and autographs later, Kasey finally managed to escape the small breakfast diner, sliding in behind the wheel of his rental truck. Pulling the ball cap off his head, he tossed it into the passenger seat next to him.

Lot of good it did me in there, he thought, but then smiled. He'd had the cutest kid, little blonde-haired, blue-eyed boy come up to him with his dad and ask for a photo. The kid, Oliver, the dad had said his name was, had been clutching a *Hot Wheels* toy replica of his car, painted with the number 33 on it.

Plugging Free's address into the GPS in his phone, he pulled out of the diner parking lot and headed in the direction that he was instructed. He looked around as he drove, awed by the fall colors that surrounded the area on three sides. From the top of the hill, he could see the bay in his rearview mirror, and it stretched beyond to Lake Michigan.

Ten minutes later his GPS told him to make a right turn into a long, gravel driveway. As his truck rumbled along, the trees on his right opened up into a field where a small ranch-style house sat, a white Jeep Compass parked in front.

He climbed out and then reached into the backseat for his overnight bag just as the front door opened and Jodi Kendall stepped out, waving.

"Hiya, doll," he called up the steps to her as he ascended them.

"Hi! How was your flight?" she asked as he reached the top of the steps. He draped one arm over her shoulders and squeezed, making her laugh.

"It was fine, we made good time with no headwind. Hope I didn't wake you guys up when I messaged Free to meet me for breakfast," he said and let her lead him into the house.

"Oh, not at all, we were up," Jodi said and waved her hand. "He called and said you would be on your way over. I'll be out of the house, so it'll be nice and quiet for you to sleep."

He nodded and yawned broadly. He *was* exhausted. Kasey followed Jodi down a hallway and into a guest bedroom with a bed that looked way too damn comfortable piled with a thick, fluffy down comforter and a pile of pillows he couldn't wait to sink into. The windows faced east, which meant the sun was shining directly into the room as the sun was still making its ascent. Jodi crossed the room and drew the shades down, which darkened the room considerably.

She pointed back through the doorway across the hall and

said, "The bathroom is just through there and help yourself to anything in the kitchen. Free should be home around five, but I'll be out until close to six. I'm sorry the room isn't available to you for the weekend, Roxy called dibs first."

Kasey laughed, then stifled another broad yawn. Free, Kasey, and Roxy had been an inseparable trio while they all lived in Texas, before Free moved back to Michigan after finally admitting he was head over heels in love with the oldest Kendall daughter. Freeman's brother, Shane, was standing as his best man, while Kasey and Roxy were groomsman and 'grooms-maid'. Jodi's younger brothers would stand as groomsmen as well.

"I don't mind. I'll just crash for a few hours and then head over to the hotel once they'll let me check in. What time is Roxy getting in? I'll make sure to be out before she gets here," he said.

"I think she said her flight is coming into Traverse City at two this afternoon, so she should be here around four or five," she said and stepped to the second window, pulling the shades down on that one as well.

"How are things with Roxy?" he asked, setting his bag down on the foot of the bed.

"They're fine," Jodi said and smiled over her shoulder at him. "It was a little awkward at first, I won't lie. She's very intimidating and seriously *gorgeous*. It took some time to get used to the fact that she and Free used to…"

"Do the nasty?" he provided when she stalled, and she laughed at his exaggerated accent.

"Yes, that," she said and rolled her eyes at him. "But Free assured me there was never any emotional feelings between them. It was just physical. Roxy and I have had many heart-to-heart chats about everything. I believe them."

"That's the honest truth," Kasey said and nodded to the ring on her finger. "I've never seen him the way he is with you, doll. You were like this missing piece in him. I've never believed in that whole 'soul mates' mumbo jumbo. But if I did, you two would be the exception."

"That's so sweet," Jodi said and smiled, her blue eyes lighting. Kasey couldn't help but notice just how similar she and Shaun were in appearance. They shared the same brunette curls and sapphire blue eyes, but Jodi was petite while Shaun was nearly six feet tall. And Jodi was softer, sweeter, while Shaun was brash and fiery and stubborn.

He yawned again and Jodi laughed as she moved toward the door. "I'll let you get some sleep." She paused at the door and said softly, "Thank you for being here. I know it means a lot to Free to have you here. To me, too."

"I wouldn't have missed it," he said and smiled, then winked. "I'm just glad he found someone to put up with his ornery self."

Jodi laughed, rolling her eyes, which made him think about Shaun again. "Get some sleep, Kasey!"

"Yes, ma'am," he drawled as she pulled the door closed behind her as she left. He laid down on the comforter, not even bothering to take his jeans off, and as soon as his head hit the pile of pillows, he was out.

SIX

"Do you need any help?"

Shaun glanced up from under the hood of the Toyota Camry she was working on, meeting the intense, dark brown-black eyes of Nate, one of her coworkers and fellow mechanics at Rodney's Auto. "Uhh, no. Thanks, though."

Nathaniel LaVictor was a guy in his late twenties, shorter than Shaun by about four inches, with a beefy build. He had black hair that could use a cut or a wash or even a comb, and a thick black beard that covered all of his lower face and most of his neck. He'd hired in at Rodney's two months prior and had been asking Shaun for dates pretty much weekly since then. He was attractive in a husky, blue collar sort of way, and seemed nice enough, but something about him gave Shaun the creeps.

Like spine tingling, watch over your shoulder kind of creeps.

He was *always staring.* Like now, even as he walked away to another vehicle parked in the mechanic bay directly next to her, he just *never stopped staring.*

Shaun ducked her head back under the hood, glad when

she was hidden from that piercing black gaze.

Reaching into the engine cavity, she grunted, wiggling her fingers around a bolt that she couldn't get with the wrench. Buried to her armpit, she made the mistake of meeting Nate's eyes from across the garage, quickly turning away before he decided to come back over. She shuddered.

She'd caught him staring at her in the most inappropriate ways, too. His favorite thing to look at was her ass, second was her breasts, which for the summer months had been encased in sports bras and loose-fitting t-shirts with the arms cut off to combat the heat and humidity. She refused to layer up just because he couldn't keep his eyes to himself.

Her cell phone rang from her back pocket, and she fished it out as she withdrew from the engine, swiping right to answer the call. "Hey, how's my favorite preggo?"

"Miserable," her best friend, Zoey Manning, whined from the other end of the line. "Someone needs to tell this baby to get ouuuuttt of meeee."

"You let that baby bake in there as long as he wants," Shaun teased, leaning her forearms against the car. "I want my nephew to be nice and well-cooked."

"Verity was nine pounds! If this baby takes after Chase, he's going to be ten pounds and two feet long!" Zoey laughed, though Shaun could hear the worry in her voice. "And I still have six weeks left. I already can't see my feet."

"Are the doctors concerned with his size?" Shaun asked, her eyebrows drawing together.

"No, she said he's measuring right on schedule," Zoey said, but then laughed. "But so did Verity, and she was a monster baby."

"I am never getting pregnant," Shaun laughed and shuddered. "I don't think I even want babies."

"Really?" Zoey asked, and Shaun fiddled with a hose near her fingers. "You and Tommy never talked about it?"

"Sure we did," Shaun said, standing upright and turning to lean her back against the side of the car door. "That was just something that was way down the road for us. It wasn't something I was even ready to consider. And I have no intention of dating again, so I think any future of being a mom is long gone. My parents are just going to have to get grandkids from the other four."

"You really don't think you'll ever date again?" her friend asked quietly from the other end of the line, and Shaun swallowed past that lump in her throat.

"Zoey… I don't think I'm made for being in a deep relationship. Please don't hate me for this, you know I loved your brother, but… something was missing." Glancing around the garage, she sighed. "We were great friends—best friends—and we had a great time together… I don't know. It just didn't feel right at the end. At the time I thought it was because he had changed, but now I'm not so sure..."

"It's okay to take time, Shaun," Zoey said quietly from the other end of the line. "And it's okay to grieve the loss of that even if it wasn't some grand love."

"But it makes me sound heartless," Shaun whispered.

"No, it makes you sound like you weren't willing to settle for something less than exactly what you deserve," Zoey said gently. "I love my brother, you know I do, but he... is flawed. He struggled with what happened to me, and with Mom's death so close behind, he developed crappy and unhealthy coping mechanisms because of it. He hurt a lot of people because he didn't want to deal with what was going on. You were one of them. You decided what was best for you, and I think it was best for him, too."

Shaun swallowed hard again and whispered, "Have you heard from him?"

"Not in a few weeks. Last I heard he was downstate staying with a cousin. He refused treatment, again." Shaun scuffed the toe of her boot into the concrete at her feet, staring down at the floor. "I gotta run, but I'll see you tomorrow at the engagement party?"

"As maid of honor, I think Jodi would skin me alive if I missed it." Then she groaned out loud. "You'll have to save me from Kasey, though."

"He's in town?" Zoey gasped. "I didn't think he was

coming up for the party."

"I hoped he wouldn't," Shaun grumbled, pacing away from the vehicle out into the parking lot in front of the building. The mid-October sun felt good, the weather unseasonably warm. "We ran into each other at the gas station this morning. He's as insufferable as ever."

"I thought he was nice," Zoey said, then giggled. "And don't tell my husband, but Kasey is a hottie! And he's totally into you."

"Gag," Shaun grumbled. "Besides, I am closed for business. No-freaking-thank-you. Especially that arrogant bastard."

Zoey laughed out loud and then said, "I'll see you tomorrow! Try to behave yourself."

"Never," Shaun laughed. "See you tomorrow."

Hanging up and sliding the phone back into her pocket, she turned on her heel in the gravel and nearly collided with Nate, who had walked up behind her on nearly silent feet.

"Shit, Nate!" she exclaimed, backing up a step to avoid making contact with his body. "Give a girl some warning!"

"Sorry," he said, his dark eyes intense on her face, squinting slightly because of the bright sunlight. "You uh, you have a party tomorrow? Do you need a date?"

"Uhh—" Shaun stammered, glancing over his shoulder before shaking her head. "I do have a thing tomorrow, my sister's engagement party, but no, I don't need a date. Besides, I've told you, I don't date coworkers. Or anyone."

"Come on," he murmured, sidling slightly closer to her, reaching one meaty hand out to touch her forearm, and she jerked away from his touch. "You don't want to go to a family wedding event alone."

"Actually, I do," Shaun snapped, taking another step backward, putting extra space between them. "My answer is no, Nate."

Fear tingled down her spine when his dark eyes flashed with something sinister, but then he just grinned and said, "Okay, sure thing. Just thought I'd offer. Should probably get back to work."

As he walked away, Shaun breathed a sigh of relief, then headed back into the garage, keeping one wary eye on Nate from across the room.

SEVEN

"How dressy is this supposed to be?" Shaun asked, her phone on speaker where it sat in the middle of her bed.

"Dressy casual," she heard Jodi's voice come from the phone. "I thought you said you had an outfit already picked out?"

"*I did*," Shaun muttered, rifling through the clothes in her dresser before stepping over to the closet and sliding hangers around on the bar. "But that was before I knew Kasey fucking Corcoran was going to be there. I can't wear *that* outfit now."

"Why not?" Jodi asked. "Too sexy?"

Shaun scoffed and said, "No. I was leaning more toward the *casual* part of dressy casual."

"So now you need to find something sexier? Because Kasey will be there?" Jodi asked and Shaun rolled her eyes. Damn nosy woman.

"You know what, never mind. I don't know why I called you," Shaun snapped. Why was she worried about what she was going to wear? Why did she care so much about what Kasey would think of her? *She didn't.* Jodi laughed out loud and

Shaun clenched her teeth together in aggravation. “I’m hanging up on you!”

“I’ll see you in an hour!” Jodi laughed again, and Shaun lunged across the bed to disconnect the phone call. Rolling to her back, she stared up at the ceiling.

Kasey had refused to leave her mind all day. It’s like having him in the general area made it so it was impossible to get him out of her head. He was by far the most attractive man she’d ever seen, but also the most infuriating.

“Fuck it,” Shaun muttered and rolled into a sitting position, standing and striding over to the closet. Grabbing a skintight pair of black jeans that she knew did wonders for her ass and legs, she tossed them onto the foot of the bed and then rifled through the tops until she found the one she was looking for.

Peeling the t-shirt she’d pulled on after her shower over her head, she let it fall to the floor, standing in the middle of the room naked. She pulled a simple black thong out of the drawer and slid them up her legs, then fastened a matching strapless bra at her back, adjusting her breasts in the cups. Stepping into the tight jeans, she jumped and wiggled until they were over her thighs and wide hips. The top she chose was black, in a buttery soft material. Fitted at her waist, it highlighted her narrow waist and shapely hips, but was loose at the top, the neckline wide enough to let it drape over one shoulder, leaving it bare. The sleeves were loose and wide, floating around her arms.

She had let her curly hair dry naturally, which meant her curls were rioting around her head. She had smoothed curl cream into it after her shower, taming them slightly, but the fullness bounced around her shoulders and down her back. A pair of simple silver earrings adorned her ears and her make-up was simple but alluring. She had taken extra time on her eyes, making the blue of them pop. Staring at herself in the mirror in the bathroom, she turned this way and that, checking her reflection. Reaching into her cosmetic bag, she pulled out a tube of dark red lipstick, staring at it for a long minute before uncapping it and gliding it onto her full lips.

"Eat your heart out, you arrogant prick," she muttered to her reflection, smiling just the slightest.

Leaving the bathroom, she slid her feet into her favorite sky-high black heels, but then kicked them off, opting for a strappy option with low, chunky heels instead. She then grabbed her purse and keys, and was out the door moments later.

Driving the familiar roads to her parent's home, she parked her truck alongside several other vehicles already in the driveway. Sliding out of the truck, she carefully picked her way across the gravel driveway to the wide front steps, taking them one at a time, when a long, low whistle sounded.

Whipping her head to the right, she swallowed hard as the owner of that whistle appeared from the shadow of the covered porch.

"I was wondering what you'd wear tonight," he said in that low drawl that made her belly do somersaults. "I've been torturing myself all day imagining it."

"You're a pig," Shaun snapped, taking the final steps up onto the porch, where she stopped. He continued forward, slowly, and for a brief second Shaun felt very much like she was prey, and he a predator.

"I just appreciate a beautiful woman," Kasey murmured as he stopped several feet away from her, his hands tucked into the pockets of his dark wash jeans. A black t-shirt stretched across his chest, and a mouthwateringly sexy black leather jacket hung open. His blonde hair looked freshly washed and tousled, like he'd towel dried it and then left it alone to dry haphazardly. Or like eager hands had been shoved through it—

"Well, don't," Shaun snapped, shaking the intrusive thoughts away, at the same time tossing her curls away from her face, revealing that bare shoulder.

Kasey's lips tightened and then he murmured, his voice low and slightly bitter, "Right. You just love to remind me."

"What—"

"Oh, you're here!" her sister's voice met her ears as the front door opened. "I need a Sissy Cocktail, though don't tell

Freeman!"

Shaun laughed, stepping forward through the open door, letting her gaze slide over to Kasey's for just a heartbeat before linking her arm with Jodi's. "Well, we can't let the bride go thirsty. Let's go get you a drink."

Shaun let Jodi lead her through the house and into the kitchen, where a vast selection of beverages had been arranged, along with several trays of charcuterie that were ready to be set out when the guests arrived. Stepping toward the drinks, Shaun first poured Jodi a cocktail, then mixed one for herself.

Levi Kendall, their father, walked into the room wearing his usual jeans and a clean white dress shirt. His collar had been left unbuttoned and his sleeves were rolled to his forearms. He lumbered toward the two of them, his cowboy boots clicking on the tile floor. His hair was dark, sprinkled with white strands at his temples, and his dark, full beard had more white than it had just a few years ago, but Shaun had always thought her dad was one of the most handsome men she'd known. He was six foot four and solidly built.

"Heya, girls," he rumbled as he stopped next to them. He leaned down and pressed a kiss to each of their cheeks, and Shaun inhaled the familiar mix of cedar, pine, and musk that clung to him. Reaching for two highball glasses, he poured several fingers of bourbon into them. "You both look beautiful."

Jodi smiled and Shaun shrugged, though they both said, "Thank you." Jodi fixed one side of his collar and said, "You look very handsome, Dad. Did Mom pick this out?"

Levi grumbled and took a sip from one of the glasses in his hands. "At least she didn't make me wear a tie."

"I had one laid out, and he refused to put it on," Serenity Kendall muttered as she entered the kitchen and Shaun laughed. Her mother looked beautiful in a simple, flowy dress that hit just below her calves, the material light and fluttery as she moved. The v neckline dipped to the middle of her chest, the sleeves flowy to where they buttoned at her wrists. Her dark, wavy hair had been secured into a loose French twist at the back of her head, several tendrils slipping out to frame her face.

"Oh, Jodi, you look gorgeous!" Seren said and beamed. Her sister had chosen a white lace maxi dress that was a little whimsical and slightly bohemian in style, and her long curly hair had been swept into a loose Dutch braid that fell over one shoulder. "Shaun, you look stunning!"

Levi took another drink of his bourbon as the doorbell rang, to which Seren disappeared out of the kitchen to answer.

Levi bobbed his eyebrows at the two of them before sidling back out the door. Jodi and Shaun followed. Levi exited the house to the expansive back patio, where a smattering of handcrafted Adirondack chairs dotted the porch. A fire had been built in the large fire pit in the middle of the yard, and Shaun could just make out the shapes of several bodies in the growing dusk.

"I should have just worn boots," Shaun grumbled, stepping out onto the porch. "I'm going to break my neck walking around in the dark in heels."

"You'll be fine," Jodi said, waving her hand.

"Says the woman in sensible flats," Shaun muttered, and Jodi laughed.

"Guilty," Jodi chuckled. "I also didn't expect it to be warm enough to have a fire outside. It's a pleasant surprise."

A smattering of people had already gathered around the roaring bonfire set in a giant fire-ring of masonry blocks. At least a dozen handcrafted Adirondack chairs circled the fire, some empty, some taken. In the golden glow of the fire, she could make out the faces of those surrounding it. 90's country drifted over the yard from the hidden surround sound from the back porch.

Shaun saw Jodi's two best friends and fellow bridesmaids, Tessa and Kit, who sat in chairs side by side to the right of the fire, clear plastic cups in their hands filled with cocktails. Tessa's wavy blonde hair shone brightly in the firelight, and she had on her classic red lipstick. She took a drink from her cup and pushed her red-rimmed glasses up with one finger. Kit sat with one leg crossed over the other, leaning back in her chair, her honey brown hair piled high on top of her head and a comfortable looking sweater wrapped around her curvy frame. The woman was *voluptuous* in all the right places.

Levi had walked up to Free, handing over one of the highballs of bourbon. Freeman stood facing the fire, wearing a black Carhartt vest that had been left unzipped over a black button-down shirt. The cuffs were buttoned at his wrists, and a black ball cap covered his dark brown hair, though the brim had been turned backward. The lower portion of his face was shadowed with a dark beard as usual, but it was trimmed short and well-groomed. Well-worn, well-fitted jeans encased his legs down to the black cowboy boots on his feet.

Shaun recognized Roxsanna Roberts' vibrant red hair where she stood next to Freeman, her backside close to the fire, and she was bundled up in what looked like several layers of jackets. Roxy was one of Free's best friends and was standing with Free as a 'grooms-maid' in their wedding in December.

Shaun stumbled slightly when she realized the man standing next to Roxy was Kasey, his back to the fire, facing Free. His back was to her and Jodi as they approached, and she took just a moment to admire the way the dark jeans he wore fit his long thighs and cupped his ass. His black leather jacket covered his back, but made his broad, hard shoulders look even broader. He turned his head slightly, and she watched him in profile as he took a drink from a clear plastic cup in one of his hands. His fingers were long and held the cup loosely. She swallowed hard and hated that she started to imagine what those fingers could do to her, how they would feel against her skin, fisting in her hair—

Shaun skidded to a halt, snapping to herself, *dammit woman, pull yourself together! Just because you haven't gotten any action in seven months doesn't mean you need to jump on that bandwagon!*

Jodi stumbled to a stop, too, her arm still linked with Shaun's. She saw Jodi glance up at her before twisting her head back to where Kasey stood.

"Are you going to be okay?" Jodi asked.

Taking a drink of her cocktail, she nodded. "Yep."

"There's my beautiful bride," Free said then, and Shaun's throat closed at the apparent adoration in his voice. Roxy and Kasey turned, and though she steeled herself, she was not fully prepared for when Kasey's eyes met hers from across the flames. The temperature had dropped into the mid-sixties as the sun went down, and although she only had on jeans and a sweater, she suddenly felt like it was ninety degrees inside her clothing. Jodi disengaged her arm from Shaun's and walked around the fire to her fiancé, who held out one arm to let her slide beneath it. Free leaned down and pressed a kiss to the top of Jodi's head.

A light breeze rustled her hair, and she reached up to tuck it behind her ear. She watched as Kasey lifted his cup to his lips again, his eyes never leaving hers. Pulling her cell phone out of her back pocket when she felt it vibrate, she sighed heavily and let her shoulders drop. It was a text from Zoey, apologizing that she and her husband Chase wouldn't be able to make it to the party after all, as their one-and-a-half-year-old daughter had developed a fever. She tucked the phone back into her pocket and lifted her eyes to the crowd once more.

Roxy waved from across the fire and Shaun lifted her free hand to wave back. "Hiya, Shaun," the redhead said, coming around the fire to stand next to her. Roxy was tall, but still stood several inches shorter than her. Kasey's eyes never left her as Roxy made her way toward her.

"Hey," Shaun said, lifting her glass to her lips again, willing the alcohol to calm her frazzled nerves. *Why did he have to affect her so!* Turning to look at Roxy, she asked, "How was your flight?"

"It was fine," she said, her Texas accent heavy as she spoke. "Layover in Chicago wasn't too long, thankfully. And the little puddle jumper flight to Traverse City was a breeze."

Shaun nodded and took a drink of her cocktail, turning slightly so that she wasn't looking directly at Kasey, who still stood across the fire from her. He was talking with Jodi, Free, and Levi, and over the music and the sound of the crackling of the fire, she could hear that low drawl that made her knees weak.

"How are things down south?" Shaun asked Roxy.

The redhead shrugged her shoulders, taking a drink of her own cocktail. "They're alright. Calmed down some, finally."

"No more trouble from the ex?" she asked, her brows drawing together. Jodi had confided in her the harrowing story of how Roxy's ex-boyfriend had gotten physically abusive at the end of their relationship. Roxy had left him, moved in with Free down in Texas, and had gotten a restraining order, but while Free was in Michigan for his brother Shane's wedding last fall, her ex had accosted her one night on her way home and beat her into a bloody mess.

"He hasn't shown his face in over a year," Roxy said, shifting from one foot to the other, and Shaun saw the way her mouth tightened just the slightest. "Good riddance, if you ask me."

Shaun motioned awkwardly to her face and said, "Looks like everything healed."

Roxy snorted and took another drink of her cocktail before saying sourly, "For the most part, yes. I still have this scar—" she said and pointed to the left side of her bottom lip, where Shaun could see a jagged white scar that bisected her lip and down below the pink fullness of it to her chin, "—and the vision in my left eye is still a little blurry. He rocked my shit pretty hard."

"Don't you get nervous being alone?" Tessa asked from

where she sat in the chairs to their right.

"Nah," Roxy said and lifted one shoulder. She motioned toward Kasey, and Shaun's eyes found his again. "Kasey checks in pretty regularly, when he's not on the road, anyway. And Bobby, the landlord, checks in a lot, too."

"It would be a helluva lot easier to check in on you if you ever answered your damn cell phone," Kasey grumbled over the fire. The redhead stuck her tongue out at him.

"You know our offer still stands, too," Free said then and Jodi nodded.

"What offer?" Shaun asked, pulling her gaze away from Kasey. He had hunkered down, pouring a hefty portion of what looked like expensive bourbon into his empty cup before standing.

"They're trying to get me to move up here," Roxy said and laughed while shaking her head. "I'm not made for the cold."

"You're also not made for a body bag," Free muttered, but it was good natured. The friendship between the three of them was obvious. "Kasey is gone most of the year and I'm up here full time now."

"I'm perfectly capable of taking care of myself," Roxy snapped, and Shaun almost laughed. She liked Roxy. She seemed to keep Free and Kasey on their toes.

Levi's deep voice rumbled over the fire from where he stood beside Jodi and Free, addressing Roxy, "As a native Texan myself, I can assure you that you will get used to the cold. I back Free and Jodi's offer. If you ever feel unsafe, please don't hesitate to take them up on it. As a father, I'd rather see you have to bundle up in extra layers than the alternative." Gesturing around them to the gathering crowd, he rumbled, "This here is family. You're a part of that, now. We take care of our own."

Shaun's nose tingled slightly with emotion, and she smiled over at her dad at his heartfelt words. Jodi cleared her throat and wrapped her arm around Freeman's waist and said to them all earnestly, "We are so glad that you all were able to make it this weekend for our engagement party, and we cannot wait to have you all standing with us in a month and a half when we say 'I do'. It means the world to us, you guys."

Kasey winked over at Jodi and said, "I'll have the getaway car on standby if you need it, doll."

"Fuck off," Free laughed then, reaching out and shoving Kasey hard on the shoulder. "Get your own Kendall woman. This one is mine."

Shaun's breath hitched in her throat when Kasey's gray-blue eyes found hers across the fire, and she could read the message in them loud and clear; *Don't mind if I do.*

EIGHT

He was having the damndest time keeping his eyes to himself.

Everything she did was maddening. The way she tipped her cup to her lips, the way those full, kissable lips pressed to the rim of the cup, the way the cool air had made her cheeks and the tip of her nose pink, the way she threw her head back and laughed, the way her straight white teeth looked as they clamped down on her bottom lip every time she failed at keeping *her* eyes to *herself*, too.

They maintained the fire-widths distance from each other at all times, but he didn't mind, because that meant he could watch her no matter where she was. The black jeans she wore hugged her mile long legs and cupped her fantastic ass in ways that made it hard to concentrate on what was going on around him. He was also fighting a near constant chubby and had to keep readjusting his jeans because fuck was she gorgeous in the firelight.

Kasey took another swallow of the bourbon he'd brought with him as an engagement gift for Freeman, the rich, smoky liquor turning the slow burn in his belly into an inferno as he continued to watch Shaun. His eyes kept skittering over to the patio door every time it would slide open as more guests arrived, waiting for the moment when that douche bag fiancé of hers would make his appearance.

His cousin Shane and his wife Cassie had joined them, her pregnant belly extending out in front of her. He watched as Serenity, who he'd met earlier in the evening, fussed over the younger woman, forcing her to sit in one of the more comfortable chairs surrounding the fire before insisting that Levi run inside to grab an extra blanket, just in case she got cold. The older man nodded in agreement before sauntering across the darkened lawn, returning a couple minutes later with the blanket for Cassie. He liked Shaun and Jodi's parents and felt very comfortable around them, though the way Levi watched him watching his daughter was a good deterrent to staring at the woman unabashedly like he wanted to.

Levi and Serenity had settled into a wooden bench swing across the fire, and the older man's arm was draped over his wife's shoulders, tucking her securely into his side. His booted toe rocked them continuously, and Kasey could see where Freeman had learned a lot of his mannerisms from, as he'd spent nearly a decade with the Kendall family growing up. The friendship between the older man and Freeman was obvious, too. He had a better understanding of why Freeman had fought so hard against the attraction he'd felt for the eldest

Kendall daughter for as long as he had. Camaraderie like what Levi and Free had was hard to come by and he understood not wanting to betray his friend and mentor by pursuing the man's daughter.

Glancing at the watch on his wrist, he was surprised to see it was after eleven. The evening had flown by. Roxy excused herself into the house, along with the two women he'd been introduced to earlier, Jodi's other bridesmaids. The three of them made their way across the yard, giggling and chattering until the patio door slid closed behind them.

Shaun had settled herself into one of the Adirondack chairs across from him and had pulled her knees to her chest. She had tucked her feet up onto the seat and wrapped her arms around her legs. Her chin rested on her knee as she stared into the flickering flames between them. Her eyes looked like glittering sapphires in the low glow of the fire. Taking another sip of his bourbon, he made his way slowly around the ring of the fire, stopping at the chair Roxy had vacated beside Shaun.

Sinking into it, he sighed heavily and leaned back against the smooth wood. Stretching his legs out in front of him, he crossed one ankle over the other and turned his head to look at her. She stared straight ahead into the flames, but he could see the way her breathing had kicked up a notch, and he watched as she swallowed hard. His own heart was beating like a drum in his chest. Just being near her did things to him.

Finally, she turned her head just enough to look at him, her chin still resting on her knee, and those sapphire eyes hit him all over again. Damn was she gorgeous.

And so fucking unavailable.

He held out his cup toward her. "Want a sip?"

She glanced at his fingers wrapped around the cup and then back to his eyes. "I probably shouldn't. I'm still supposed to drive home."

He nodded, bringing his arm back and taking a sip of it, his eyes still on hers. "I don't think I'll be driving tonight." Then he motioned with his head over to Jodi and Free, and Shaun turned her head to look. Free had settled himself in one of the chairs and Jodi was sitting across his lap, her head leaning against his chest, his arms wrapped around her. They were murmuring quietly to each other, Freeman's lips moving against her temple, and then Jodi laughed. Kasey's chest ached with a mixture of longing and envy.

Shaun turned her head back toward him and smiled gently, and it made his heart do double time in his chest. "They're always like that. So gross."

"I'm just glad to see him happy finally. Not that he wasn't happy in Texas," Kasey said quietly, low enough for just her to hear. "But we could tell something was missing for him. Roxy always knew there was someone up here that he left behind. I was clueless. I just thought he needed to get laid more." He nodded his head toward the two in the chair again. "Sounds like she needed him, too."

Shaun rested her cheek on her knee and nodded as she looked at him. "Her ex was a piece of shit. She'd been in love with Free for over half her life. She deserves the happiness that he gives her. And he's so good to her. I couldn't hope for something better for either of them."

Glancing at her hands, he noticed her fingers were bare, that engagement ring he'd seen on her finger back on New Year's Eve not in place. His heart quickened, but he shot it down. *Just because she's not wearing it doesn't mean shit, you jackass. She works on cars all day. She can't wear it without losing that finger if she gets caught in a machine. Better that she doesn't wear it.*

"What about you?" he asked, clearing his throat, unable to resist digging for information.

"What about me?" she repeated, her brows drawing over her eyes.

"Is your relationship everything that you deserve?" he asked, swiveling his head forward to stare into the flames. His heart was pounding, dreading her answer. *Fucking masochist.*

He watched her out of his peripheral vision and saw when she turned her face to look forward into the fire, too. "I'm content with where my life is now," she whispered softly. They were silent for a few moments before she sighed and uncurled her arms from around her legs, setting her feet on the ground. Pulling herself forward, she stood, glancing down at him before speaking to the few that still gathered around the fire, "I should probably head home."

Jodi looked up from Free's chest and then stood, crossing the few feet to hug Shaun. Kasey almost laughed at the height difference between the two sisters.

Serenity called over the fire, "Please let me know when you get home safely." Jodi returned to Free, who enveloped her in his arms a moment later. "Are you sure you don't want to stay?"

"I will, I promise, Mom. And no, I'm fine," Shaun said, glancing in his direction again. "I only had two drinks. Good night, you guys."

Kasey saw Levi sit up straighter in his seat and then that gruff voice traveled across the fire as he murmured, "Kasey can walk you to your truck, Shaun."

"Oh, no, that's really not necessary," Shaun stammered, whipping her head from her dad's face to his own and then back again like a ping-pong ball in a volley. "I don't need an escort to go across the yard, Dad."

"Humor me," Levi rumbled, and Kasey took that as his cue, pushing himself to his feet. Setting down his drink on the armrest of the chair he'd just vacated, he had to fight the urge to smile when Shaun rolled her eyes and huffed out an annoyed sigh.

Shaun stomped away from the fire, her arms crossed over her middle. Kasey fell into step beside her, his long legs keeping stride with her angry ones. They were almost to the corner of the house when she stopped.

"I left my keys on the kitchen counter," she said, glancing over at him. "You really don't have to walk me to my car. I know my way."

Kasey just put his hands in the front pockets of his leather jacket and raised his eyebrows, notching his chin toward the back porch that would lead into the house. Shaun huffed again and started across the lawn, climbing the two steps onto the large back deck. Kasey followed, trying not to grin at how annoyed she was. He and Free had done damage to the bottle of bourbon he'd brought, and he was feeling the effects of it.

Sliding the patio door open, she entered and walked through the living room and into the kitchen, and he could hear her swipe her keys off the counter into her hand. A moment later he heard her heels clicking on the hardwood floor as she stalked back out of the kitchen where he waited in the entryway. He followed her to the front door, right behind her, and pulled the door closed as they exited out onto the covered front porch. It was shrouded in inky blackness, and he knew he couldn't let her leave without saying what was on his mind.

"Shaun, wait."

Kasey's fingers wrapped around the upper part of her bicep, stopping her before she could take a step down the porch stairs, and she stared down at the fingers there before raising her eyes to his.

He stared down into her face, partially shadowed in the darkness that surrounded them, half of her face illuminated by the silvery glow of the moon that had risen into the sky. His fingers flexed around her upper arm and his face lowered toward hers, until only inches separated them. He stared into those stormy sapphire blue eyes; the world silent around them except for the sound of their breathing.

He watched her as he licked his lips, then swallowed, his throat moving with the motion, before he whispered, "Don't… Don't marry him."

"What?" Shaun snapped, though it was breathless and made his cock twitch in his jeans. Those dark, raven wing eyebrows dipped low as she frowned, and the look of shock and confusion on her face would have made him chuckle if it weren't for the urgency to get the words out before she walked away from him again. That tool bag wasn't here with her, and he wasn't going to pass up the opportunity to make her understand how badly he didn't want her to marry that prick. She *couldn't* marry that loser. Whether she knew it yet or not, she was *his*. Had *always* been his.

"Don't marry him," he repeated, his throat going dry, and

then his eyes dropped to her mouth. Dammit he wanted to put his mouth on hers. Taste her lips, her tongue, feel it against his—

Her lips parted and her eyes went wide, and he nearly groaned with the effort it took to not duck his head and press his lips to hers. The bourbon had made him brave, but he held still, and the next second he heard her whisper, "What?"

Kasey shook his head, just barely, before raising his eyes to hers again. His fingers flexed around her bicep, nearly wrapping entirely around it. *God dammit she's infuriating.* "You heard me," he breathed huskily.

"I have no idea what you're talking about," she whispered, raising her chin haughtily.

"Yes, you do, Shaun," he growled, his voice dangerously low. His self-control was rapidly fading. "Don't marry him. I know you don't—"

He saw anger flash in her eyes, and she shoved him with one hand against his chest, though his fingers tightened around her arm, refusing to release her. "You don't *know* anything, Kasey," she hissed, trying again to pull her arm out of his grasp. He held tightly to her, pulling her closer as his face descended toward hers.

"I know that you feel… whatever this is, Shaun," he growled low through clenched teeth. He inhaled the scent of bonfire and a hint of cherry blossom, and he closed his eyes briefly before opening them again. "I know you feel it, just like I do. You can lie all you want, but I know you feel it, too. You want me as badly as I want you. He didn't even show up, Shaun. Left you alone all night."

Pain shuttered her eyes and her breath stilled. He hated the hurt he saw on her face, and it made him hate that douche bag even more. "I'll ask you again: Is your relationship with that tool bag everything you deserve? Are you happy? Because if you were, you wouldn't be thinking about how it would feel to have my cock buried inside you right now."

"You're an asshole," she spat, but it didn't hold the weight he was sure she meant it to.

"No, I'm *right*," he breathed, his lips dangerously close to hers. "You can't stop yourself from thinking about it anymore than I can. You wanna know how I can tell, darlin'?"

Her eyes dropped to his mouth, and he nearly lost it. He wanted nothing more than to slant his mouth over hers and kiss her, then bury his cock inside her so deep and so hard she forgot all about that limp noodle of a fiancé. Her breath was coming in short, rapid puffs against his face. He knew her body well enough to know she was just as turned on as he was, even if she didn't want to admit it.

He watched as she swallowed hard, and he grinned. Letting his mouth flit over the softness of her cheek, just outside of the curve of her mouth, he squeezed his eyes shut when he felt her head tilt to the side. Biting back the groan as her breath fanned over him, Kasey fought for the control that was very nearly gone.

"You have… several tells, Shaun. And every single one of them is like a drug to me. I can't… I can't get enough. Your breathing gets choppy, and I can see your breasts move with each breath you take. It makes this—" he touched the fabric that covered her chest with just the tips of his fingers, terrified if he touched anything else he wouldn't stop, "—flutter against your skin. This mouth, *Christ this mouth*," he groaned deep in his throat, sweeping the pad of his thumb over the curve of her full bottom lip, making her gasp lightly, "you bite this lip and I lose my mind a little more each time. Whether you like it or not, your eyes give you away, too. You give me that 'Come fuck me' look and it takes every ounce of self-control I have not to give you exactly what you're asking for." Shaun opened her mouth as if to protest, but he let his hand drift down, sliding his palm along the curve of her hip, and he could sense her own inner struggle that matched his own. "And you clench your thighs together when you're turned on, Shaun. Just like you're doing right now. Because you *ache* for me," he breathed, sliding his palm around her to press flat against her lower back, bringing his hips to hers so that she could feel his reciprocating arousal, "to fill you up so full you can't stand it. You ache for it, just as much as I do, darlin'. I'd bet my next race that you're wet for me right now."

Shaun's breath hitched in her throat again as he pressed against her, and he knew he was going to lose the fight with his self-control. She was too beautiful. Too sexy. Too close. He was painfully hard behind the fly of his jeans.

"I promise you if you were mine, darlin', you wouldn't be thinking about any other man," he breathed, his lips brushing once, twice, over the corner of mouth. Touching, but not quite…

He ached to press his lips to hers. Had wanted to taste her from the moment he'd seen her walking through that event tent at his cousin's wedding over a year ago. He knew she wanted it, too. He needed her to understand who she belonged to.

"But I'm not yours," she whispered back, her husky voice taunting, as if reading his thoughts.

"You want to be," he breathed on a grin, his lips flitting over hers, just barely. *Fuck* they were so soft. "*Don't marry him, Shaun.*"

"Why are you doing this?" she asked, her voice a mix of desire and anguish. She shifted her weight from one foot to the other, sliding her body directly against his erection. He groaned out loud this time, unable to stop the rumble from escaping his chest. He watched as one corner of her lips lifted in a seductive smile, the anguish from moments ago lifting from her eyes, and he just about lost it. Spreading his palm wide at the small of her back, he guided her even closer, fairly growling at the breathy gasp that escaped those perfect lips when she felt how hard he was against her, even as she whispered, "Kasey."

"Because I can't stay away from you," he breathed, his words choppy and uneven. He was milliseconds away from losing control and crushing her to him, crashing his mouth down onto hers like they both wanted. "And I can't stand the thought of his hands on you. He doesn't deserve you."

But Shaun shook her head, letting her lips brush across his. She wanted him to say it out loud, the damn minx. "And you think you do?"

He stared down at her, his own breathing harsh, his fingers rubbing along her back through the softness of her sweater. She pressed closer and he groaned, clenching his teeth together. He was about to give her exactly what she was asking for. He'd spin her around, put her hands on the railing of the porch, bend her over and—

"Why are you doing this?" she breathed, repeating her question from earlier, cutting off the fantasy that had just been running rampant through his mind, and tilted her head slightly closer. Their lips brushed again, lingering slightly longer, and he growled low in his throat. She was *killing* him.

Fucking *hell.*

Back off, man. She's still engaged, even if it is to a worthless prick that doesn't deserve her. Even if she wants this as bad as you do... she's still engaged and you'll both hate each other if you don't stop right now. She's not yours yet, *asshole.*

He felt her fingers as she slid her hand along his side, up his ribcage, before slipping around to press against his back, bringing her breasts into contact with his chest. Pushing the thoughts away, he nipped at her full bottom lip, making her gasp, and his cock throbbed in his jeans. "Tell me, Kase."

"Dammit, Shaun—"

The front door opened as the light from the entryway illuminated them, and Shaun jumped back, forcing him to release her. Roxy stopped on the threshold, her eyes bouncing from his face to Shaun's, before she grinned and then shut the door, shrouding them in darkness once more.

Kasey turned back to Shaun just as she whirled away, racing down the porch steps. "Shaun, stop!"

"No," she snapped, yanking her arm away as he tried to grasp her wrist in his hand. "I don't know what game you're playing, but it's not funny. Leave me alone!"

"Game?" he asked, stunned, stopping in the middle of the driveway as she yanked the driver's door of her truck open.

She waved one hand from his general direction to the porch where they'd just been, and he hated that guarded, hurt look that shuttered her eyes once more. "Yes, *game*, Kasey.

Whatever cruel game this is, I'm not playing it."

"Shaun—" he started, his voice dropping with regret.

"You did what you were supposed to; I've made it to my truck. Good night," she asserted, climbing up into the truck and slamming the door shut. He watched as she turned the truck on and then the tail lights came on as she backed up before pulling out of the driveway.

"Fuck!" he muttered darkly, spearing his fingers through his hair as he stared at the tail lights as they faded out of sight.

NINE

"Mornin."

Kasey grumbled something unintelligible to the fiery redhead sitting at the counter on one of the stools pulled up beneath it. Free stood with his hips against the kitchen counter, a cup of coffee sitting beside him.

"Did you guys finish off that bottle of bourbon last night?" Roxy asked them, leaning forward on her elbows, her hands clasped around a mug of steaming coffee. Sunlight filtered in through the sliding glass doors that led to a small back porch, and through the window over the sink, casting the kitchen in golden light. He glanced at the clock on the stove and grimaced. It was well into the morning. He'd slept later than he'd wanted to, probably due to the amount of liquor he'd consumed last night, before and after Shaun had left the party.

Kasey groaned and opened cupboards until he found one that housed the coffee cups, taking one down and pouring himself a hefty portion of black coffee. "No, I did that on my own." Sitting down on the empty stool next to Roxy, he sipped the coffee. "Where's Jodi?"

"She had to run a couple errands this morning– she should be back any moment," Free said, shifting from one foot to the other and reaching for his coffee. Bringing it to his lips, he took a drink, then nodded to the couch, where Kasey had just been sleeping. "So much for that hotel room you booked."

Kasey scrubbed his hands over his face and then shoved all ten fingers through the shaggy mess that was his hair. His head was pounding. "I don't even remember leaving the party last night. I didn't drive, did I?"

"Lord no," Roxy laughed, and he groaned at the sound. "Jodi's brother Tristan drove us all back here last night. You said you would just crash on the couch."

"No, what he said was 'Ughhshleep coush'," Freeman said in his best impression, chuckling when Kasey groaned again. "Wanna fill us in on what happened out on that front porch last night with a certain Kendall woman?"

"Nope," Kasey grunted, taking another drink of his coffee, staring straight ahead.

"Fair enough," Free chuckled again, taking another drink of his own coffee. "I warned you to stay away from her."

"Yeah, well," Kasey grunted, staring into the dark liquid in the cup clasped in his hands. Straightening his back, he looked first at Free then at Roxy. "When do you fly out?"

"Not until Tuesday morning," Roxy said, swiveling in her barstool to face him, bracing her bare feet on the rungs of his stool. "What about you?"

"I promised Charlie I'd be in Alabama by Tuesday. I fly out tomorrow afternoon."

"Always on the go," Roxy mumbled sourly, but she smiled gently. "You're doing really well this season."

Kasey shrugged. "The team has had a lot of success this year."

"You sound like you're not part of it," Free said from where he stood.

"It's just a very hectic schedule," Kasey admitted, swirling his coffee in his cup. "There's not much time for life outside of racing during the season. I'm ready for the off-season to start, ready for a little break. I like being able to hide away at home with no screaming fans or reporters shoving cameras and microphones in my face."

"Kasey Corcoran, ready for a break from being famous?" Roxy teased, shoving him gently in the shoulder.

He laughed then, nodding. "I'm not that famous," he mumbled humbly. "I'm no *Tony Stewart* or *Dale Earnhardt Jr.*"

"You probably get so much action on the circuit," Roxy sighed wistfully.

Free laughed out loud, crossing his feet at his ankles where he remained leaning against the counter. Kasey shrugged again. "We've got groupies that follow the circuit. Easy, but not all that worthwhile."

"Nah, you want something else," Roxy said and waggled her eyebrows at him. "A tall, dark-haired, blue-eyed bombshell that won't give you the time of day. You just like the chase, Kase."

Kasey admitted to himself that for most of his adult life, he had fully enjoyed the thrill of chasing women that played hard-to-get. Was that all this was with Shaun? Because she wasn't fawning over him like most other women did? He doubted it. There was something more about Shauntelle Kendall that drove him damn near insane.

"I need to shower," Kasey mumbled, rising from the barstool. "I smell like a bonfire."

"Towels are in the cupboard in the bathroom," Free said, pushing away from the counter. "Extra toiletries are in the bottom drawer of the vanity, help yourself."

"Thanks," he said as he refilled his coffee, raising it in a salute as he made his way out of the kitchen and down the short hallway to the bathroom that Jodi had shown him two days before. Closing the door, he turned the taps of the shower on, then stripped, folding his clothes and placing them on the sink. He hated the idea of putting the smoke infused clothes back on after his shower, but his things were back at the hotel that he hadn't stayed at the night before.

Stepping into the shower and under the warm water, he thought back to the night before, standing on the porch in the dark with Shaun, her body pressed close to his, and it wasn't long before his dick had hardened in memory of how she'd felt against him, how good she smelled, or how incredibly soft her lips had been as they'd brushed against his just the slightest.

Gnashing his teeth, he fisted his cock in his hand, willing it to go away, but the memory of her was too strong, too potent. Swearing silently, he let his hand move up and down the hard length, wishing it were Shaun's hand, her mouth, that sweet pussy, instead of his own hand. It didn't take long for him to come all over the floor of the shower, hissing in an unsteady breath as he emptied his balls.

Bracing one hand on the shower wall, he let his head hang until his chin almost touched his chest.

'I don't know what game you're playing, but it's not funny. Leave me alone!'

Game? he wondered again. Her statement had confused him last night, and he still didn't understand it this morning. The pain in her eyes before she shuttered them still made his chest ache. What was this damn minx doing to him? Scrubbing his hair clean, he ducked his head beneath the spray of the water.

She wanted him to leave her alone? Fine. He'd spent the last year trying to convince her of something she didn't want. He was done.

He scoffed to himself, hanging his head again.

Yeah right.

TEN

Doing her best to ignore the shadow that was Nate to her right, Shaun fumbled with the wrench in her hand, dropping it with a clang to the concrete floor beneath her back, narrowly missing her head. Swearing under her breath, she gave him a tight-lipped smile when he reached out to pick up the dropped tool and hand it back to her. "Thanks."

"You really ought to be more careful," he said, and she gritted her teeth, waiting for the next sentence she knew was coming. "A woman like you shouldn't be out here doing this dirty work. You could get hurt."

Reaching up to fasten the wrench around the bolt again, she grunted out, "I've been working on cars for a decade, Nate. I know what I'm doing. But thank you for the concern."

"If you were my girlfriend, you wouldn't even have to work, you know," he replied with what was probably supposed to be a disarmingly charming smile, but the dark look in his eyes bellied the charm, making her shiver in revulsion.

"Ugh, no thanks," Shaun muttered, turning her eyes away from him. "I don't date coworkers. And I'm not some damsel in distress. I don't need a man to take care of me. Besides, I like the work that I do. I'm good at it."

Nate laughed, and she turned her head to glare at him. "You're a novelty, Shaun. The only reason you get requested for jobs is so they can ogle you."

"No, I get requested to be put on jobs that you fucked up the first time," she snapped, sliding out from under the vehicle and sitting up, bracing her hands on her widespread knees, feet flat on the concrete floor. When his eyes dropped between her legs, she snapped her fingers in his face and snarled, "Hey, asshole, my eyes are up here, thank you."

A muscle twitched in his jaw as he clenched it and that dark, foreboding look in his eyes returned, making Shaun's heart feel like it was falling into her stomach.

"I was going to ask if you needed a date for that wedding you're going to, but fuck you," Nate sneered as he stood from where he had been kneeling beside her.

"And I've already told you a dozen times; *I don't date coworkers*. Or chauvinistic douche bags," she snapped as she stood, too, dusting her hands off on the thighs of her jeans. "I guess it's hard for a guy like you to understand that 'No' is a full sentence."

"I'm sure I can change your mind," Nate coaxed on a low murmur, though his eyes had taken on that darkness in them again, making her shiver.

"Don't bet on it," she muttered, turning away from him. "I have work to do, Nate."

Shaun waited until she heard his heavy footfalls fade away across the garage before letting herself take a deep, restorative breath in, bracing her hands wide on the edge of the work bench that covered a massive tool chest beneath it. Hanging her head between her shoulders, she closed her eyes.

What a fucking day. And it's only ten in the morning on a Monday.

A throat being cleared to her right startled her, and she opened her eyes, whipping her head around at the sound. She sagged against the bench, groaning audibly.

"What is it about men not taking no for an answer?" she asked out loud, straightening and crossing her arms over her chest, ridiculously self-conscious of the fact that she was wearing stained jeans and an old, long-sleeved *Petoskey Northmen* shirt that had motor oil, grease, and a little bit of jelly doughnut filling that had dropped onto her chest that morning all over it. Dammit did he look good, though.

His jeans were clean, and the army green, long sleeved Henley shirt he wore was unfairly well fitted to his chest, shoulders, and arms. The sleeves were pushed to his forearms, his hands tucked into the pockets on the front of his jeans, pulling them tight across the front. She raised her eyes to his, hating the knowing smirk on his too handsome face.

Notching one hip out, she asked acerbically, “Is there something I can assist you with, Kasey? I’m really not in the mood to spar with you this morning.”

Pulling his hands from his pockets, he took several steps forward, only stopping when he was just a couple feet from her. He hitched his chin toward the opposite side of the garage, and when she glanced over, she saw Nate watching them intently. “Was he bothering you?”

Shaun sighed heavily and shook her head, no. “He’s harmless.”

“Does he do that often?” Kasey prodded, his voice low and earnest. His eyes scanned hers and she felt a blush rise up her chest into her cheeks. Dammit.

Licking her lips, she shrugged. “It’s not a big deal, Kasey.”

“It is if you’ve made yourself clear and he’s not respecting that.”

Shaun laughed out loud at that, cocking one eyebrow high. “You do hear yourself, right?”

Kasey had the decency to look chagrined, his lips tilting up in the slightest smile, making his eyes crinkle at the corners, but his next words made her belly do flip-flops. “You and I both know there’s a difference, darlin’. You wouldn’t have almost kissed me Saturday night if you didn’t want it. You don’t want that sleazebag anywhere near you, that’s obvious.”

“I didn’t almost kiss you,” she whispered, her face flaming

as she stared up into those stormy, rain cloud blue eyes.

"Yes, you did," he whispered back, leaning slightly closer, so that less than a foot separated them. "And you're thinking about it right now."

"I am not," she argued, though it came out breathless.

"You're a terrible liar, Shaun," he chuckled, his eyes dropping to her lips. Then, he whispered, "Does your fiancé know that you think about me?"

Growling low in her throat, she shoved her hands into his chest, pushing him away from her with all her might, making him stumble back a step. "God you're such an *asshole*! Did you come here just to make fun of me? Get out, Kasey. Leave me alone."

"What? No," he murmured quietly, a look of confusion passing over his face briefly before taking that step forward again. She glared up at him, her lips pressed into a thin, hard line. "I can't leave you alone. I've fucking tried."

Her mouth opened in a silent gasp, her eyes going wide. "Try harder," she pleaded breathlessly, and his eyes dropped to her mouth before raising once again to hers. "Kasey, please."

He raised one hand, reaching out to tug on one stray curl that had fallen out of the messy bun she'd piled her curls into that morning, and she held her breath as he tucked it behind her ear, letting his fingers drift along her cheekbone. Then, his thumb trailed over her chin, before rising to sweep along the ridge of her bottom lip, making her gasp. Her heart thundered in her chest.

"I'm going to taste this mouth eventually, darlin'," he murmured huskily, and she believed him undoubtedly. "Tell me you don't want that."

"I don't want that," she whispered, but even she didn't believe the words.

He chuckled again, sweeping his thumb across her bottom lip one more time before letting his hand drop back to his side. "You're a liar. But I forgive you. Because I'm going to make you take back every lie you've told me, doll."

And then he was gone, sauntering back out the main garage bay door and out of sight while she struggled to remember how to breathe.

ELEVEN

"He's absolutely insufferable," Shaun muttered sourly, dropping down into the middle of the couch. Jodi laughed, rounding the corner of the couch to sink into it, two glasses of red wine in her hands. Shaun took one with a thank you, taking a long drink of it. Roxy followed, a glass in her hand, and she lowered herself into the far corner of the couch. "He thinks he's God's gift to women or something."

"Sounds like Kasey," Roxy muttered dryly, making Shaun nod in agreement.

"I mean, he is outrageously good looking," Jodi murmured, her tone light and teasing.

"I heard that," Free called from the kitchen, and the three women laughed.

"He's still got nothing on you, babe," Jodi called back, and then they heard Free chuckle. Turning back to Shaun, she asked, "So he just showed up, out of the blue? And what is this with that Nate guy?"

Shaun folded her legs beneath her and swirled the wine in her glass, staring into it. "He's been on this kick asking me out a lot lately. I've tried to explain to him that I'm not interested, and that I don't date coworkers, but he's not taking the hint." She shuddered then, remembering the darkness that sometimes lurked in his eyes. "He sometimes acts like I already belong to him. It's creepy."

Freeman rounded the corner from the kitchen into the living room, sitting on the arm of the couch next to where Jodi sat. "You don't think he's dangerous, do you?" he asked, and Shaun smiled at the protectiveness that hinted in his deep voice.

"No, I don't think so," she said hesitantly. "I'm never alone with him, though, so I'm really not worried. He's just a little overzealous."

"If you ever feel unsafe—"

"Dad made sure all of us kids took firearm safety classes, Free," Shaun said gently, cutting him off. "I have my concealed carry permit. I know how to disassemble, clean, and reassemble my pistol, and I'm a decent shot. It stays in my glovebox. He's harmless though, I promise."

"Keep it on you, if it's in the glovebox it doesn't do you any good," he said gruffly, and Jodi reached out to place a hand on his thigh, squeezing gently. Glancing over at the other end of the couch at the redhead that reclined in the corner, he said gently, "I just had to have this talk with Roxy, too."

"Yes, Dad," Shaun quipped dryly, but softened it with a

grin when he glared over at her from under dark brows. She laughed out loud. "I will keep it on me, I promise."

Free nodded and stood, retreating to the kitchen, and Jodi reached out to take a notebook off the coffee table in front of them. Opening it, she scanned it, running her finger down a long list written on it. "What do you want to work on tonight?"

"What do we have left?" Shaun asked, leaning over to read the list of 'to-dos' of wedding projects. Jodi and Free had decided on a small, intimate destination wedding at a secluded resort in the mountains of Colorado, so fortunately the on-site wedding coordinator was taking care of the majority of the planning, but Jodi had insisted on doing some of it herself, recruiting Shaun's help when necessary. Roxy had volunteered to help, so the three of them had made the plan to meet for wine. Pointing to one item on the list, Shaun said, "How about we package and seal all the sparklers for the send-off?"

"Perfect," Jodi said, setting the notebook down and rising from the couch, disappearing down the hall into the extra bedroom. She came back a minute later with a box laden with sparklers and little cardboard tabs that she had had designed to match their New Year's Eve wedding theme. Setting out the sparklers, the cardboard tabs that they would need to attach to each sparkler, and an extra box to put the finished products, they got started. "I can't wait to see the fireworks over the mountain at midnight."

"It's going to be great," Shaun agreed, taking a break to take a sip of her wine, which was very nearly empty. A brief wave of sadness washed over her, realizing that she and Tommy had never even made it this far in the planning of their own wedding before she'd called it off. But then the realization dawned that she wasn't necessarily sad about not getting married to Tommy, but more so she missed the friendship they'd had. Standing, she excused herself to the kitchen to pour herself another glass of wine, then leaned her hips back against the counter as she took a sip.

Roxy came around the corner into the kitchen, smiling as she reached for the almost empty bottle of wine, topping off her glass and reaching for a second bottle that was on the counter, waiting to be opened. Shaun handed her a corkscrew bottle opener, and after the cork had been pulled from the mouth of the bottle, Roxy set it aside to let the bottle breathe for a few minutes.

Leaning back against the counter across from Shaun, Roxy took a sip of her wine, then used her glass to motion toward her as she said, "Kasey isn't as bad as you might think, you know."

Shaun sighed, rolling her shoulders as tension filled them. "I'm sure he's not… but he makes me literally insane, Roxy. From the moment we met at Shane and Cassie's wedding… It's been volatile."

"Kasey has a very strong personality," Roxy admitted, her heavy Texas twang making Shaun smile. "He doesn't half-ass anything. I have the feeling you're the same way."

Shaun shrugged, taking a drink of her wine. "I'm just not the kind to be pushed around, and all Kasey seems to do is push my damn buttons all the time. I know what I won't settle for."

"Don't take this the wrong way, but can I ask why you were with your ex?" Roxy asked, crossing one arm over her middle, setting the wine glass on the counter beside her. Shaun's eyebrows rose in surprise at the boldness. "You say you know what you *won't* settle for, but it just seems out of character for someone so strong willed as you to… I don't know… *settle* for something that wasn't wholly fulfilling."

Taken aback, Shaun could only stare at the woman for a long heartbeat before blinking several times. "Who ever said it wasn't fulfilling?"

Roxy gave her a dubious look over her wineglass as she took another drink. "Intuition." Raising one crimson brow over her hazel eyes, she asked dryly, "Can you tell me that it was fulfilling, Shaun?"

"We were best friends," Shaun said defensively.

"Were you?" she asked. She pointed to the living room, where they could hear Jodi and Free murmuring to each other.

"That man in there has been my best friend for years. But our friendship is child's play compared to what those two share. What you and your ex had was the same as that?"

"Well, no—"

"He was your best friend, or were you just dating your best friend's brother?" Roxy asked, shifting from one foot to the other.

"You're kind of a pain in the ass," Shaun grumbled, crossing her arms over her chest.

"Did it just make sense?" Roxy pressed, and Shaun sighed, rolling her eyes.

"I guess you could say that," Shaun said sharply, glancing around the kitchen to avoid the other woman's knowing eyes.

"Was the sex good?" Roxy asked, and Shaun raised her eyes to the other woman's, her mouth dropping open, before glancing at the entrance to the living room. Roxy waved her hand and said, "They can't hear us. Well? Was it?"

"Tommy was the only one I've been with," Shaun said quietly. "It wasn't *bad.*"

"Did he make you come?"

"Jesus, Roxy," Shaun huffed out a breath, hating the blush that crept up her cheeks. "What does that matter?"

"Oh, trust me, it matters," Roxy laughed, taking a drink of her wine. "And that's probably why you're wound so tight around Kasey."

"For fucks sake," Shaun snapped, pushing away from the counter. "Did he put you up to this? Poking more fun at me?"

"Poking fun at you?" Roxy asked, her eyebrows shooting up in surprise. "That doesn't sound like Kasey. He doesn't joke about orgasms."

Shaun thought her eyeballs were going to explode out of her head as she stared at the redhead. "Did you and Kasey...?"

"Oh, fuck no," Roxy laughed gustily. "Kasey is like my third cousin twice removed or something, that's just nasty. I might have slept with Free a million years ago, but no, I didn't make a habit of sleeping around with all my guy friends." Still chuckling, she shook her head and that knot seemed to loosen in Shaun's stomach. Is this what Jodi had felt when she found out the gorgeous redhead had slept with Freeman prior to the start of their relationship? *Ugh, what an awful feeling,* Shaun thought as Roxy continued. "Kasey is brutally honest, always has been. He doesn't have it in him to beat around the bush, and as much of an ass as he can be, he doesn't have a deceptive bone in his body. So if he's pushing you, it's because he sees something worth pushing *for*."

TWELVE

"Where is your tux?"

Kasey notched his chin toward the front door and said, "Already hanging up in the car. I didn't forget it, Roxy." In the six weeks since the engagement party, she had sent him weekly reminders to pick up his tux.

The redhead nodded once, scanning her eyes over a handwritten list in her hand. He pointed to a garment bag hanging by the door and asked, "Is this your dress? Want me to take it to the car? Where's your suitcase? I can take that, too."

"That would be great," she said and walked into the bedroom, coming back a moment later with a rolling suitcase in tow. Kasey took the handle from her and picked up the long garment bag with his index finger, holding it aloft so it didn't drag on the ground. "Is this all you packed?"

"I'm only staying the weekend," she murmured, picking up her jacket and pulling it on before swinging her purse over her head and adjusting the strap that rested between her breasts. Glancing around the house one last time, she muttered, "I can't believe Freeman is getting married in the middle of the Colorado Rockies. In winter. I'm going to freeze my ass off."

"It's not like they're having the ceremony or reception *outside*," Kasey chuckled, heading toward the door with her suitcase and dress. "You'll be fine, you crybaby."

Roxy followed Kasey to the door, double-checking the lock as they exited. Loading her things into the trunk next to his, she climbed into the backseat of the Uber that was going to make the twenty-minute drive to the Fort Worth International Airport from her house in Melody Hills. She pulled out a pair of aviators from her purse and put them on, the sun shining directly into her window as the Uber pulled away from her house. Roxy had booked their flights, managing to seat them next to each other on the flight to Denver, a miraculous feat with the busy holiday travelers heading to Colorado for skiing during Christmas break.

Roxy was unusually quiet during the short ride, but Kasey was lost in his own thoughts as they got closer to the bustling airport. Freeman had called him early that morning as he was finishing packing, and he'd answered it, tucking the phone between his shoulder and ear as he zippered his suitcase closed. "Hey, man, how's it goin'?"

"Just getting settled into the vacation rental," Free had said. "Levi spared no expense, man. This place is awesome. I just wanted to call and let you know that Shane and Cassie had their baby last night."

"No way!" Kasey exclaimed, standing up straighter and switching the phone from one ear to the next. "That's awesome! Everyone doin' alright?"

"He says Cassie did great," Free said warmly, and then continued, "baby boy is doing just fine. Little smaller than they anticipated, but healthy set of lungs from what I could hear on the phone."

Kasey chuckled. "That's awesome, I'm glad to hear it."

"Uhh," Free began then, and the hesitancy in his voice made Kasey's brows draw together in worry. "I need a favor, though, Kasey."

"Anything," he said, pacing from the bed to the closet.

"Shane won't be making the trip out this weekend, so he can stay with Cassie and Samuel. I would really appreciate it if you could stand as my Best Man in his place, Kase," Free said gruffly, and Kasey smiled.

"I'd be honored," Kasey said and laughed when Free sighed in relief. "Were you worried I'd say no?"

"Not exactly," Free chuckled. "It just means that you'll be a little more hands on with Shaun than originally planned. She's Jodi's Maid of Honor. So that means—"

Kasey swallowed hard and muttered on a sigh, "Yeah, I know what that means."

It meant he would have to stand next to her, walk with her on his arm, *dance with her* throughout the evening. It would be Heaven and Hell all rolled into one.

Especially if that douche of a fiancé was with her. He squeezed his eyes shut and pinched the bridge of his nose with his thumb and forefinger.

"Will you guys be able to behave for a few hours?" Free asked and Kasey laughed, though it wasn't exactly a pretty sound.

"I'll be the perfect gentleman," Kasey murmured, tipping his head back to stare at the ceiling. Free laughed out loud.

"You wouldn't know the first thing about being a gentleman where she's concerned, but I appreciate it nonetheless," he laughed, and Kasey couldn't help rolling his eyes. "You're welcome to take over Shane and Cassie's room, that way you don't have to stay at the main lodge. There's plenty of room."

"I don't mind," he said gruffly, grabbing the garment bag that held his tux and laying it over the suitcase. There was no way he was staying in the same house as her and Tommy. Fuck that. He'd rather gargle shards of glass than be around to witness them together at such a romantic setting.

"Earth to Kasey..."

Yanked out of his reverie, he swung his head to look at Roxy, who grinned slyly. His mouth tightened in annoyance at being caught thinking about Shaun, again. "Huh?"

She pointed out the front windshield and said wryly, "We're here."

He turned his head and sure enough, the Uber was just pulling up under the massive parkway at the doors of the airport. She snickered and shook her head as she climbed out of the car, and Kasey took a deep, steadying breath before stepping out of the vehicle.

Pulling their luggage out of the trunk, he carried both of their garment bags on one crooked finger over his shoulder, his duffel bag over his other shoulder as Roxy walked ahead of him with her rolling suitcase trailing behind her.

"Have you decided what you're going to do?"

Standing in line waiting to check in, he glanced down into the hazel eyes of the one woman that knew him better than just about anyone. Her fiery red hair had been pulled into a messy topknot. Once inside the building, she'd shoved her sunglasses up to sit on the top of her head.

Kasey just wrinkled his nose and turned back to face forward, giving a barely noticeable shake of his head. "We'll see where the weekend takes me."

THIRTEEN

"Nope. No way."

Jodi smiled gently. "It won't be that bad."

"The answer is still no," Shaun muttered darkly, slicing her arm across her in the air. Jodi was dropping this bomb on her *the day before the wedding?* "I am not walking down the aisle with him. We'll kill each other. It's bad enough that you've shoved us together in this secluded mountain resort, and I refuse to walk with him or have to dance with him again. No."

Jodi sighed and crossed her arms over her chest. "Cassie had the baby last night; Shane can't leave them to come to the wedding. Kasey has agreed to step in as Best Man in his place. But that means—"

"I said no," Shaun snapped, standing and striding to the wide window that overlooked the snow-covered Rocky Mountainside beyond. It was gorgeous, and for a moment took her breath away, just like it had that morning when they'd arrived. The final six weeks leading up to the wedding had flown by, and before she'd known it, they'd been on the flight out to Colorado, bridal bags in tow.

"I wasn't asking, Shaun," Jodi snapped back, and Shaun turned to stare at her sister, who had placed her hands on her hips, her stance fierce. "Are you really telling me you can't be a mature adult for a few hours? After the wedding, *by all means,* go ahead and kill each other. But can you please put aside this ridiculous vendetta you have against Kasey long enough to be my sister and Maid of Honor? This is my *wedding*, Shaun. Please."

Shaun's shoulders sagged and she sighed in defeat. Her sister deserved the wedding of her dreams to the man of her dreams, after everything she had gone through. Shaun could at least pretend to get along with the cocky and arrogant bastard for a few hours. "Fine… Consider it your wedding gift."

Jodi beamed a smile and Shaun couldn't help the reciprocating one that tugged at her mouth. "I'll take it," Jodi said animatedly. "Thank you, Shaun. I couldn't do this without you standing up there with me."

"Yeah, yeah," Shaun muttered, though she softened it with a smile and a wink. "I'm getting drunk on your dime, just so you know."

"Dad's paying for the open bar," Jodi laughed. "So you're technically going to get drunk on his dime."

"Perfect," Shaun chuckled, reaching out and hugging her sister tightly. "I still can't believe we're in Colorado and you're getting married tomorrow!"

"I hope everyone can get here," Jodi fretted as they pulled away, glancing nervously out the window at the steadily falling snow outside. Levi and Serenity had booked a large vacation rental, and the first thing the girls had done when they arrived was to run through the massive house, checking out the gorgeous log cabin home. The massive house was set just a few hundred yards away from an expansive resort hotel, where the ceremony and reception would take place the following day.

The guest list for the wedding was small, close family and friends only. The house was large enough that the entire Kendall family, including Shaun's Uncle Micah and Aunt Summer, and the Storm clan, which consisted of their Uncle Spencer and Aunt Sadie and their Gram and Papa, along with the entire bridal party, would be staying under one roof. Rooms had been delegated, couples received their own room, but Shaun was bunked with Jodi for the night, keeping with tradition to keep the bride and groom separate the night before the wedding. Shaun had been surprised and thrilled that she would get the room to herself after the newlyweds left for their honeymoon the following day. Freeman and Kasey were sharing a room for the night despite Kasey being offered the room that Shane and Cassie would have been using, instead relinquishing it to Roxy so she could have her own room instead of bunking with Tessa and Kit or the three teenage girls in the Kendall and Storm family. Their brothers Warren and

Tristan had been bunked together, along with two other male cousins. It was a full house.

"This place is so pretty," Jodi whispered as she walked around the great room, walking over to the floor to ceiling windows that overlooked the mountainside. Skiers raced down the snow-covered slopes in the distance to their left. Directly out the double French doors, a large, rough-hewn, covered wooden porch extended out along the entire length of the house. Off to one side, Shaun could see steam from a massive hot tub sunken into the porch rising into the cool winter air. "Even better than the pictures."

"I can't believe you're getting married tomorrow," Shaun sighed, stepping forward. For being full of people, the house was surprisingly quiet, most of the occupants hiding away in their designated rooms after hours of traveling. Jodi and Free had decided on a New Year's Eve ceremony, and the resort was heralded to have a truly magical fireworks display at midnight. "Are you nervous?"

"No," Jodi said and smiled. "Just excited. I hope we remembered everything."

"We went over that checklist a dozen times," Shaun heard her mother say as she came up behind them. "And the wedding coordinator will be meeting us in a few hours to go over everything. Tonight and tomorrow are going to be perfect, sweetheart." Shaun watched as their mother hugged Jodi to her side. "I just can't believe it's already here. My little girl is getting married."

"I wish this was the first one," Jodi whispered wistfully, and Shaun watched as she fiddled with the diamond ring on her left hand.

Serenity squeezed Jodi's shoulders. "It will feel like it is, I promise. You and Free are right where you are supposed to be, at the right time. I'm just so glad you're finally happy. I always hoped you and Free would get here."

"We just took a little detour," Jodi laughed on a smile, and Shaun smiled back. Jodi then clapped her hands excitedly and asked, "What time are we supposed to be at the spa?"

"In about an hour," Seren said after glancing at the clock on the wall. "Shaun, why don't you start rounding up the girls?"

"Sure thing," Shaun said and gave her mom a mock salute, which earned her an eye roll from the older woman. The wide staircase that led to the second floor was made out of massive tree trunks and polished slabs of wood, and Shaun ran her hand along the smooth handrail as she climbed them. Lifting her chin, she stared up at the cathedral ceiling above her, swiveling her head this way and that to look at everything as she ascended the stairs.

Knocking on an open door of the first room she came to, she peeked her head in and said, "Tessa, Kit? We're going to be heading to the main lodge in a bit for the spa. Mom sent me up to gather everyone."

Tessa's blonde head popped around the corner and she smiled. "Fabulous. We'll be down in a few!"

Shaun continued down the hall, knocking on the next open door. She could hear all four of her aunts and uncles in the room, Uncle Micah and Uncle Spencer discussing the wildlife in the area while Aunt Summer and Aunt Sadie were busy packing a tote to take to the spa. "We're almost ready," Aunt Summer called, and Shaun kept on to the next room.

"Fallon, Cate, Kylee," she called in when she opened the door after a quick knock. All three teenage girls were laying on their stomachs across the multiple twin mattresses lined along the farthest wall, chatting animatedly. "We're leaving in about ten minutes."

The three girls squealed in excitement and gathered their bags, heading out the door and down the wide staircase moments later. Shaun rolled her eyes when she heard her cousin Cate say, "I wonder if we'll find any hot guys here this week!" and then Fallon's response of, "There was that cute guy at the lodge when we checked in!"

Continuing down the hall, she stopped at the next door, which was open.

"Roxy, are you ready to head to the lodge for the spa?" she called as she stepped into the room. When no response came, she rounded the corner and frowned when it was empty. Stepping back out of the room, she collided with a naked chest, her hands flying out to press against the smooth expanse of wet skin as strong hands gripped her upper arms to steady her. Her pulse quickened and she knew without raising her eyes who she was pressed against.

"Hiya darlin'," he drawled, and she could smell spearmint on his breath as it fanned over her face. She hadn't seen or spoken to him since the day he'd come to her shop, and dammit if he didn't still make her weak at the knees. She made to pull away, but he tightened his grip, muttering, "Don't move. Your body is the only thing keeping my towel on right now, doll."

Gasping, she jumped back reflexively, and the next second she felt the towel drop from around his waist to land at their feet. Her heart hammered in her chest knowing he was completely naked in front of her. She swallowed hard, keeping her eyes focused on his Adam's apple.

"I said *don't* move," he chuckled, though it was strained, then squeezed her arms once more before releasing them as he took a step back. Shaun slammed her eyes shut as he bent at the waist to retrieve the fallen towel, and she could hear the rustle of the fabric and the whoosh of air as he wrapped it around his waist again. "You can open your eyes, Shaun. I swear you won't go blind if you look."

"I don't need to see anything of yours," Shaun snapped, though she did open her eyes, only to raise them to his and glare up into those gray-blue eyes that were crinkled at the corner with laughter.

"Did you get a good feel, then?" he asked quietly, ducking his head close to her ear.

Shaun rolled her eyes and snapped, "Feel what? That twig between your legs?"

Dropping his voice, he whispered, "You and I both know that's not what I'm working with, darlin'."

"You're such an ass," she sneered, pulling away from him. "Why are you walking around naked anyway?"

Kasey shrugged, readjusting the towel so it was more securely fastened around his waist. "Is it a crime to take a shower?"

"No, but what if it was Fallon that had run into you instead of me? She's only seventeen, you perv."

Kasey grimaced, then nodded. "True. I'll keep that in mind. I'll be out of here tomorrow anyway."

"What? Why?" she asked, surprise drawing her brows together.

Shaun was sure her heart was going to pound its way out of her chest when he stared down at her with those intense storm-cloud blue eyes, as if he was trying to see all the way through her. His lips thinned then, and he said quietly, "You know why, Shaun."

She swallowed hard, and he nodded, then excused himself as he stepped around her, shutting himself into one of the rooms without looking at her again.

FOURTEEN

Shutting the door, Kasey leaned with his forearm braced above his head, his forehead pressed into the wood of the door and took deep, steadying breaths until he heard her footsteps fade down the hallway.

He'd agreed to stay in the bridal party house for the night at Free's request, but it was turning out to be pure torture.

She was going to be in the same house, just a room away. And sometime today or tomorrow that douche bag was going to show up, put his hands all over her, kiss her, probably make love to her in that big bed with that amazing view of the mountain… he couldn't stay and be a witness to it, when he wanted nothing more than to be the one doing those things to her. Fucking Christ, if purgatory were a place, this was it.

He hadn't had the balls to ask Free when Tommy would be showing up, but he knew it had to be before the ceremony tomorrow. The idiot had missed the engagement party, but only a fool would choose to miss a wedding of the family he was marrying into.

And then Kasey would have to endure the entire wedding

watching her being fondled and kissed by that useless tool.

From inside the door, he heard the women of the house convening in the great room to head over to the main lodge for a spa excursion. He was grateful that Shaun was going to be gone most of the day. He wouldn't have to see her again until the rehearsal.

Fuck, he thought mulishly as he padded over to his suitcase, pulling out a fresh pair of clothes. He pulled on a pair of boxer briefs, then shoved his legs into a pair of jeans. Tugging a white Henley over his head, he ruffled the towel over his still damp hair as a knock sounded on the door, then a second later it opened and Free entered.

"The girls all left for their spa afternoon," he said and shook his head. "You'd think they'd won the lottery with how excited they all are."

"Something about a sauna, hot tub, massages, and champagne just makes women batty," Kasey chuckled, running his fingers through his hair to push it away from his forehead. He sat down on the foot of one of the beds, pulling a clean pair of socks on his feet before sliding them into a pair of black work boots. He tied the laces and then stood, stretching his arms high over his head. "What's the plan for us manly men while the women get pampered?"

Free laughed and said, "Levi said for us to meet at the bar at the resort in a couple hours. We're eating lunch and then I guess there is a lounge with billiard tables and darts. After that we'll come back and get ready for the rehearsal dinner and then meet everyone at the main lodge around six o'clock." Freeman glanced over at him and eyed him knowingly. "Please don't be an ass to Shaun until after Jodi and I leave for our honeymoon."

Kasey crossed his finger over his chest, drawing a large X. "I swear, I'll behave." Free gave him a dubious look, and Kasey laughed as he turned toward the closet, where he had hung up his tux for the following day and a pair of dress slacks and two button-down shirts. Changing the subject, he asked, "Dress code for tonight?"

Free shrugged, walking toward a garment bag that had been draped over the foot of the other bed. He picked it up and carried it to the closet, too, where he unzipped it, rifling through the clothes on the hangers. "I've got black slacks and a white button-down for tonight. I'm not wearing a tie for rehearsal."

Kasey held up the two dress shirts he'd brought with him, holding first one up to his chest and then the other. The first was a grayish blue, the second was a simple white. Free pointed to the grayish blue one, and Kasey nodded in agreement. The slacks he had chosen for the evening were a deep navy, his shoes a cognac brown leather. A matching belt was inside his suitcase.

Stepping back over to his suitcase, he unrolled a t-shirt,

revealing a bottle of twenty-five-year bourbon, handing it over to Free, who took it with a long, low whistle of appreciation before passing it back. "Jesus, Kasey. That's some good stuff."

"My cousin and best friend only get married once," he said, opening it and taking a deep inhale. Crossing to the dresser where he had placed a couple highball glasses from the kitchen downstairs, he poured a finger into each glass, then held one out to Freeman. "To the same woman every night for the rest of your life."

"Damn straight," Free said and laughed, then they both took sips of the amber liquor. Free made an appreciative hum in the back of his throat and Kasey nodded in agreement, taking another swallow. "May your wedding be the next one we have."

Kasey laughed, shaking his head. "That's farfetched, Free. The closest I got was with Savannah, and we both know how that ended."

"Have you seen her since y'all split?" Free asked, taking another sip.

Kasey shook his head. "Nah. She's somewhere in California with her new hot-shot fiancé. Good riddance. Models are a fucking nightmare."

Finishing the bourbon in their glasses, they made their way down into the great room, where the men of the house had started to gather. Levi and his younger brother Micah Kendall, who was married to Serenity's younger sister, Summer, had claimed two large recliners in front of a massive stone fireplace that had a roaring fire already built in it.

Four younger guys, who Kasey had been introduced to as Jodi and Shaun's brothers and cousins, were fighting over the remote of the tv. Summer and Micah's youngest, a six-year-old little boy, was running around with a toy car, zooming it across every conceivable flat surface in the place.

"Guys," Levi barked when the teen boys' bickering got louder, and the lot of them went silent. "Come on. You're not kids anymore. Can we not do this? Are you all ready to go in a bit?"

Kasey grinned. He really liked Levi Kendall. He was a no-nonsense, call it like he sees it kind of guy, and he respected that immensely. He reminded him of his own dad.

An older, white-haired gentleman had fallen asleep in a lazy-boy recliner, snoring gently. Kasey knew that was Paul Storm, Shaun and Jodi's maternal grandfather. Levi woke him several minutes later to ask if he was joining them, but the older man declined, saying he'd rather stay in and enjoy the quiet of the house.

It seemed like moments later that Levi's booming voice thundered through the room to announce that the resort shuttles had arrived to transport them to the main lodge, and the whole group of them filed out and climbed into the transit vans waiting for them. Depositing them at the front doors of the massive log cabin inspired resort, it didn't take them long to locate the lounge. Billiard tables, dart boards, shuffleboards, air hockey, foosball… you name it, and they had it. Kasey could hear old fashioned pinball machines along the farthest wall, and a wide bar made of one massive tree slice had polished, black leather barstools tucked up to it. Too many beer taps to count and hundreds of bottles of liquor sat along a mirrored wall behind the bar. Kasey could smell burgers, hot wings, and freshly made popcorn. It was a man cave on steroids.

The hours passed quickly, pool games won and lost, someone's finger got caught between an air hockey puck and the side of the table, and after the third beer Kasey declined another from the smartly dressed bartender. When Levi sidled over toward him and Free as they set aside their billiard sticks, the older gentleman said gruffly, "We should start rounding up and heading back. The girls will shoot me dead if we're late to rehearsal."

After the lot of them clambered back into the shuttles that returned them to the massive vacation rental just down the road, they all climbed the wide staircase up to the second floor to their respective rooms to shower and change for the evening.

The girls had returned from the spa all giggly, rejuvenated, and relaxed, and when Kasey passed Shaun in the hallway, he nearly lost his mind at how fucking good she smelled; like coconut lime verbena body oil and pink Himalayan sea salt. Even the hint of chlorine that still clung to her skin from the hot tub smelled intoxicating. Her hair was curlier than normal, tied up on the top of her head in a loose knot, tendrils falling freely around her face and the back of her neck.

Kasey made quick work of the erection that ensued while taking a brief shower, positive that he was going to lose his ever-loving mind by the end of the weekend.

Dressing in the dusty blue button-down shirt and navy slacks he'd set out earlier, he was putting on his shoes just as Free was sliding his feet into a highly polished pair of black cowboy boots. Crossing to the dresser where he'd left the bottle of twenty-five-year bourbon earlier, he poured some into the two glass tumblers he'd snagged earlier and turned, handing one to Freeman.

"Nervous yet?" Kasey asked after they clinked glasses. Raising it to his lips, he took a swallow, humming in appreciation at the aged bourbon. Free did the same, swirling it in his glass several times, shaking his head.

"Not at all," his best friend said quietly, and Kasey could hear in his voice the conviction of his words. "I've never been more sure of something. Jodi is everything I'll ever need in this life. I pray that I can always be that for her, too."

Kasey clapped Free on the back, squeezing his shoulder

tightly before dropping his hand. "If the way that woman looks at you is any indication, I'd say you're doing just fine, my friend."

They drained their glasses and set them down before heading out the door together. They'd just made it to the top of the stairs when Kasey realized he'd left his watch on the counter in the bathroom and said, "I'll be down in just a second."

Strapping the watch to his wrist as he walked, he nearly barreled into Shaun as he exited the room. The audible gasp that escaped her as his hands circled her upper arms went straight to his dick and he nearly groaned; a lot of good that jerk off session had done. The little navy-blue dress she wore should have been outlawed.

Releasing her as soon as they both had their balance restored, she stepped back, her eyes flying to his.

"I'm sorry—"

"I wanted to—"

They both stopped talking at the same time, and Kasey said gruffly, "Sorry, go ahead."

Shaun bit her bottom lip, a sheen of shimmery gloss coating them, before sticking her hand out to him as if to shake his. He stared down at her extended hand, one brow rising quizzically.

"I promised Jodi that I would behave this weekend. This

is her wedding, and she deserves nothing but the best. I am willing to put aside whatever this—" she waved at the space between them, "—is, if you are. No snarky comments, no sexual innuendos, no shitty attitudes."

Taking her hand in his, he said, "Deal."

She made to pull her hand out of his grasp, but he held tightly, pulling her slightly closer as his lips tilted up into a grin. Leaning down until his lips brushed against her cheek, he murmured, "But the second those two leave for their honeymoon, deal is over, darlin'. I'm not leaving this mountain without tasting you at least once."

FIFTEEN

"If you keep your face like that for too long it's going to get stuck like that."

Shaun turned to glare at her father, who had just sidled up to her while they waited for the wedding planner to finish walking the groomsmen through their roles.

"You said the same thing about sitting too close to the TV when we were kids. Yet not one of us went cross-eyed," she muttered sourly as she turned back to face forward, crossing her arms over her middle.

Levi's low chuckle both calmed her and irritated her. She didn't want her dad to be funny, not when Kasey was driving her absolutely insane.

She'd tried to be the bigger person. She'd sought him out, shaken that stupidly strong hand of his that made butterflies whip around in her belly, and said she'd behave if he would.

"I'm not leaving this mountain without tasting you at least once."

Those huskily whispered words—a dark promise—his lips moving directly against her cheek, damn near touching the corner of her mouth, all of it combined to cause an awful, delicious ache in the deepest part of her.

He was being a perfect gentleman. Not one sly glance, not one provocative remark, not a single ungentlemanly touch had come her way from the man since he'd stepped away from her and sauntered down the staircase at the vacation rental. She'd stood at the top of the stairs, as if in a stupor, for long minutes, willing her heart to slow its frantic pace in her chest, or the trembling in her hands to cease. He was doing exactly what she asked of him.

So why was she so irrationally angry that his eyes never lingered on her in the skintight bodycon dress that she *knew* highlighted her full hips, the narrowness of her waist, and the roundness of her breasts?

"Okay, let's run it from the top again, please," the wedding planner called to the room, and Freeman, Roxy, and the groomsmen made their way back down the aisle from where they'd all been stationed where the altar would be the following day. A set of double doors stood open at the entrance to the ceremony space, where the bridal party would enter through. Jodi and Free had chosen to say their vows in front of a massive set of floor to ceiling windows overlooking the snow-covered mountain beyond. "Ladies, please get in line in the order that you will be walking down the aisle. Jodi and Mr. Kendall will be last."

The drop-dead gorgeous blonde, giant ipad in hand, smiled coquettishly at Kasey as he made his way back down the aisle. He winked at the woman, which made her smile seductively, and Shaun gnashed her teeth together at the flash of irrationally intense jealousy that rampaged its way through her body. Her lips tightened into a hard line as she made a half turn away from him, but not before she saw Roxy elbow him hard in the side, making him wince and clutch his ribs with an audible, "Ow!"

As the women lined back up on the other side of the double doors, the wedding planner cued the music to start, and they were off again. They ran through it twice more before both Jodi and the wedding planner were confident that everything was nailed down and running smoothly. At the end of each run-through, when Kasey would extend his arm to her to take as they made their way down the two small steps from the raised dias in front of the windows, Shaun would steel herself as she placed her hand in the crook of his elbow. The entire walk back down the aisle was pure torture; her hand tucked into his elbow, her fingers stiff against the soft fabric of his shirt.

As soon as they made it down to the end of the aisle, he would release her, turning away from her as if she didn't exist.

Dinner went much the same.

They were seated in a private room of one of the

restaurants at the resort, served by impeccably dressed waitstaff. It was evident her father had spared no expense. The food was phenomenal, the wine divine, the company some of the best. Her sister was relaxed and radiant with Freeman by her side. Her mother was having a hard time keeping tears from her eyes, and her father routinely reached out to kiss them away with quiet murmurs. Roxy was flirting shamelessly with one of the handsome waiters to Shaun's left, and across the table from her, Kasey was deep in conversation with his father and younger brother who had flown in earlier that afternoon. Not once did he look her way.

By the end of the night, Shaun had worked herself into a fine fit. She'd wanted him to *behave*, not ignore her completely!

The wine had put a flush to her cheeks after her third glass, and as they all climbed into the shuttles that would take them back to the vacation rental for the night, Shaun shrugged out of her jacket, too warm from the wine and the heat in the vehicle.

"I know it's an exciting night, but please don't stay up late!" her mother called to the group of them. Levi already had her hand in his, pulling her toward the wide staircase. Shaun prayed that the walls in this house were soundproof.

Free motioned to the bridal party as a whole, and the group of them circled a giant marble island in the kitchen as he produced a bottle of tequila and several limes. Roxy grinned and said, "Oh hell yes," as she began lining up plastic shot glasses that Free set on the countertop. Tessa found a cutting board and a knife and began slicing the limes as Free poured out enough shots for the group—all but Fallon and Tristan, anyway, who were still underage—and once everyone had a shot in hand, Free looked around the room.

"I want to thank you all for being here with us. We wanted this weekend to be for close family and friends only, and to have this group of people here, standing with us tomorrow as I marry the most beautiful woman in the entire world... Thank you. We wouldn't want anyone else standing with us tomorrow," he murmured earnestly, and then raised his shot.

"Here here!" Kasey called, reaching his shot glass out to clink it against Free's, and then Jodi's. The rest of them followed suit before tossing back the clear liquor. It burned Shaun's throat as she swallowed, chasing it by sticking the lime between her lips and sucking.

It wasn't until she brought her eyes to Kasey's that she nearly stopped breathing, the intensity of his stare burning straight through her. His eyes dropped to her mouth as she plucked the lime wedge from between her lips, licking them nervously.

Jodi waved her hand when Free made to pour out another round, saying, "No more for me! I don't want to be hungover tomorrow!"

Shaun lowered her eyes from Kasey's as Free gathered her sister in his arms, kissing her soundly. Jodi came up laughing from the kiss, pecking her lips against her fiancés again sweetly.

Whispered murmurs drifted from the two of them, but the group ignored them, trickling away from the island countertop, leaving them alone. Roxy and Kasey walked together toward the staircase, Kit and Tessa following behind. Warren and Tris plopped into the two giant leather recliners and turned the TV on, finding a replay of an NBA broadcast.

"Not too loud," Shaun muttered as she walked past them, and Tris saluted her, which made her smile.

Doors along the long hallway were closing, others left open with a dim lamp lit, which sent beams of light into the dark hall. Tessa and Kit were sitting cross legged on their beds, Roxy lay flat on her stomach next to them. Roxy waved, getting Shaun's attention as she walked past. "Hey, come in for a few!"

Shaun entered, crossing the floor until she reached one of the beds, falling back onto it with a flop and a heavy sigh. "I want to go sit in the hot tub but I'm too tired. I'm afraid I'd fall asleep sitting in the water and drown. Then one of you would have to give my speech tomorrow."

"Nope," Tessa laughed, shaking her head adamantly. "I don't do public speeches. No dying tonight."

Kit was scanning over a printed itinerary of the next day's

schedule that the wedding planner had handed to the entire bridal party after rehearsal had ended. “We have plenty of time to relax tomorrow morning. We don’t have to start hair and make-up until one in the afternoon, since the ceremony doesn’t start until sundown.”

“It’s going to be such a long day,” Shaun groaned. “I don’t know if I’ll make it to midnight to watch the fireworks.”

“Anyone taking bets on Jodi and Free sneaking out in the middle of the night to see each other?” Roxy asked, swinging her head to look at the other three.

Shaun laughed, still laying on her back, staring up at the log ceiling. “One hundred percent going to happen.”

The other three women laughed, and Shaun rolled into a sitting position. “I’m heading to bed. Y’all should think about it, too.”

A chorus of “Okays” from the other three met her as she crossed to the door, exiting into the hallway and heading down to the room she would be sharing with Jodi for the night.

Slipping out of the skin tight bodycon dress, she left it on the floor and stripped off her thong and matching lace bralette, padding naked over to where her suitcase was still laying open on her bed. Rifling through the clothes, she found a pair of boy short underwear and pulled them up her legs. Next, she pulled on a well-worn t-shirt that hung clear to mid-thigh. She was fairly certain it had belonged to Tommy, left behind after he’d left town. At first, she'd kept it for sentimental reasons, but now it was just a comfortable sleep shirt.

Taking her hair down from the high topknot she'd pulled her curls into, she shook her head, running her fingers through it enough to detangle some of it, before securing it into a loose French braid over one shoulder.

She had washed her face and was brushing her teeth when Jodi finally came into the room, looking well-kissed, her curls a finger tumbled mess around her head. She closed the door and leaned back against it.

"Jid ou uys oo iht ihn dhe kishen?" Shaun asked around her toothbrush, leaning out the bathroom door to glare at her sister.

Jodi rolled her blue eyes that were so similar to her own and shook her head. "Not entirely."

"Eww, grosh," Shaun groaned before going to the sink to rinse. Putting her toothbrush on the bathroom counter, she turned the water off and flipped the lights off. Crossing to the bed, she jumped into the middle of it, bouncing as she landed. "I hope we can't hear Mom and Dad tonight. They're always the worst."

"The worst," Jodi laughed, crossing the room to stand at the edge of the bed, then turned her back, pulling her hair to one side. "Can you unzip me?"

Shaun rolled to the edge of the bed, reaching up to unzip

the pretty white cocktail dress Jodi had chosen for the evening, before flopping back onto the bed when Jodi thanked her and walked into the bathroom.

Shaun was almost asleep, still on top of the covers, when Jodi exited five minutes later, dressed in a pair of white lounge shorts and a button-down, short sleeve sleep shirt in a buttery soft material with 'Bride' embroidered in gold thread over her left breast. Her hair had been pulled into a high knot on the top of her head and her face was clear of make-up.

"Where are the maid of honor pj's I got you to wear?" she heard Jodi ask petulantly, slapping her on the back of the thigh.

"I'm going to wear them tomorrow to get ready," Shaun mumbled into her pillow without turning her head. Yawning broadly, she said, "You're lucky I'm wearing clothes at all."

"Scooch *over*," Jodi whined, pushing hard on Shaun's deadweight body that was taking up the entire bed, since she'd laid on it diagonally.

"You have a whole bed over there," Shaun whined back, but smiled when Jodi shoved again, rolling her over onto her back until her head was hanging off the edge. "Sleep in your own bed!"

"No," Jodi grumbled, pushing Shaun's feet aside and climbing into the bed under the covers, snuggling down into them. "I want to sleep with you tonight. *Move over!*"

Laughing, Shaun righted herself on the bed and slid under

the covers too, rolling to her side and stacking her hands beneath her right cheek, Jodi facing her in the same position. "You're getting married tomorrow."

"I'm getting married tomorrow," Jodi whispered reverently, and Shaun watched as her blue eyes shimmered with tears. "I love him so much."

"I know," Shaun whispered back, reaching out to tuck a strand of hair behind her sister's ear. "You're going to be the most beautiful bride, sis."

Jodi caught her hand as she made to bring it back, squeezing it three times, their secret way of saying, 'I love you'. Shaun squeezed back four times, 'I love you, too' the response. "Thank you for being here."

"I wouldn't miss it for the world," Shaun said quietly, then yawned again. "Now go to sleep. You need all the beauty rest you can get."

"You're a brat," Jodi laughed, but snuggled deeper into the pillows. Within minutes, Shaun knew Jodi was asleep by her slow, rhythmic breathing.

She was asleep in minutes herself but awoke only a couple hours later. Glancing at the clock, she saw that it was only two in the morning. She knew without rolling over that Jodi was no longer in the bed and rolled her eyes, not in the least surprised. She sighed quietly into the dark before sliding from beneath the sheets and padding to the door.

The giant house was dark and silent, except for the quiet noises coming from Free's room, and Shaun hurried down the hallway and down the wide staircase. Crossing to the kitchen, she opened the fridge, taking a bottle of water out and drinking half of it before closing the fridge door, once again ensconcing the room in darkness. There was faint moonlight filtering in through the wide windows in the great room, the snow having finally given way to a cloudless, star filled sky.

"Is that *his* shirt?"

Shaun squeaked in alarm at the husky growl that came from somewhere in the dark behind her. Spinning on her bare feet, she swallowed hard when she saw the outline of Kasey sitting in a high-backed armchair across the room. The moonlight cast him half in shadow, half in pale light. He was slouched slightly in the chair, reclining on his tailbone, his thighs widespread. One arm lay along the arm of the chair, his long fingers clasped around a crystal glass with several inches of amber liquor. He wore a pair of dark sweatpants and a black sleeveless tank top that clung to his upper body. His arms were well muscled and bare for her to stare at.

"Wh-what?" she asked, the word coming out way more breathless than she'd intended. Her heart hammered in her chest.

"Is that *his* fucking shirt?" he asked again, the darkness in his voice making her nerves skitter.

"So what if it is?" she asked, straightening slightly.

In the faint glow of moonlight, she watched his chest expand with a slow, deep breath in and his fingers shifted around the highball glass that glittered in the silver light.

"Take it off."

"Excuse me?" Shaun gasped in outrage.

"I didn't stutter, Shaun."

"No," she snapped, setting the water bottle down on the island she stood next to, placing her hands on her hips defiantly.

Fear, dread, excitement, she wasn't sure what it was, snaked through her when he stood in one fluid motion, lifting the glass to his lips as he prowled—yes, *prowled*—toward her. Setting the glass down on the marble countertop as he reached her, he leaned closer and snarled through clenched teeth, "*Take. It. Off. Shaun.*"

"I can't," she whispered, heat rising to her cheeks. "I'm not wearing anything under it."

"You can take it off or I will take it off for you," he continued, leaning forward until she backed up against the edge of the counter. His arms reached out, bracing his hands on either side of her.

"I'm not taking my shirt off in front of you, Kasey," she breathed.

Stepping back a half step, he reached up and gripped the

collar of the tank top he wore, pulling it up and over his head in one motion, until he stood in front of her with his entire upper body and torso naked to her. Her mouth went dry, and she had to fight the urge to reach out her hands and run them over the muscles that rippled along his abdomen. The muscles of his abs arrowed down in a V into the waistband of his sweats, slung indecently low on his hips, and the sight made her mouth water. He held out the shirt to her at the same time he muttered darkly, "Take off that fucking shirt, Shaun. I won't say it again."

Growling at him, she slapped his hand away that held out his shirt and grabbed the hem of Tommy's t-shirt, pulling it over her head and then dropping it to the floor. She snatched his tank top out of his hands, ignoring her heart as it pounded out a beat in her chest. Her breasts were bare, but he held her gaze. Glaring at him through the darkness, she slid her arms into the tank top and tugged it over her head, letting the soft material conform to her breasts. It was long, covering her bottom in the boy-short underwear she wore. He bent at the waist, picking up the discarded shirt and balling it up in his hands.

"That's better," he murmured, reaching out and letting the back of his index finger trail down her side, over the ribbed material of the shirt. Slapping his hand away, she glared up at him in the dark.

"You're a bully," she hissed as he backed away.

Holding the shirt that had very clearly offended him so badly out in front of him, he shook it in his fist as he growled, "If he's not man enough to show his fucking face, you don't get to wear his clothes in front of me."

Shaun spluttered in outrage, but he was already striding across the room, his feet carrying him up the stairs until he disappeared from sight.

SIXTEEN

"You're in a foul mood this morning," Roxy drawled as she crossed the room, and he grunted from the tufted armchair he'd slept in for the latter half of the night to give Jodi and Free their privacy when she'd knocked on the door at one-thirty in the morning. "Guess Shaun and I won that bet."

"What bet?" he grumbled as he rolled into a sitting position from the slouch he'd been resting in.

"We knew Jodi and Free wouldn't stay apart last night," Roxy laughed, coming toward him with a steaming cup of coffee from downstairs. "You should have kept this room. Or you could have slept on the bed. I don't bite."

"You were sprawled across the whole damn thing," he muttered as he accepted the mug from her. "Just because I couldn't sleep didn't mean I needed to keep you up, too."

"Oh, darlin'," Roxy drawled, winking at him, which made him roll his eyes, "you only wish."

"Gross," he muttered, but his lips tilted up in a half grin.

"What is this?" she asked, picking up the shredded remains of the t-shirt he'd conned off of Shaun the night before. He made to swipe it from her hands, but she jumped back with a devilish laugh, holding it up the best she could with how badly he'd mutilated it in his rage. She pointed to his bare chest, one red eyebrow arched knowingly, as she murmured, "So, this is why Shaun was downstairs wearing your tank top."

It wasn't a question, but a statement, one he didn't deign to respond to. Standing, he dropped the throw blanket he'd tugged off the foot of the bed after sneaking into her room back onto the chair he'd just vacated. Striding on bare feet to the door, he opened it and exited into the hall, grinding his teeth at the sound of Roxy's laugh. He found perverse pleasure in the fact that Shaun had worn his tank top for the rest of the night, sleeping in it. His dick twitched at the thought.

There was a flurry of activity down in the great room, but he turned and headed further down the hallway to the room he was supposed to have shared with Free the night before. The door was open, so he walked inside to find Free standing at the window staring out over the mountain beyond. When he heard Kasey enter, he turned, grinning sheepishly. "Thanks for uh—"

"What's the best man for if not facilitating a late-night rendezvous with the bride?" Kasey chuckled, waving his hand. He nodded his head toward the door. "Did you get any coffee yet or are you quarantined up here?"

"I've been instructed to stay up here until the girls leave

for the main lodge in an hour," Free chuckled.

Kasey set his coffee down and rifled through his suitcase until he found a clean shirt, pulling it over his head. "I can run down and grab you some."

"Thanks, I appreciate it. I thought Levi was coming back with some, but that was like fifteen minutes ago," Free said and rolled his eyes.

"I'll be right back," Kasey said and exited the bedroom, carrying his coffee with him as he descended the stairs. The noise from below got louder as he got closer, and he realized most of the women were in the kitchen. Hanna, Summer, Sadie, and Seren were dishing up massive amounts of food. Scrambled eggs, bacon, sausage links, pancakes, a pile of fresh fruit, and assorted bagels covered the marble countertop island in the kitchen. A stack of paper plates and plastic cutlery were stationed at the head of the counter.

Keeping his eyes on what he was doing, he poured a cup of coffee for Freeman, then topped off his own before turning from the far side of the kitchen to face the room. Tristan had Ben on his shoulders while the six-year-old held a toy airplane high in the air, and they raced around the room, making the little boy giggle happily.

The bridesmaids and Jodi were surrounding the massive dining table to the right, and Kasey let his eyes wander over Shaun while she was talking to Kit and Tessa. She had on a short sleeved, button-down sleep top that had Maid of Honor embroidered over her left breast, but it was left unbuttoned, the sides hanging open, revealing the ribbed material of his black tank top as it conformed to her breasts in a way that made his dick jump.

Shaun turned and caught him staring, and though her blue eyes shot fire at him, she didn't say a word. Jodi turned her head and blushed furiously, smiling shyly. He winked at her and he saw Shaun roll her eyes and huff in annoyance, which just made him grin as he wandered over closer.

"Happy wedding day," he murmured and bent to kiss the top of Jodi's head. She giggled and swatted him away.

"Thank you. Are you taking coffee up to Free?" she asked, motioning to the two cups of coffee in his hands. "Dad wouldn't let me take it up."

Wiggling his eyebrows, he made the table laugh as he whispered loudly, "Are you trying for round two?"

Tessa cackled from the other side of the table and muttered dryly, "Ha. Try round four."

"You hussy," Kasey teased, winking at her again, making her blush to the roots of her hair. "But yes, I am taking coffee up to your betrothed. Ladies," he drawled, notching his chin at the women sitting around the table.

It took every ounce of willpower he possessed to walk away from the table and not stay to stare at the sight that was

Shaun wearing his shirt. He liked it far too much.

He shoved down the memory of seeing her topless in the faint glow of moonlight last night when she'd yanked that tool's shirt over her head. Not exactly the way he'd hoped to see her naked for the first time, but the image was burned into his brain, nonetheless. He'd seen the flash of something metallic in the sliver of moonlight and had nearly died at the knowledge that he'd been right after all; her nipples *were* in fact pierced, and he wanted nothing more than to touch, to taste, to tease.

After ripping the shirt to shreds with his bare hands, he'd disappeared into the bathroom to take care of the erection he'd been unsuccessful at keeping under control.

He did the best he could to shove all thoughts of Shauntelle Kendall from his mind. Today was about Freeman and Jodi. He handed the cup of coffee off to his friend and cousin and grinned widely.

Roxy poked her head into the room a while later after a quick knock. "I'm going to hang out here for a while, and then I'll meet Jodi and the other women at the main lodge for hair and make-up and photos."

"You can head over with them now," Free said, but she shook her head.

"I'm your grooms-maid. Grooms-woman? Whatever, you know what I mean. I'll hang out with you guys, then head up there. Though I should come back and make sure you guys are ready on time," she muttered the last part sternly, making the two men chuckle. "Is it too early to crack open that bourbon?"

SEVENTEEN

"You actually look like a girl, Roxy," Kasey murmured on a sardonic drawl.

The vivacious redhead did a small curtsy in her floor length black gown and batted her eyelashes up at him, at the same time flipping him off. He laughed out loud as she said with false sweetness, "It's known to happen on occasion."

Kasey fidgeted with the knot of his tie at his throat, pulling at it with his index finger hooked into it. *Damn uncomfortable things.*

"Stop fidgeting," Roxy muttered, eyeing him shrewdly.

The groom's party had arrived at the main lodge of the resort, and Levi had insisted they make a stop at the bar, to which Freeman had agreed. Levi had downed his whisky before thumping Free on the back, squeezing his shoulder once, and then he disappeared out of the bar, surely to head upstairs to the bridal suite to find his daughter. The bartender was passing out drinks to the group of them just as Roxy had walked up to them. Kasey raised his glass to his lips, grinning when Tristan elbowed his cousin Tanner hard in the ribs, the teenagers' eyes nearly popping out of their skulls as they stared at Roxy.

"You're going to make those kids have coronaries," Kasey chuckled, leaning down closer to Roxy. She shrugged, grinning. Her dress was simple in design; a strapless top that was fitted snugly to her chest and torso but flared out and flowed around her legs from the waist down. A high slit let a leg peak out when she walked or turned, and Tristan and Tanner hadn't missed it. Heels adorned her feet and her red hair had been pulled into a loose updo at the back of her neck. Teardrop crystal earrings hung from her ears and a thin crystal choker was around her throat. A simple bouquet of white florals was clasped in her hand.

Tugging at his tie again, he glanced around the bar. Always perceptive, Roxy noticed and grinned, then whispered, "She's not down here. They're still up in the suite."

Kasey grunted, turning his eyes back to the bar. "I don't know what you're talking about."

"Mmhmm," Roxy drawled knowingly, grinning up at him. "You're not looking for a tall brunette bombshell?"

He raised his glass to his lips again, choosing not to respond.

"If I was a lesbian, it would be for her for sure. Just wait til you see her," Roxy continued, sliding her arm through the crook of his elbow as she leaned closer. She opened her mouth just as the wedding planner found them, telling them that they were needed. As they made their way toward the door, Kasey admitted they made a handsome looking group. The black-on-black tuxes that Jodi and Free had picked out were striking. Black slacks, black dress shirts, black vests, black jackets, and black neckties made a luxurious and chic statement. The bridesmaids had all been dressed in black as well, from what Roxy had said.

Kasey could feel the swish of Roxy's dress around their feet as they exited the bar, making their way to the private ceremony space. The double doors were propped open, and inside at the end of the aisle he could see out the floor-to-ceiling windows, the sun beginning its decline over the snow-covered mountain beyond. The sunset was painting the sky in golden yellow, brilliant orange, and crimson red with just a hint of fuchsia pink at the edges. A crystal chandelier had been strung directly above where Jodi and Free would stand. The room was lit dimly, with candles in tall hurricane jars lining the wide aisle on either side. Soft, romantic instrumental music drifted out of the doors.

Spencer, Micah, and his own father, Adam, were acting as ushers for the small guest list, and as family and friends from either side began to arrive, the three men took turns leading them to their seats. Once everyone had arrived, the blonde wedding planner came around the corner, stopping in front of Freeman to adjust his boutonniere of a single white rose before saying gently, "She's waiting just around the corner. We'll start whenever you're ready."

Kasey clasped his cousin on the shoulder as Free nodded, taking a deep breath in before releasing it slowly. Serenity came around the corner wearing a floor length, glittering gold gown, a brilliant smile on her face, though admittedly looking a little misty eyed. As she reached Free, she held her arms out, stepping into a tight embrace. Kasey saw the older woman's lips moving against Free's ear, too soft for anyone else to hear, and Free's arms tightened around Jodi and Shaun's mother as he smiled. His eyes got suspiciously wet looking before she pulled away and squeezed his hand, putting her arm through Spencer's as he led her down the aisle to her seat.

Tablet in hand, the wedding coordinator cued the music to start with one quick touch to the screen. At a nod from her, the officiant started his walk down the aisle to stand directly beneath the glittering chandelier hanging over the raised dais. The coordinator touched Free's sleeve, and he started his walk down the aisle as well; Kasey, Roxy, Warren, and Tristan followed behind. Stepping to Freeman's left, they lined up beside him.

The double doors at the entrance had been closed after the men had made their march down the aisle, but they opened now as Fallon stepped through them in a much more modest black, floor length dress than Roxy had chosen, a bouquet of white florals in her hands. Kit followed, then Tessa, both in floor length black gowns in different silhouettes that fit their bodies and personalities.

Kasey swallowed hard, his mouth going uncomfortably dry as Shaun stepped around the edge of the door. Gliding toward him on sky high heels—he hadn't expected anything less from her—she was breathtaking in her black evening gown. Thin straps over her shoulders that cut down into triangles covered her breasts, and the neckline plunged between them nearly to her navel. He had the insane urge to run his tongue down that groove between her breasts—

He made an effort to steel his expression, worried his eyes just may bug out of his skull, much the way Tristan and Tanner's had when they'd seen Roxy earlier. The bodice was fitted snug to her torso, but large swaths of skin were bare under her arms down her ribcage, and from her waist to her knees the dress was form fitted to that intoxicating hourglass figure he'd fantasized about for over a year. From her knees to the floor the chiffon material flowed around her legs, and a mouthwateringly high slit nearly up to her hip left the majority of her right leg bare with each step she took. Her long, curly hair was fashioned into a loose waterfall braid over one shoulder, curls left to frame her face. The low lighting made the dozens of crystals hidden in the curls glitter. Sparkly, crystal earrings dangled from her ears and a wide crystal bracelet was strapped around one wrist.

Those full lips he couldn't wait to taste were painted a deep red and looked velvety. He wondered hazily if they would feel as soft as they looked.

As she stepped up the two steps onto the dais to the spot designated to her, that right thigh was bare clear up to her hip and he thought he may just black out from the eroticism of it. He wanted to run his hands, his fingers—fuck, his *tongue*—along every exposed inch of smooth skin showcased. That slender foot encased in a sky-high black heel that had a thin strap wrapped around her ankle was sexy as hell. He wanted to remove them with his teeth.

She turned to face him, the folds of her dress billowing around her legs and feet as she moved. Her fingers were clasped loosely around the same style of white floral bouquet as the other bridesmaids, and then her eyes raised to meet his.

Those dark sapphire eyes… *Fuck.*

He was grateful when those blue eyes cut away from him back down the aisle, as the music changed into an instrumental version of Elvis Presley's '*Can't Help Falling In Love*'. The double doors opened once more, and Free's bride stepped through them on her father's arm.

He glanced at Free, who had his head tilted down slightly, staring at a spot between his polished black cowboy boots, his hands clasped tightly together in front of him. Free raised his head and Kasey reached out his hand to clasp his cousin's shoulder in a tight squeeze as Free caught sight of his bride for the first time.

As she glided toward them in a white gown that glittered like starlight in the candlelit room, a brilliant smile on her face as she stared at Freeman, Kasey felt Free's chest heave, and his shoulders shook with emotion. His own nose tingled at the raw emotion and undiluted love and joy he could sense between the two of them.

His eyes cut over to Shaun again and his lips tilted up in a grin when he saw the wide, adoring smile on her face as she watched her sister come down the aisle toward them. Damn was she gorgeous.

Jodi and Levi stopped at the bottom of the steps to the dais and Free stepped down them to shake Levi's hand. Kasey's nose tingled suspiciously when the older man's eyes watered, too, as he gave Jodi's arm to Freeman to take.

Free guided Jodi up the two steps until they stood beneath the chandelier above them, and once they were in their places, the officiant began his welcome.

Kasey let his mind drift, back to when he'd thought he'd found the person he'd spend his life with. He'd proposed, enamored with the drop-dead gorgeous model. Little did he know, she'd only been after his money, recognizing that he was up-and-coming on the circuit and wanted to cash in on all that she could. When Kasey's parents had insisted on a prenup, Savannah had found herself a rich doctor instead, leaving him just months before they were supposed to be married.

His attention was brought back to the beautiful brunette that stood across from him when she stepped forward to take Jodi's bouquet from her, bending slightly to straighten the train of Jodi's gown. Kasey barely stopped himself from groaning out loud at the expanse of cleavage she unintentionally showed off, his eyes cutting away quickly, only to get caught on another pair of intense blue eyes that were glaring daggers at him. Levi hadn't missed his reaction to his daughter, and Kasey swallowed hard before returning his gaze to the back of Free's head, clasping his hands tightly in front of his crotch to hide the fact that he was in fact growing hard from the sight of Shaun.

"Jodi and Freeman have chosen to write their own vows, and I'll ask them to state those now," the officiant said, and Kasey watched as Free pulled a small black booklet out of his pocket, opened it, then stuffed it back into his pocket, taking both of Jodi's hands in his tightly. When he spoke, his voice was steady, but fraught with emotion.

"Jodi Leigh, I vow to be your rock, your safe haven, and your home, no matter where life takes us. I promise to always be your biggest fan, to celebrate your accomplishments, and to comfort you in your defeats. I will always be your partner in creating the life we want, together. I vow to love you unconditionally, without end, and cherish you for all of eternity."

Jodi tugged one hand from Freeman's, taking out a lace edged handkerchief and dabbing at her eyes, before turning to Shaun, who held out a small white booklet. Turning back to face Free, she said, "Freeman Jon, I vow to you my deepest love, my fullest devotion, and my tenderest care through the pressures of the present and the uncertainties of the future. It is clear to me now that everything in life has led me to you. I vow to always give you the best of me without condition. In a hundred lifetimes, in a hundred worlds, in any version of reality, I would find you, and I'd choose you. For this forever and the next."

Well damn, Kasey thought, blinking the tears out of his own eyes. He didn't know how Freeman was still standing.

The officiant asked for the rings, and as Free turned toward him, Kasey dug in his pocket for the sparkling diamond and band he'd been entrusted with earlier. Placing them in his cousin's hand, they smiled at each other before Free turned back to his bride to place them on her finger and allow her to slide a simple gold band on his own.

"It is truly an honor to stand here and pronounce you husband and wife. Freeman, you may kiss your bride," the officiant said warmly, and a heartbeat later Freeman had pulled

Jodi into his arms and lowered his mouth to hers in an ardent kiss. The small crowd erupted in loud applause, several wolf-whistles ringing in his ears.

When the newlyweds finally came up for air, Jodi laughed breathlessly, before Free took one of her hands in his as Shaun reached out to hand Jodi her bouquet once again. The officiant then called across the room, "I am honored to present to you for the first time, Mr. and Mrs. Thorp!"

Free guided Jodi down the steps, the two of them heading back up the aisle to the double doors. Kasey looked over at Shaun as he stepped forward, offering her his hand to assist her down the stairs, his heart thudding triple time as she stepped toward him, that smooth expanse of thigh making its appearance and stealing his breath. When her hand slipped into his, the heat of her touch scorched him, igniting something fierce inside of him.

When those blue eyes lifted to his ever so briefly, his heart fell into his stomach at the flash of sadness he saw in them. Glancing around, he realized then that he hadn't seen Tommy Chandler in the small gathering of guests, and in that moment, he'd never hated someone as fiercely as he hated the man that hadn't shown up for the woman whose hand was clasped within his.

EIGHTEEN

Shaun's fingers tightened around Kasey's as he led her down the steps of the dais, releasing as soon as she was back on the main floor. His touch was like an inferno on her skin, sending sparks along every inch of her straight to her middle, and she bit her lip as she squeezed her thighs tightly together against the onslaught of desire that coursed through her.

Kasey extended his elbow to her, and she hesitated only a heartbeat before she slipped her hand into the crook of his arm, and then they made their way down the aisle to where Jodi and Free were waiting just outside the doors, locked in another heated embrace.

Fleeting, momentary sadness had crept in as she'd watched her sister and her new brother-in-law, so ridiculously in love it was sickening... in the best way, of course.

How could you not be outrageously happy when in the presence of *soul mates* of true love?

Kasey's other hand came up and covered hers where it was clasped around his elbow, his long, strong fingers closing over hers with a gentle squeeze. Taking a risk and raising her eyes to his, she had to admit that whatever she had been fighting against so adamantly was quickly beginning to crumble at her feet.

Especially with the way his fingers were caressing the back of her hand softly, and the way those gray-blue eyes of his stared into her own as if trying to read every single thought in her mind. Or the way he made her feel alive in her skin for the first time in ages…

She hated to admit it, but she had begun to love the witty banter that volleyed between them, and looked forward to it even. He drove her absolutely insane, but she certainly was never bored when he was around.

Okay… maybe he's marginally tolerable… and certainly not bad to look at, she thought, letting her gaze rove over every nuance of his face; the strong, defined jaw, the lips that were slightly too thin but damn-it to hell did she want to know what they felt like against her own, the tapered, straight nose and those damn captivating storm cloud eyes that she could admittedly stare at for hours at a time and never get tired of them, to the dark blonde hair that looked clean and soft to the touch.

He looked absolutely mouthwatering in his black-on-black ensemble, though his tie was slightly crooked, as if he'd been fidgeting with it before the ceremony started.

He finally released her when they reached Jodi and Free,

quickly followed by the rest of the bridal party behind them. Kasey stepped away from her and she felt an immediate sense of deep loss, which was ridiculous because he was still within reach.

Not that he was hers, anyway. Because she absolutely *was not* his.

She'd made a point of arguing that for over a year.

She reached out and embraced Jodi tightly, hugging her fiercely and kissing her cheek, whispering, "I'm so happy you found this, Jodi. You deserve all this happiness and more," before turning to hug Free just as fiercely.

After a brief receiving line of the guests as they filed out of the ceremony space, the bridal party was ushered off for photos in the growing twilight, while the guests were shown to a separate, private hall where the reception would be held. Shaun thought for sure she was going to die of overheating when Kasey's hand settled low on her back as they stood for the photographer to take pictures.

When the rest of the party was preoccupied with being shifted from one set up to another, she was shocked her knees didn't give out when she felt him lean close from behind her, and then his warm, whisky fragrant breath hit her ear as he whispered huskily, "God dammit, I promised I'd behave, but fuck I can't stop thinking about the way your breasts looked last night, or how you looked wearing *my* shirt, darlin'." His hand slid around her waist, his fingers grazing the exposed skin of her ribcage and she sucked in her breath sharply, her mouth falling open as heat flooded her. "You are stunning, Shaun. That idiot doesn't deserve you."

And then he was gone, headed off to join the other groomsmen and Free as they lined up for photos of just the men. Shaun turned away from the group, taking long moments to pull herself together.

"You look like you need a drink."

At the sound of Roxy's heavy Texas twang, Shaun turned with a grimace. "That obvious?"

Roxy rolled her hazel eyes and shrugged. "You two should stop fighting it and just get it over with."

"I don't do casual sex, Roxy," she murmured, fingering the petals of one of the roses in her bouquet in her hands.

Leaning close, Roxy muttered, "Doll, if he wanted casual, he could find it anywhere else, starting with that wedding coordinator that's had her eyes on him since yesterday. He doesn't want casual. He wants you."

"Did he put you up to this?" Shaun muttered wryly, turning to look suspiciously at the redhead.

Roxy laughed out loud, causing several people to turn and look at them. "Girl, the sexual tension between you two is thick enough to cut with a damn butter knife. I think your daddy is getting tired of the lustful looks Kasey's been sending your way all weekend. Better to hole up in a room and bang it out and save the rest of us from having to be a third party to it."

Shaun's face flamed scarlet, and she couldn't stop the laugh that escaped her, earning her that baleful 'Mom look' from her mother for being too noisy.

Roxy nudged Shaun in the arm, and she glanced down, grinning when she saw a flask in her hand. Shaun took it, tipping it up to take a short pull, before making a face and breathing heavily through her mouth after the burning swallow. "Good lord, Roxy. What the fuck is that?"

"Moonshine," Roxy chuckled.

Shaun shuddered, goosebumps erupting over her entire body, and shifted her arms to cover the peaks of her nipples through the bodice of her gown. When she felt heat spread over her, she lifted her eyes to find Kasey's hot gaze on her, and she knew he'd seen the evidence against the material of her dress.

When the photographer dismissed them, having gotten all of the shots requested, the small bridal party made their way toward the reception hall, where music and chatter could be heard through the closed double doors. Kasey was several steps ahead of her, his head lowered slightly as the wedding coordinator said something close to his ear. He grinned, that devilish smirk tilting up the corners of his mouth and revealing those damn near perfect white teeth, his eyes crinkling lightly in the corners. His hand clasped lightly around the backside of her bicep, near her elbow, and the woman smiled up at him coyly.

Jealousy stampeded its way through Shaun, unbidden and unwelcome, but there nonetheless. Steeling her face into one of indifference as Kasey and the pretty blonde turned, she raised her chin slightly as his eyes met hers.

"Okay everybody! Please line up in couples in the order that you will enter the reception and be introduced by the emcee," the coordinator said cheerily, and the group split, pairing up. They made their way into a haphazard line, all of them chattering excitedly. "I'll enter first and tell the emcee we are ready."

Shaun didn't glance over at Kasey as he took his place beside her, but watched out of the corner of her eye as he extended his hand to hers, palm up. Hesitating for a long time, she finally reached out and slid her hand in his, trying her damndest to ignore the sparks that flew between them at the contact.

The doors opened and through them they could hear the emcee as he gathered the guests attention. The song playing on the speaker was Bruno Mars' '*Marry You*'. The emcee called out, "It is my pleasure to present to you the bridal party! Please welcome the parents of the bride, Serenity and Levi!"

Shaun's mouth tugged into a smile when her mom and dad entered the lavishly decorated space, her mother's arm tucked into her father's elbow. The crowd cheered in welcome. Next, Fallon and Tristan were introduced, followed by Kit and Warren, and then Tessa and Roxy entered together, both women doing an extra little dance on their way in.

Shaun and Kasey stepped closer to the door, awaiting the emcee's introduction. "Best Man Shane Thorp is unable to attend tonight, home with a brand-new baby! So I introduce you to Interim Best Man, Kasey and Maid of Honor, Shauntelle!"

They stepped forward together into the room to applause, and Kasey raised the hand that held hers captive, spinning her lithely beneath his outstretched arm, and she couldn't help the laugh that escaped her as she glanced up at him, her dress flowing around their feet. His eyes, those beautiful storm cloud eyes, were gentle as he stared down at her, bringing her in close as he walked them toward their seats.

Her hand still clasped in his, she gasped audibly when he squeezed her fingers gently, then rubbed the back of her hand with his thumb slowly. Thankfully, the emcee's voice boomed over the speakers at the same time as he said, "And may I present to you, for the first time, Freeman and Jodi Thorp!"

The guests erupted in applause, and Shaun disengaged her hand from Kasey's to do the same as her sister and new brother-in-law came through the doors, hand in hand, brilliant smiles on both of their faces. Free twirled Jodi under his arm, much the way Kasey had done to her, and when Freeman pulled Jodi back to him, he clasped her around the waist and kissed her to another eruption of cheers.

Kasey held her chair for her to sit, then moved to take his seat directly next to her as Freeman led Jodi to their sweetheart table. She reached for the crystal water glass in front of her as his impossibly hard thigh brushed hers under the table, her hand trembling, making the ice clink in the glass as she brought it to her lips.

The next twenty minutes were a blur. She somehow stumbled through her maid of honor speech, managed to make the guests laugh and even drew a tear or two from her sister and mother. She barely registered Kasey rising to his feet next to her as she sank shakily into her seat. She purposely kept her eyes away from the tree trunks that were Kasey's thighs encased in the black slacks of his suit, or the way they molded to the curves of his ass. She heard none of his speech, just the low timbre of his voice as he spoke. She was transfixed by the graceful way his hand moved as he spoke, the wide wrist that peeked out from the cuff of his suit, the wide band of his watch glinting in the candlelight on the table in front of them.

As Kasey resumed his seat beside her, the emcee announced dinner as the handsomely dressed wait staff appeared to serve the wedding guests.

"Would you like a drink?" he asked, leaning close to her, and she was intoxicated by his nearness and the scent of his cologne.

"Umm," she mumbled lamely, staring into his face, her mind a jumbled mess. One corner of his mouth tilted up slightly and she bared her teeth in a snarl. *The bastard knew what he was doing and was laughing at her!* "I'm fine, thank you."

"How about another sip of moonshine?" he murmured low, at the same time drawing one finger up the length of her exposed thigh. Her mouth parted and all thought escaped her as goosebumps erupted over every inch of her. The tip of his finger toyed with the flowy edge of her dress where it V'd open high on her thigh. Hidden from view behind the black tablecloth, no one else would know that his fingers were sliding beneath the material to cup the soft flesh of the inside of her thigh. His voice was a tortured groan when he spoke next. "I can't stay away from you."

And as she watched as he slowly pulled away from her to face forward once again, Shaun wasn't so sure she wanted him to.

NINETEEN

Keeping his hands off of Shaun was proving to be impossible. He had no self-control, no will to even try. She called to him like a goddamn siren, and he was powerless against her. He'd promised Freeman to leave her alone until after the wedding… but nothing short of his own death—or Shaun choosing to stab him in the back of the hand with the tines of the fork resting on the black tablecloth—could have stopped him from sliding his palm over the smoothness of that bare thigh.

And when she shifted her leg toward him just a hair, seeking more, he knew he was in far more trouble than he'd realized.

The long, loose braid that her hair was pulled back into fell over her shoulder, tendrils framing her face as she went back to pretending he wasn't there. She sipped her champagne, ate the delicious meal in front of them, chatted and laughed and drove him damned near crazy.

The lights in the private room dimmed as the waitstaff cleared the dinner plates from in front of the guests, and their attention was directed to the emcee as he called to them as Free led Jodi out to the center of the dance floor. True to the nature of their relationship, they'd chosen a classic 90's country ballad for their first dance as a married couple. John Michael Montgomery serenaded them to '*I Can Love You Like That*' as they watched Freeman take his bride into his arms like she'd always belonged there.

Shaun had risen from her seat, making her way around the tables to stand closer to the dance floor, and he watched her as she swayed to the music. Levi stepped up beside her and draped a burly arm around her shoulders, drawing her into his side as he spoke directly to her. Kasey was too far away to hear what was being said, but his heart did something painful in his chest when she reached her arm around her father's back and hugged tightly. Levi's hand rubbed down the outside of her bare arm, then reached out his other hand and took her left hand in his, drawing it to his bewhiskered mouth and kissing the bare knuckles there.

Was that why that douchebag hadn't shown up? Was all not well between Shaun and Tommy, despite her insistence that she was happy? Was that why she didn't wear her ring? Hatred for the man that had abandoned her when he should have been here with her bloomed fierce and ugly inside his chest. As happy as he was that Tommy Chandler *hadn't* shown up, the cowardice of the man who had this woman's heart when it should belong to *him*… it burned inside his entire being.

Levi turned her in his arms, spinning her gracefully, and when she looked up at her father and bestowed him with that hundred-watt smile, Kasey knew he needed her to grace *him* with that smile. The smile that blinded anyone near her. Her sassy, snarky attitude was maddening, yes, but the heart that beat beneath those breasts was fierce and wild and he'd give anything to be the one to tame it.

As the song came to a close, Kasey watched as Shaun danced lightly with her father on the edge of the light, just far enough in the shadows to not take any attention from the bride and groom in the center of the dance floor. The emcee asked Levi to join Jodi in the center of the dance floor then, and Levi leaned down to press a kiss to his second born daughters' cheek before ambling out to meet his eldest. Freeman walked to the edge of the polished dance floor and extended his hand to Serenity. The older woman took it with a dazzling smile, though Kasey could tell it wouldn't be long before tears would be sliding down her cheeks.

Sauntering over to the bar, Kasey ordered two highballs of bourbon, then crossed to where Shaun still stood. Holding one out to her, he grinned lopsidedly down at her when she glanced up at him. "Truce?"

He loved the skeptical side eye she bestowed upon him, the way those red painted lips pursed in deliberation before finally reaching up and accepting the glass he offered her. They clinked the glasses together lightly, but before she raised it to her lips, she said dryly, "I don't believe your truce for a second, Kasey Corcoran."

Fuck if he didn't love the way his name sounded coming off her lips. He wanted to lean down and kiss her, taste his name on her lips while he did deliciously decadent things to her.

But again, that awful reminder that she wasn't his, didn't belong to him no matter how badly he wanted her to, came unbidden to his mind.

"But thank you for the drink," she continued, giving him a reluctant smile, her dark sapphire eyes sparkling in the low light of the room, surrounded by hundreds of candles. The candlelight caught the tiny crystals pinned into her curls, and he could just imagine running his fingers through her hair to find every last one of them while her head rested against his chest as they lay in bed.

Anger and bitterness at the unfairness of it all, how badly he wanted her when she wasn't his, how she belonged to someone that clearly didn't appreciate the absolute fucking *goddess* he had in his hands... The one woman that he couldn't get out of his mind couldn't be his.

Of course the woman he had fallen in love with had to be engaged to someone else.

TWENTY

Shaun could sense the anger as it radiated off of Kasey in furls. His fingers clenched around the crystal glass in his hand, his knuckles turning white. His jaw tightened, the muscles clenching in that sharp jawline that just begged for her tongue to run over it. His shoulders were tense, his mouth pulled into a tight line, where moments ago he'd been using that disarming grin to charm her.

Downing the dark liquor, she reached behind her and set it down on a nearby table before murmuring, "I—" but when those stormy gray-blue eyes sliced over to hers, the words stuck in her throat. She swallowed hard, then tried again. "I need to—"

Without finishing the sentence, she turned and made her way across the room, rushing out an exit into a deserted and dark hallway. A sliver of light cut across the floor, and she made her way toward it, finding a shallow alcove with a window that looked out over the now darkened mountainside. There was only a tiny sliver of moon visible, the stars making a stunning display in the navy sky.

Sucking in several long, deep breaths as she stared out the window, she willed her heart to steady its frantic beat, willed her body to stop reacting to Kasey's like he was the most delicious man she'd ever laid eyes on. Which was the truth, but dammit, her body needed to listen to her *brain*, not her lady bits.

Turning, she gasped, startled to find Kasey standing in the alcove doorway. He was silent, his eyes dark and intense as he stared at her. She hadn't heard him follow her, and the predatory way he was watching her made her heart race and white-hot desire shoot directly to her core.

Yes, was all that crossed her mind.

Taking a step forward, Kasey gave her a soft shove and Shaun found herself with her back pressed against the wall of the intimate niche in the wall, his forearm coming to a rest along the wall above her, allowing him better access to press his body in close to hers.

She made to push him back, but he just pressed closer to her, not touching, but she could feel his heat *everywhere*.

Ensconced in the dark alcove along the private passageway, they were completely hidden from view, not that any passersby would be coming this way anyway.

They were alone. In the shadows of the alcove, Kasey loomed over her, his head descending toward hers. Tilting her head up, she was all but waiting for his lips to meet hers. She gasped out loud when she felt his mouth on the curve of her shoulder, instead.

"You are… *killing me* in that dress," Kasey breathed on a growl, even as his nose trailed up the side of her neck, just beneath the curtain her hair made from the loose braid. His lips brushed her throat, so light she might have imagined it before his head tipped up again, this time fluttering against the space behind her ear. Shaun's breath came in soft, quick pants. She was on fire. "Fuck, Shaun. The things you do to me. The things you make me want to do to you…"

His right forearm still pressed flat against the wall above her head, his hand curled into a loose fist, the fingers of his left-hand trailed feather light down the outside of her arm, making goosebumps erupt over her skin. His body, so tall and outrageously attractive, was close enough that their clothing was rustling against each other, but their bodies never connected.

Kasey's breath was uneven as he continued, stirring her hair, "And you know exactly what you're doing to me, don't you? You've been strutting around this party all night for me, darlin'."

"I've done no such thing," Shaun whispered, her eyes fluttering closed as his nose dragged up her temple, his mouth following. She felt more than heard his breathy chuckle as it drifted over her face.

"Yes, you have," he murmured, cocky as ever.

The hand that had been idly trailing over her bare arm slid down until she sucked in her breath at the first touch of his fingers against the skin of her thigh, an open invitation to him by the tantalizingly high slit of her dress. The backs of his fingers brushed lightly, again and again, moving inch by inch toward the soft inner part of her thigh, and she nearly fainted at the eroticism of it. She was impossibly wet, aching.

Kasey's mouth had lowered back to the soft underside of her jaw, and she tipped her head back, granting him better access even as she shifted her leg just slightly, and she felt his grin against her skin as his fingers moved again. His fingertips grazed the lacy edge of her thong, and Shaun panted into the dimly lit room as those fingers found her, wet and warm and ready.

"Christ, Shaun..." he groaned, and she sensed his breathing change, felt his chest as it heaved like a bellows. Felt his grin against her neck as his fingers explored higher, deeper, sinking into her. Her eyes rolled back into her head at his ministrations. "You're fucking perfect. Perfect, darlin'."

He chuckled darkly when her breath hitched in her throat, his mouth finally moving until it hovered over hers. His storm cloud gray-blue eyes were luminous as he stared down into her own. It was rare that Shaun ever had to look up at someone, and his height compared to her own, even in her heels, was intoxicating. His finger flicked inside her and she bit her lip to stifle a throaty moan.

Those eyes darkened as they watched her teeth clamp down on her red painted lips, and he did it again, this time adding a second finger. Moving her hips against his hand, he delved deeper, the heel of his hand grinding against her clit, and she gasped against his lips that were so close to her own, but still not touching. She was about to shatter, every nerve ending zinging with anticipation as he continued to move his fingers inside her, stroking her, tugging her toward that precipice that waited for her. Moving his hand, his thumb found her clit and circled it, nearly causing her knees to buckle. She was so close…

Her hands finally found the edges of his suit jacket, fisting them in her fingers, holding him to her as she began to tremble. He growled low in his throat, his mouth so close to hers, and the sound, along with the magic his fingers were working, completely undid her.

Fire exploded in her veins, and she came hard, squeezing his fingers. Her needy cry was instantly muffled by his mouth as it slammed down onto hers. She returned his kiss weakly, her mind short circuiting with the intensity of the orgasm rushing through her. His own growl of pleasure as he let her ride out that high as he continued to stroke vibrated against her lips, and she let out a half moan, half sob.

Holy. Shit.

Achingly slowly, he pulled his fingers out, at the same time breathing against her lips, "Does that sorry excuse of a fiancé of yours ever make you come that hard, or did you save that just for me?"

His words registered through the haze of pleasure, and it was as if he'd dumped an entire bucket of cold water on her. She gasped in outrage and shoved the heels of her hands against his muscled chest with as much strength as she could muster. He braced for it, only falling back a step as he reached up and placed those two fingers in his mouth, grinning wolfishly as he tasted her. She couldn't stop the blush that stained her cheeks, which made her all the more furious.

"You bastard," Shaun seethed, her chest heaving, her blue eyes fierce. Humiliation clawed at her, making her nose sting with tears.

"I'd say by the time it took…" he muttered darkly, that haughty grin widening, "you haven't been taken care of in a while, darlin'."

"I hate you," Shaun gritted out through clenched teeth, her entire body taut with rage, those damn tears rising to line her lower lids.

Taking a measured step closer, Kasey leaned in and whispered on a taunt, "Do you hate me? Or do you hate that I'm right?"

She made to shove past him, but he gripped her upper arm in a vicelike hold, stopping her and hauling her close. She glared up at him even as his head lowered toward hers again. "Do you hate *me*, or do you just hate how much you loved that?"

All of the above, she wanted to scream at him. He grinned then, as if reading the thought as it crossed over her face, still bristling with fury and humiliation. But his eyes softened, just a touch, when she knew he saw the tears that lined her eyes.

Forcing the unwanted tears back and pushing the heel of her hand into his shoulder hard, she dropped her eyes to the floor and stepped away from him, surprised when he let her go. Raising her eyes to his once more, she saw the regret in his gray-blue gaze as he stared down at her, which made her even angrier. She didn't want a pity orgasm. Shoving past him, she snapped, "You're such a jerk, Kasey. Just… just leave me alone."

Her heels clicked on the tiled floor as she pushed past him, leaving the intimate little alcove as she rushed toward the doors back into the reception. She never looked back as she struggled to hold back the tears of mortification.

TWENTY-ONE

"Can I get a shot of tequila?" Shaun asked the bartender as she stepped up to the smartly dressed woman. "Actually, make it three. Or can I just have the bottle?"

The woman smiled at her and set out a shot glass, filling it with the clear liquor. Shaun reached for it and tossed it back quickly, setting it down on the bar for the woman to refill. Downing the second one, Shaun took a deep breath before setting it down again. The bartender arched one brow at her, and she nodded, tapping the polished bar with one manicured nail. The woman laughed, shaking her head slightly, but filled it again, and a moment later, Shaun had downed that one as well.

Setting the shot glass down, she pushed it away from her and slid a twenty out to the woman, saying a quiet, "Thank you," before turning back to face the small crowd of the reception. Jodi and Free were in the middle of the dance floor surrounded by guests as they all danced to the Macarena. As it finished, she heard the beginning notes of the Cupid Shuffle come on from the DJ booth over the speakers, and Jodi rushed forward, spotting Shaun.

"Come on, you're not missing this one! This is our favorite!" Jodi laughed as Shaun protested weakly, already feeling the effects of the three shots of tequila. Once out in the center of the dance floor, Shaun laughed and shoved all thoughts of that douche Kasey freaking Corcoran out of her mind. Pity orgasm. Pfft. It wasn't really *that* amazing.

That was the hardest O you've ever had, sister, her mind reminded her dryly.

"*—To the right to the right to the right, to the left to the left to the left to the left. Now kick now kick—*" the group of them danced along to the popular line dance, following the instructions. As Shaun kicked first her right leg, then left, then chacha'd in place as she rotated ninety degrees, she knew Kasey's eyes were on her because she suddenly felt hot all over

Swaying to the music, they made three ninety degree turns before she saw him from across the room, his intense gaze riveted on her.

Damn him! she thought angrily, but she continued to smile and laugh as the song wound down, the crowd applauding before the next song came on.

The tequila had set in, making her feel just relaxed enough, but anger and hurt still tumbled around inside her.

At five minutes to midnight, the DJ asked the guests to please head toward the balcony doors, where the resort would be setting off a display of fireworks as they rang in the new year. Baskets of soft blankets had been arranged by the doors, and several women took one to wrap around their shoulders as they made their way out to the balcony.

The music stopped at one minute to midnight, changing over to the live feed of the countdown to the new year. Jodi and Free were front and center, Jodi wrapped in a white cashmere shawl, Free's arms wrapped around her as they all waited, counting down together with their family and friends that surrounded them.

"Ten… Nine… Eight… Seven… Six… Five… Four… Three… Two… One… Happy New Year!" rang out in a chorus of cheers just as the first of a truly spectacular firework display erupted over their heads with a chest rattling boom.

Shaun glanced around her, taking in the many couples that surrounded her; the newlyweds, her parents, her aunts and uncles, grandparents… Last year she was engaged. Now she was single and getting pity orgasms from too-sexy-for-their-own-good-groomsmen. Ugh.

Spun around roughly, she only had a heartbeat to comprehend what was happening before her face was captured in both of Kasey's hands, his mouth dropping down onto hers, hard and insistent and oh-so wonderful. She fought for all of a heartbeat before sighing in defeat. She was still pissed at him, but she was too tired of fighting this, fighting him. She'd wanted this for as long as she could remember and didn't have the willpower to stop it.

Because… *Finally.*

He kissed her until she was breathless, his tongue sinking into her mouth, his lips twisting over hers deliciously. He took his time with this kiss, whereas their first kiss in the alcove had merely been a pressing of mouths to keep her quiet as she came. She met his kiss fiercely, wanting all of him. He tasted like bourbon, and she moaned into his mouth lightly, her hands flattening on his vest. And still he continued kissing her, claiming her mouth. Claiming all of her.

Her mind and her body were a trembling mess when he finally released her mouth, one of his thumbs stroking over her kiss roughened lips, and she'd never been more thankful in her life for smudge proof lip stain. Her entire body was on fire, his kiss zinging over every nerve like the fireworks still dancing in the night sky.

His breathing was harsh as he leaned close to her and whispered, "I didn't kiss you last year at midnight out of respect for you and for your relationship, but if he's too much of an idiot to be here to do it himself, damn straight I'm going to."

The haze of desire she'd succumbed to vanished in an instant, but he was gone before she could open her mouth, weaving through the crowd and disappearing back into the reception hall.

Fury, outrage, bitterness, all of it roiled through her violently and she rushed after him, flinging open the door and striding across the now empty dance floor. He'd already made it out the other doors and was down the hallway toward the main part of the lodge and had stopped at the elevators when she caught up to him. The doors swished open, and he stepped inside.

Damn near sprinting the last few steps forward into the elevator, she skidded to a halt in the sky-high heels, somehow miraculously not breaking an ankle or her neck in her mad dash to follow him.

Grabbing his arm roughly, she yanked him around to face her as the doors closed, letting her fists fly into his chest in rage. "Fuck you, Kasey, you arrogant, heartless bastard!"

"Shaun? What—"

"Why do you keep bringing up Tommy? I knew you were a jerk, but I didn't think you were as callous to purposely make fun of me like you have been for months! Why are you being so cruel, Kasey!"

"Make fun of you?" he asked, wrapping his fingers of both hands around her upper arms. "As overjoyed as I am that that prick didn't show up, I want to rip him to shreds for not being here with you—"

"*Why would he be here with me?*" she exclaimed on a shout that echoed in the small elevator. She was trembling as she cried, "We broke up in February! Why would he come to my sister's wedding with me? What is the point of this cruel game, Kasey? To make fun of me for ending an engagement? Or is it to remind me that I'm fucking single and that I never got this far in the planning of my own wedding? Don't you think I know that?!"

Shaun watched as shock registered on his face, and then she shivered when his jaw tightened, his eyes darkening as he hauled her closer, until her breasts were flattened against his chest. One hand released her arm and tangled in the hair at the back of her head roughly, tilting her face up to his. The sting of pain as he tugged tight made her mouth drop open, and she didn't stop the moan that escaped her.

"*You're. Single?*" he growled through his teeth, and Shaun swallowed hard, her eyes never leaving his. She nodded, just barely, the hand at the back of her head holding tight enough to hinder her movement.

"I—" she whispered, her voice trembling, and her teeth clamped down on her bottom lip as he tightened his fingers in her hair, "—I thought you knew."

The doors of the elevator swished open, and he moved them out of the elevator into a deserted hallway of the hotel. Never releasing his handhold in her hair or the hand clasped around her upper arm, he backed her against the wall and pressed close, angling his body directly against hers. His breathing was harsh, ragged, his eyes dark and dangerous.

"Do you think I would have waited this long to kiss you if I'd known?" he rasped, the sound of it making her ache, and she pressed her thighs tightly together.

"It didn't stop you five minutes ago," she whispered on a taunt, her lips brushing against his as he leaned closer. "Or an hour ago, when you made me come with your fingers."

His eyes squeezed shut and he let out a shuddering breath. "I've never gotten involved with a woman that was taken," he murmured, opening his eyes, and for the first time, Shaun saw the torment in them. "From the second I saw you the first time, you were someone else's."

The hand still clamped around her upper arm loosened, trailing his fingers down her arm until he slid his arm around her waist, his large hand fairly burning her through the layers of fabric of her dress as he pressed his palm to the curve of her ass, urging her closer. She moaned when she felt him, rock hard and ready, against her middle. The fingers still tangled in her hair pulled tight, causing her to twist her head more in his direction, bringing her mouth to his. He nipped her bottom lip sharply and she gasped audibly. Soothing it with his tongue, she groaned, her eyes sliding shut of their own accord.

His voice was rough as gravel as he breathed, "But you were mine the second I laid my eyes on you, Shaun."

"I'm not yours," she hissed through clenched teeth, the

haze of desire lifting slightly, her eyes opening to glare up at him.

A sharp slap to her ass made her cry out in shock, her eyes widening just as his mouth crashed down onto hers ferociously. This kiss was fierce, carnal, hungry, and she reveled in it. She had waited so long to taste him, to feel his lips fully against hers, to know what his tongue tasted like as it spiraled into her mouth, claiming all of her. The hand that had spanked her gripped the stinging flesh, kneading it. She moaned into his mouth, her arms wrapping around his neck as he pressed her back against the wall again. The hand at her ass slid down to the back of her thigh, his fingers curving around until he hauled her leg up around his hip, at the same time grinding against the apex of her thighs, right where she wanted him the most.

"You. Are. Mine," he growled menacingly as he released her lips, the hand in her hair pulling taut, making her throat arch back. Lowering his mouth to her throat, he suckled and nipped until she was a writhing mess, her fingers clutching at his back, his perfect ass. "Do you hear me? *Mine*."

"I'm not yours," Shaun repeated, though this time it came out on a breathy pant, her eyes closed against the onslaught of ecstasy coursing through her at the feel of his hands, his mouth, his everything, on her.

The dark chuckle that reached her ears made goosebumps

break out along her entire body, just as he forced her head to lower back toward his. "Keep telling yourself that, darlin'."

Releasing her, he stepped away, extending his hand toward her. She hesitated only a moment before placing her hand in his and allowing him to draw her down the hallway, stopping at one of the closed hotel room doors. Reaching into his pocket, he pulled out a keycard, passing it over the mechanism to unlock it. It whirred as it unlocked, and he pushed the door open, moving them into the dark hotel room.

"When did you get this?" she asked quietly, almost too scared to speak too loudly, worried if she did, she might break whatever spell this was. She didn't want it to end.

"I thought Tommy was joining you this weekend. I didn't want to be at the same vacation rental as the two of you… so I booked a room elsewhere," he murmured, moving them further into the dark room. He reached out and switched on one dim lamp, casting the majority of the room in shadows.

Shocked by the vulnerability in his words and not entirely sure how to feel about his admission, she reached out to touch the sleeve of his jacket with her fingertips, whispering, "Kasey—"

But he had other ideas, because his mouth covered hers again then, and damn did the man know how to kiss. Soft and agile, then swift and rough, he changed tempos often, leaving her guessing what was coming next. His hands slid over her, one skimming up her back to press her against him, the other smoothing over the curve of her ass to palm it, then squeeze it. When his hands left her body entirely, she let out a mew of disappointment. That dark chuckle reverberated through the semi-darkness of the room again, a heartbeat before she was hauled up and into his arms, their chests pressed tightly together as he crossed the room to the bed, his hands cupping her backside, her legs wrapped around his waist.

"I can fuck you in this dress or I can tear it off of you," he growled. "Because I will be fucking you tonight, you understand that?"

"Don't you dare ruin this dress," she warned, but there was no heat in her words as his mouth lowered to her throat again, his tongue dipping into the deep V between her breasts that the revealing dress left bare for him. Her fingers slid into the dark blonde hair at the back of his head, holding him to her as she moaned quietly. "Fuck, Kasey."

"That's the plan, doll," he murmured as he nudged the triangle of fabric that was covering her right breast with his nose until he found her pierced nipple, sucking it greedily into his mouth. Her back arched, her hands clasping his head against her as sparks shot from the nipple in his mouth straight to her core. "Christ, Shaun, you're perfect. I knew the second I saw you that these were pierced. I saw them last night and nearly died. I wanted to see them so bad. Taste them. God damn I've fantasized about this."

He set her on her feet and her legs wobbled slightly beneath her as his mouth and hands left her feeling bereft again. He shrugged out of his suit jacket, tossing it away. She watched as his fingers deftly released the cufflinks at his wrists, dropping the black titanium links onto the jacket he'd just discarded, before methodically rolling first one sleeve, then the other, up to his forearms. She bit her lip and he growled a heartbeat before his hands came to rest on her shoulders, turning her so that she faced away from him.

His hand swept her long, plaited hair over one shoulder to allow him to find the zipper at her back. When she felt his mouth on the curve of her shoulder, at the same time that his deft fingers began to pull down on the zipper that started halfway down her back, she let out a breathy, "Oh my god."

His mouth followed the line his fingers made down the column of her spine as more of her skin was revealed, until the zipper stopped just above the slope of her backside. His fingers were hot as they trailed, featherlight, back up the exposed skin of her back, sliding under the thin straps that held her dress up over her shoulders, pushing them down her arms.

The bodice of the dress pooled at her waist, leaving her breasts bare to the room, her nipples pebbling in the coolness of the air. She heard him drop to his knees behind her, his hands skimming down the curve of her waist on either side until they met with the fabric of her dress at her hips. His mouth was hot as he pressed it to the exposed skin of her back, and Shaun let her head fall back when she felt his tongue at the dimples at the small of her back. He slid the dress over her wide hips until it fell to the floor around her feet, still clad in the sky-high black heels.

Then his mouth was on the curve of her backside, his hands sliding freely over every inch of her thighs, her calves, then back up to hitch his thumbs into the scrap of lace that was her thong. She had never been adored like this before; he paid homage to every inch of her as it was revealed to him. She couldn't stop the blush that covered her entire body when he slid her panties down her thighs, leaving her completely naked in front of him.

"You smell so good," she heard him murmur from behind her, felt his nose as it traveled over her. She let out a soft gasp when his fingers slid between her thighs, parting them. One of his fingers teased her clit, making her sway on her feet, and then those fingers speared into her as deep as he could go, crooking them inside her. Shaun's knees nearly gave out when he found that special spot, manipulating it effortlessly.

He must have felt how unsteady she was on her feet, because a second later his other arm had banded around the tops of her thighs, and his mouth was once again pressed hotly against the top curve of her ass. She was powerless against the magic of his fingers, reaching blindly behind her until one hand clasped his hard shoulder, steadying herself even as she circled her hips against his hand.

Her muscles began to shake, her stomach fluttering uncontrollably, her chest heaving. Her head fell back and she cried out to the ceiling as she came around his fingers again, her inner muscles convulsing wildly as he continued to pump them inside her, prolonging her orgasm for what felt like forever. She panted into the dim room as she came down slowly, her legs shaking against the arm banded around them tightly. Shaun moaned when his mouth trailed along the skin at her back, her hand clutching his shoulder with trembling fingers.

"Kasey," she whimpered, her legs shaking. She was terrified she was going to break an ankle, her feet still strapped into the four-inch heels. "I need to take these shoes off."

"Mmm, no," he murmured huskily, and she felt him shake his head behind her. His fingers strummed inside her again and she shuddered, biting her lip to keep from crying out at how incredible it felt. "The heels stay on. I want to wear them as earmuffs."

"Oh my god," Shaun moaned throatily, his filthy words erotic to her ears. "Please."

"We've got all night, darlin'," he murmured, though he did pull his fingers from inside her, teasing her clit again before sliding his hand from between her thighs as he stood. Reaching around her, he pressed one palm flat to her abdomen, the other taking a handful of her breast as he pulled her back against his front, circling his hips into her. "I'm going to make you come on my fingers, on my tongue, my cock. Over and over. Hmmm," he rumbled against her back, and she let her head fall back against his shoulder as his fingers tugged at her nipple, rolling the piercing between his thumb and index finger. "Christ, I've wanted this for so long. You're so fucking beautiful. Should we see how many times I can make you come? We've already got two. How many more can you give me, Shaun?"

"You're going to kill me," she groaned as his hand drifted down from where he'd pressed it flat against her stomach to the apex of her thighs again, his fingers finding her clit easily. She clutched at his forearm with one hand, the other covering his and moving with him as she ground her hips back against him. He growled low in his throat, rocking his hips against her and she reveled in the feel of him against her. "Death by orgasms is one helluva way to go, I guess."

He chuckled against the skin of her neck as he pressed his mouth there, and she gasped when he bit her lightly, at the same time his fingers pinched her clit sharply, making her knees buckle as she came again with a shocked cry. "That's it, darlin'. Fuck I love making you come. I can't tell you how long

I've waited to do this."

Her entire body was trembling violently, her breaths coming in short, soft pants. She wasn't going to survive the night. Her lungs would give out, or her heart would explode inside her chest from how hard he was making her come, or the stars that danced behind her tightly closed eyelids would simply burn her from the inside out.

"Please, Kasey," she begged, turning in his arms until she faced him. He was still entirely clothed, and she felt even naughtier since she was completely naked in front of him.

She reached for him, but he tsked her lightly, stopping her. First one, then the second, he removed the titanium cufflinks at his wrists, placing them methodically on the polished surface of the dresser. With one hand, he loosened the tie at his throat, his eyes never leaving hers, then reached up with the other hand to slip it free of its knot. The whisper of the material sliding against each other as he removed it from around his neck was the sexiest sound Shaun had ever heard.

The black vest was barely a blip, the buttons loosened, and the article of clothing tossed to the floor behind him. The buttons on his black dress shirt were quick work for his deft fingers, and when the last one had been slipped from the hole, he tugged the hem of the shirt from the waistband of his black suit pants, and to Shaun, it was quite possibly the most erotic thing she'd ever seen. The muscles of his abdomen, chest, and shoulders rippled and bunched as he worked the shirt down his arms, letting it fall to the floor with the rest of their clothes.

Shaun reached for his belt, sliding her fingers into the waistband of his slacks, the backs of her knuckles resting against his abdomen as her fingers curled around the material. The fly of his pants was tented, his arousal pressing against the material, just begging for attention. He let her slip the buckle of his belt loose but grasped her hands in his when she reached for the zipper.

"I want to touch you," she whispered, and the filthy grin that crossed his face made her heart race.

"You're going to, don't worry," he chuckled darkly, making her knees tremble where she stood. "If you touch me now, darlin', this will be over before we get started."

Dropping her hands, he toed off his dress shoes and reached down to remove his socks. Then he grasped the zipper of his slacks and pulled it down, sliding his pants and the black boxer briefs he had on down his thighs at the same time, revealing what she'd only dreamed about.

As he straightened to his full height, completely naked to her eyes, her mouth dropped open in awe. His cock stood straight and proud, rock hard and so much larger than she'd anticipated.

Oh shit.

Clasping her behind the neck, he pulled her close, angling

their bodies together from chest to thighs. Shaun's breaths were coming in short, fast, uneven pants as she finally felt him press against her belly with nothing between them. His mouth slanted over hers, kissing her fiercely, his tongue spearing into her mouth, to taste, to ravage.

Releasing her mouth and removing his hand from around the back of her neck, he pinched the point of her chin between his thumb and forefinger and forced her eyes up to his. "I'm going to fuck you, Shaun. I'm going to fuck you, hard and fast, and then I'm going to take my time with you. Understand?"

She nodded mutely and she rotated her hips in a circle against him, making them both groan. Walking her backward until her legs met the edge of the bed, she let him lower her back to it, and then he was there, a welcome, needed weight against her, over her, between her thighs. She reached for him, but he manacled both of her wrists in one of his impossibly large hands, hauling her arms up and over her head, pinning her hands to the mattress above her even as his hips settled heavily between her parted thighs. His weight was fully on her wrists, making them ache, but she ceased to care when she felt him reach between their bodies, took his cock in his fist, and rubbed the swollen head against her. He groaned, lining up and sliding in just an inch, then backed out before repeating it, this time sliding another inch deeper.

Shaun whimpered, trying in vain to rotate her hips against

his to draw him deeper. Sinking just the tip inside her, her inner muscles clenched around him, desperate for more. Her hands still manacled above her head, his other hand braced against the mattress beside her as he levered himself over her.

"Kasey," she begged, barely coherent.

"Dammit I wanted to go slow this first time, but I can't, darlin'," he groaned as he slammed inside in one long, hard, smooth thrust. Dropping his forehead to the cradle of her neck, he didn't give her time to even breathe before drawing out and slamming back inside. Again, and again.

"Ohhhh," Shaun moaned, raising her hips to meet his thrusts as he moved inside her. He levered himself up again, her wrists still bound by his fingers above her head. The angle that he was driving into her was hitting in all the right places deep inside, lighting her up like a goddamn Christmas tree. "I don't want you to go slow, Kasey. This is what I want. Yes, *oh god* just like that."

His dark chuckle above her skittered like electricity over her entire body, and he leaned down to pull one of her pierced nipples into his mouth as he continued to piston his hips between her thighs. "Say it again."

"S—say what?" she asked, nearly incoherent with pleasure. His tongue, lashing her pierced nipples, timed perfectly with each of his impossibly deep and punishing thrusts, were stealing every rational thought from her mind.

Her arms ached, her fingers flexing, itching to touch as much of him as she could, but still he held them prisoner above her head.

His teeth flashed white in the darkness, and a second later she cried out sharply as he nipped her with those teeth, the sharp sensation arrowing straight to her core, making her clamp down on him. He growled in pleasure and then breathed, "Tell me you've thought about this, Shaun. Tell me you've thought about taking this cock inside you. Fuck, you take it so well."

"Yes," she sobbed, grinding on him, desperate for more. More. "Yes, I've thought about this, about you. You know I have."

"You're mine, Shaun," she heard him growl ferociously as he pumped into her, harder, deeper, rougher, than before. She opened her mouth to protest, mostly out of spite, but another slam of his hips had her splintering, ready to fall. "So stubborn. Stop fighting, Shaun. You know it's the truth."

Too many emotions, too many sensations, too much of everything was rioting through her to speak sensibly, all coherent thought deserting her as he reached between them to flick his finger over the sensitive bud at the apex of her thighs where his body was joined with hers. Her breathing stalled in her throat as she came, stars bursting behind her tightly clenched eyelids, her entire body shaking with the intensity of the orgasm he'd just rocketed her into. Her core spasmed around his steely length, and his hips stuttered in their thrusts, his body tensing above her.

She heard the deep groan rise from his chest, his breathing erratic in her ear as her orgasm vaulted him into his own, and she felt his hardness pulse inside her, over and over.

TWENTY-TWO

Shaun wiggled her fingers, and he was positive they had to be aching and half numb by now. He released her wrists as he lowered his body onto hers lightly. Taking one of her wrists in his hand, he brought it to his mouth, pressing his lips to the redness there as she flexed her fingers.

Her breathing was still unsteady, as was his own. Still locked deep inside her, he flexed his hips, enjoying the fluttering little pulses of aftershocks that coursed through her. He was still hard, a miracle after that soul deep orgasm she'd just pulled from him, and ready for round two. He doubted he'd ever get enough of this woman. Warmth bloomed somewhere in his chest, a sensation he hadn't let himself feel in nearly five years.

Rocking into her gently, slowly, he reveled in the way her head tossed back, and her throat arched, her red painted lips falling open in a gasp that was the only sound in the otherwise silent room.

She was a goddess. And he was going to worship her.

Dropping his head to her chest, he drew one of her nipples

into his mouth, his tongue laving the piercing, suckling, nipping with his teeth. First one, then the other, he gave equal and fervent attention to each breast, until she was once again a writhing, moaning mess beneath him.

Nothing he'd ever imagined, nothing he'd ever dreamed, could compare to the woman beneath him, wrapped so tightly around him, taking him deeper than he'd thought possible.

Her fingers scraped against his back as she wrapped one arm around his side, then slid, palm flat, down his back to his ass. Releasing her nipple, he raised his head and pressed his mouth to hers, sinking his tongue between her lips even as he continued to rock against her, pulling out then slowly sinking back in.

Rising up, he tugged her to the edge of the tall bed, making her squeak in surprise. Standing at the edge of the bed, her legs draped over the side of the mattress, he reached down and clasped one ankle in his hand, still wrapped in the straps of the heels she wore. Resting her heel against his chest, he kissed the soft inside of her knee, allowing his mouth to follow the line up to her ankle, then did the same for the other foot, until both rested against his shoulders as he stared down at her, repose on her back on the bed before him, her dark curls a tousled mess of a halo around her head.

Dropping his hand between her thighs, he circled her clit with his thumb, making her clamp that lower lip between her teeth, her eyelids dropping closed. Pinching her clit, he demanded roughly, "Open your eyes. Look at me."

She did as he instructed, opening desire heavy lids, watching him with those deep sapphire blue eyes. Sinking into her again, he growled a warning when her lids dropped shut.

He let his hands drift down the tops of her legs until he could grab handfuls of her thighs where they met her hips, his fingers curling into the soft inner part of her thighs. Her ankles propped on either side of his head on his shoulders, those sexy heels still in place. Using the hands clasped tight on the meaty part of her upper thighs as leverage, he began to move again, slow at first, but it wasn't long before he was pounding into her. She grabbed handfuls of the bedsheet beneath her as she cried out, her head thrashing wildly.

Possessiveness choked him as he stared down at her as she took everything he gave her. His gaze dropped to where they were connected, watched as her body took all of him to the root, felt it as she squeezed the life out of him. He'd make her forget that motherfucker had ever touched her. He'd wipe him from her mind, her body, her heart, her fucking soul. She belonged to *him.*

He wasn't going to last much longer. She was too sexy, too hot, too tight… Fuck.

His fingers were tight on her thighs as he slammed into her, and he loosened his hold slightly, worried that he may bruise her, before she moaned brokenly, "N-no, don't stop. Don't let go. I'm going to come again, *o-oh god, Kasey...*"

Too far gone to form coherent words, he used his body to tell her what he couldn't say. The backs of her thighs and ass slapped against the front of his hips and he tightened his fingers around the thickest, prettiest thighs he'd ever seen as she fell apart in his arms again, squeezing the life out of his cock as he slammed into her, his hips jolting as he felt his orgasm rippling down his spine, drawing his balls tight. Each pulse of her pussy around him matched his own as he emptied every drop inside her with a guttural groan.

His legs shook, his heart pounded in his chest, and her breathing was a ragged pant in the darkness of the room as they came down. Her thighs trembled where they rested against his abdomen, and he turned his head to press a kiss to the inside of her ankle, before using shaking fingers to release the tiny clasp on each ankle, tossing the sexy heels to the floor behind him.

Bracing his hands on either side of her on the bed, he leaned over her, lowering his head so he could trail his mouth down the groove between her breasts, and he was delighted when goosebumps broke out along her skin, making her nipples pebble deliciously. She reached out and grabbed hold of his head, sinking her fingers into his hair and tugging his mouth to her nipple.

"You insatiable wench," he chuckled, but obliged, groaning against her skin. She hummed in appreciation when his tongue circled her, playing with the piercing. "You taste so good."

"I think I'm dead," she whispered shakily, tossing her head against the sheet even as his mouth continued to tease and suckle her breasts. "I've died and gone to orgasm heaven."

He laughed out loud, leaning up and pressing his mouth to hers once more before finally levering himself up enough to pull out of her. "Don't move," he warned, then disappeared into the bathroom. He came back with a damp cloth and caught her knees when she made to close them. "Let me take care of you, darlin'."

Throwing one arm over her eyes, she sighed heavily and let him open her thighs. Pumped full of his cum, it leaked out of her. *What a sight,* he thought with a silent roar of pride before he lowered the cloth to her. He smiled lightly when she groaned at the first pass of the warm, damp cloth against her sex. Washing her gently, knowing without asking that she had to be sore, he took extra care with every inch of her before standing to toss the washcloth into the bathroom.

Returning to the bed, he lowered his frame to it and gathered her against him as she yawned, pressing her face into his chest. Stroking her hair, he chuckled then, coming up with a crystal studded hair pin in his fingers.

"I forgot about those," she mumbled around another yawn, nuzzling her face into him. Leisurely, his fingers sifted through the mess of curls until he found all of the sparkly pins, setting them on the nightstand beside the bed. She moaned when his fingers massaged her scalp, and he chuckled again. Her arm was draped over his body, her fingers drawing small circles on his ribs on his opposite side. "I like how it sounds when you laugh like this."

How had this maddening woman so irrevocably stolen his heart with so little effort?

Nuzzling the top of her head, he spread his other hand over the naked expanse of her back as he murmured, "Glad you think so."

"I'm going to be dead in the morning, if I live that long," she whispered against his skin.

"Why's that?"

"I'm the maid of honor and I ran out of my sister's wedding before the send-off to have hot hate sex with you. She's going to kill me. Or my parents. Whoever finds me first."

"Hot hate sex?" he asked, tilting her chin up. "Do you hate me?"

"Sometimes," she whispered through the dim light of the room, and the honesty made his chest ache. "You're mean to me a lot of the time."

"I didn't know you and Tommy had split," he murmured

gently, searching her dark sapphire eyes with his own. "I would never have been that rude if I'd known."

"Yes, you would have," she mumbled, resting her chin on his chest. "You hate me, too."

"No, I don't," he whispered gently, the truth on the tip of his tongue.

He watched as she rolled her eyes and let her shift slightly, so that she could resume her position laying against his chest, her hair fanned out over his shoulder. Now wasn't the time for confessions, anyway.

Long minutes passed in the quiet of the room, the fingers of one hand stroking through her curls, the other idly strumming lazily along the bare skin of her upper arm. Her hand rested lightly on his chest.

"You know I'm going to ask, Shaun," he murmured quietly, continuing to trail his fingers from the tip of her elbow to her shoulder and back again.

Turning her face into his chest, he felt her hand still against his skin. "I'm not going to talk to you about that, Kasey," she said, her voice muffled where it was buried half in his side and half into the bed beneath them.

"I want to know what this idiot did to lose you."

Leaning up out of the warm cradle of his arm, she pulled the sheet up with her as she rolled to a sitting position, covering her chest as she turned her face forward, turning away from him. “Kasey, please don’t.”

“Don’t turn away from me,” he murmured, trying his best to keep his voice gentle, but still, a bite rang through. “Talk to me.”

“I don’t owe you an explanation,” she snapped, whipping her head around to face him. Christ was she feisty.

“No, you don’t—”

“So just drop it, okay?” she snapped again, then hunched her shoulders in on herself before scooting to the edge of the bed.

“Whoa—” he muttered, curling his arm around her middle and hauling her back into the bed beside him, ignoring her protests. “Just where do you think you’re going?”

“I need to get dressed and go back down to the wedding, to help clean up. We epically failed at our maid of honor and best man duties,” she grumbled around a huff as she tried to disengage his arm that was banded around her like a vice.

“That’s what the staff is for,” he reminded her gently, tightening his hold around her as she struggled. Slapping her ass smartly, he grinned when she gasped. “Stop moving and lay down.”

“Kasey,” she ground out through clenched teeth, and he grinned wider at the annoyance in her voice. Fuck was this fun. “Even if I don’t go back down to the wedding, I still need to go back to the vacation rental. My parents will worry when I don’t come back—"

Reaching for his phone, he opened a text thread with Roxy and shot off a message, asking her to please let the Kendall's know he'd kidnapped their daughter for the remainder of the evening, but that she was safe. Showing it to Shaun when just a second later a thumbs up emoji appeared from Roxy, he said simply, "See? That wasn't difficult."

"You have got to be kidding me," she muttered, shaking her head. "My dad is going to murder you and make me clean it up, then after that, probably murder me."

"You're a grown adult," he reminded her, stroking his hands over the smooth expanse of her back as she slowly, reluctantly, leaned into him. "I think your parents will be more understanding than you give them credit for."

"Freeman is my dad's best friend, and he still gave him a black eye when Free told him how he felt about Jodi," Shaun mumbled dryly, but finally settled back into the circle of his arms. Pulling the sheet up to Shaun's shoulders, he tucked her against his side.

"I'll take my chances," he chuckled, pressing his lips to the top of her head. "You're worth it."

He felt her heavy exhale against the skin of his chest and then heard her whisper, "Your funeral."

He grinned. "Would you mourn me? Visit my grave?"

She shrugged, nuzzling into his side again. "I guess. Those

were some pretty great orgasms. I might need a few more, just to make sure, though. For research purposes, of course."

He laughed out loud, tightening his arms around her, before resting his chin against the top of her head. "I am happy to provide you with as many as it takes, darlin'. Though I have to warn you, I have heard they are habit forming. You may become addicted."

"A-dick-ted," Shaun chuckled around a yawn. "I see what you did there."

"Go to sleep," he ordered roughly, though he gentled it with another chuckle. "You're ridiculous."

"Re-dick-u-lus," she giggled sleepily. He rolled his eyes in the dark.

"Good night, darlin'," he murmured dryly.

She didn't respond because she was already asleep.

TWENTY-THREE

The buzz of a phone vibrating somewhere nearby woke her. Pressed from cheek to toe along Kasey's sleeping form, one of his thighs was thrown over the backs of hers, an arm draped over her back. She nuzzled into the pillow for a heartbeat longer, staring at his sleeping face, repose and serene in the gray light of dawn. He was handsome when he wasn't using that filthy mouth to piss her off.

Shifting so she could reach for the clutch she'd tossed next to the bed sometime last night, she dug out her phone and swiped it open before looking at it fully. "Hello?" she whispered.

"Good morning. Why are you whispering?" Zoey's voice came over the line and Shaun slid out from beneath the weight of Kasey's leg and arm, biting her lip as she realized she had nothing to wear other than her bridesmaid gown. Slinking into the bathroom, she glanced at him, still sleeping, and shut the door.

"I'm… not alone," Shaun whispered, worried even through the door that Kasey would wake and hear her.

"Oooooh," Zoey murmured knowingly, and Shaun rolled her eyes. Looking at herself in the mirror, she groaned at the mess that greeted her. Her hair was a tangled riot of curls that had escaped the loose braid from the night before, her make-up had been fucked off of her, though the red lip stain had held up for its promised twenty-four hours. "Do I dare ask who you're not alone with?"

"Please don't make me say it out loud," she grumbled, putting the phone down on the counter and turning it to speaker so she could wash her face with a fresh washcloth that was folded on the marble top.

"A certain sexy Nascar driver, perhaps?"

"Shhhh," Shaun hissed, glancing at the closed door. Pulling her hair from the remainder of the braid, she ran her fingers through it the best she could, then secured it into another plait that draped over her still naked shoulder.

"Ohhh it is!" Zoey exclaimed, and Shaun could hear her clapping her hands excitedly. "Tell me all of it!"

"Later, you hussy," Shaun quipped lightly, making her best friend laugh.

"Oh come on! I'm so miserable and sex is so uncomfortable right now, I have to live vicariously through you."

"They say sex will help induce labor," Shaun muttered dryly, looking around the bathroom for a robe or towel or *something* to cover herself in before leaving the bathroom. "Something about semen and orgasms helping."

"That's only if your body is already ready for labor, which according to Dr. Jacobs, mine is *not*," Zoey grumbled. "We're already three days overdue and I'm just so ready. Chase has been acting like a maniac. When will you be home to help keep him sane?"

"Help keep *him* sane, or help keep *you* sane?" Shaun asked wryly, pausing with her hand on the door. Barely daring to breathe, she heard weight shift on the bed in the next room, but then all was silent again. Whispering frantically, she muttered, "I gotta go. I'll call you later, bye!"

Ending the call, she took a deep, steadying breath in, then made sure the towel she'd found to wrap around her nakedness was covering at least *most* of her before opening the door and stepping into the room. He had rolled over, his hand extending in his sleep to where her body had been until ten minutes prior. The sheet barely covered his bottom half, pushed down to his waist, revealing his naked back and just the hint of the curve of his bottom. That leg was uncovered as well, and she admired the long, muscular expanse of his thigh and calf.

Spotting his suitcase across the room, she tiptoed toward it, thanking whatever stars were above that the zipper was nearly silent as she pulled it open. Rifling through his belongings, she found a clean, folded Henley and a pair of sweatpants. Glancing over her shoulder again, she dropped the towel to the floor and stuffed her feet into the sweatpants hurriedly, nearly falling over in her haste. She'd worn no bra with the bridesmaid dress, so she'd have to do without, but she pulled the soft material of the Henley over her head and tugged the tail of her braid out of the neck to fall down her back.

The sweatpants were both too long, amazingly, and too big in the waist, so she rolled the waistband over several times, then tucked the front edge of the Henley into the waist. Loathe to put on the sky-high stilettos from the day before, she found a pair of clean white socks and shoved her feet into them.

Turning toward the bed, she was grateful he was still asleep. Picking up her dress and draping it over her arm, she snagged first one, then the second high heel from the floor where he'd tossed them in opposite directions the night before.

Dawn was creeping over the mountain outside the window, casting the room in pale gray light through the curtains.

Kasey shifted in his sleep again, making panic claw at Shaun's throat as she dashed as silently as possible toward the door. Disengaging the lock, she prayed the door didn't squeak when she pulled it open, and then pulled it shut behind her.

Getting away was all that mattered at the moment. She couldn't let herself think about what had happened, what she'd done, what they'd done, couldn't think about anything that had been said between them. It changed nothing. They still hated each other, even if the sex *was* mind blowing.

Padding in stockinged feet to the elevator, she pressed the button and waited. Closing her eyes, she took a deep, shaky breath in.

A text message dinged, and she opened it, rolling her eyes as she read.

I swear to everything holy, if you didn't have at least a dozen o's to make up for skipping out on the rest of the wedding, I'm disowning you.

The three little dots showed up at the bottom of the screen, signaling that her sister was typing again. And then:

Make sure you rehydrate and TELL ME EVERYTHING!

She typed up a quick message just as the elevator chimed that it had arrived, the doors swishing open. Stepping inside, she hit send.

Yes ma'am, but after your honeymoon.
See you in two weeks!

The elevator doors swished shut behind her and started its

descent to the lobby. She was grateful it was still early and that not many guests were mingling about yet, more than likely recovering from their New Year's Eve celebrations. Another message dinged.

You're crazy if you think I'm waiting that long to hear details!

Padding her way to the front desk, she shot off another text.

Margaritas at your house when you're back. I'll bring the chips and salsa. Have fun with your hubby!

The gentleman at the concierge desk gave her a kind smile as she stepped forward, stuffing her cell phone into the pocket of Kasey's stolen sweatpants. "Hi. I'm in need of a shuttle or taxi back to my vacation rental down the road. Is there any available this early?"

"Absolutely, our shuttles and local taxi services are on twenty-four hours for the holiday," he said, then picked up the phone in front of him. Dialing quickly, it was just a moment later that he said, "Yes, a shuttle to—"

"Oh, uhh, the Pike Lodge," she stammered, juggling the dress in her arms. She knew it was painfully obvious that she was doing the walk of shame. Lord she was going to die of shame when she got back to the vacation rental and her entire family. The concierge relayed the message, and she whispered, "Thank you."

"They'll be here in just a few minutes. You're welcome to wait in the lounge by the fireplace until they arrive," he said kindly, motioning toward a wide arched doorway where she could see a smattering of leather sofas and armchairs surrounding a blazing stone fireplace.

She nodded and said another thank you, before wandering over to the lounge, conscious of the fact that she was just in socks and no shoes. Sinking into one of the comfortable leather armchairs, she was debating whether to look like a total moron and put the heels on over the socks or suck it up and go out in the snow in just socks when a shadow fell across the floor to her left.

Before she could react, a hand clasped around her neck, tilting her head up and back. Kasey loomed over her, trembling in anger, as he curled her long plait around his other fist, holding her still as he leaned down to growl menacingly, "I thought I told you I was going to take my time with you. You said you understood. So why are you sneaking out in the dead of morning wearing my clothes, Shaun?"

"Would you rather I find some more of Tommy's clothes he left behind instead?" she taunted breathlessly. His eyes darkened dangerously, and fear, excitement, desire all skittered through her and along every nerve ending.

His fingers curled around her throat, the space between his thumb and forefinger cradling the underside of her jaw just tight enough to bite and she swallowed hard as he drew even closer, breathing against her mouth, "If I ever see you wearing anything that belonged to him or to any man other than myself, I'll turn your ass a pretty shade of pink."

"I fucking dare you," she hissed, but it didn't hold the weight she wanted it to. No, it came out all breathy and needy and oh fuck she was in trouble because that… sounded divine.

"Bet, darlin'," he growled low, his teeth bared in a snarl, but then his eyes softened, and he groaned a heartbeat before his mouth crashed onto hers. His hands still held her head captive, and she was powerless against him, instead simply clasping her hands over top of the one that still held her throat. When his mouth finally left hers, he growled low, "I haven't had any coffee yet and I barely pulled on clothes on my way to find you, you infuriating, pain in the ass woman."

Releasing her, he extended his hand down to her. She stared at it for a long moment before placing her hand in his and allowing him to pull her out of the chair.

Bringing her close to his body, he leaned in and whispered, "I'd follow you, you know."

Her dress slid to the floor, her grasp on the slinky material giving way at his huskily spoken words, and she gasped, "What?"

"You were running. I'd follow you," he murmured low, and this time she heard the warning in his voice. She had no doubts that he meant it. His lips flit over the corner of her mouth, causing electricity to zing across every nerve ending, making her shiver.

Taking a step away from her, he bent at the waist to retrieve the dress that had pooled at their feet and to take her shoes from her. "Were you seriously considering not wearing any shoes outside?" he grumbled, steering her toward the main lobby. Calling over to the concierge, he said, "The lady will not be needing the shuttle, she's staying."

"And just where are you taking me?" she hissed as his fingers tightened around hers. Her cheeks were on fire in embarrassment.

"Breakfast."

"Breakfast?" Shaun parroted dumbly.

"Yes, breakfast. It's the meal normal people eat when they wake up in the morning. Usually comes with a cup of coffee."

"Kasey, I have no shoes—" she protested as he led her toward one of the several restaurants inside the massive resort. "They're not going to let me inside. And I'm wearing your clothes with no bra on—"

"Oh, trust me, I've noticed," he muttered darkly as they

stopped at the hostess stand just inside a set of giant double doors that looked like they'd been carved from massive trees. The smell of a breakfast buffet wafted over to them, and her stomach growled. He smirked over at her. "Lucky for us, it's so early in the morning after every other human on the mountain was up late as fuck getting hammered, so we should be relatively alone."

A woman that appeared to be in her late forties welcomed them, taking in their rumpled state, Shaun's dress and shoes in Kasey's hands and smiled knowingly, then led them both to a table.

"Would it be possible to have a booth? Please?" Kasey asked, and the woman nodded, motioning to a booth situated in one corner, which held much more privacy than the table. "Perfect, thank you."

Half a heartbeat later a petite, brunette waitress had sidled over to them as they settled into the booth on opposite sides. "Coffee?" the woman asked, and the chorus of 'Yes, please' made them both smile. The waitress was back just a moment later with two porcelain coffee cups and a carafe of coffee. Pouring out two servings, she set the carafe on the table for them. "Any cream or sugar?" When they both shook their heads, no, she continued, "Alright then. Do you need a few minutes to look over the menu? Our strawberry cream cheese stuffed French toast is our special this morning."

"Oof, sold," Shaun moaned and slid the unopened menu toward the edge of the booth table with a smile. "With a side of bacon, please. Limp. It smells amazing."

Kasey's mouth tilted up at one corner as he perused his menu, and Shaun's cheeks heated again. Handing the waitress the menu, he said quietly, "I'll have the western omelet and a side of sausage gravy, please."

When the waitress had walked away, Kasey leaned forward on his elbows across the table and whispered, "Limp bacon, huh? I got the impression last night you liked your meat a little...*firmer.*"

"*You are a menace,*" Shaun hissed through her teeth, her cheeks roaring into flames to match the fireplace that blazed across the room. Kasey laughed out loud and leaned back into his seat, picking up his coffee cup and bringing it to his lips.

His hair was still messily tousled, his jaw shadowed with a days' worth of growth, and he wore a plain white long-sleeved shirt, and she'd noticed he'd pulled on a similar pair of gray sweatpants. His feet had been shoved into what looked like a beat-up pair of crocs, which made her grin. She kept his gaze, staring into those gray-blue eyes that always seemed to look like they were bringing a storm with them.

"Text your parents," he murmured, motioning with his chin toward her phone that she'd placed on the table off to the side.

"Why?" she asked, raising an eyebrow at him. "Are you keeping me hostage?"

"A willing one, yes," he drawled, setting his coffee cup down and wrapping the fingers of both hands around the mug.

"You're so unbelievably conceited," she scoffed, a sardonic laugh escaping her. "Just because—just because we—"

"Don't."

"Don't what?" she hissed, leaning over her tightly clenched hands that rested on the top of the table in front of her.

"Don't open that smart mouth of yours and try to come up with some half-cocked excuse as to why last night was a mistake, or that it wasn't absolutely mind-blowing," he murmured quietly, though she sensed the tension rolling off of him in waves.

"Why, you arrogant ass—"

Reaching across the table quick as a viper strike, he clasped the point of her chin between his finger and thumb, holding her still as he ground out, "Lie to yourself all you want, but don't lie to me, darlin'." His fingers slackened and then rubbed his thumb over the fullness of her bottom lip. "Stay with me, Shaun. Just for a little while. Let's just pretend for a moment that nothing outside of this place matters."

Well, damn. How was she supposed to say no to that?

TWENTY-FOUR

"I need to get back to the rental, Kasey," she whispered weakly in protest, but he saw the submission in her eyes. She wanted to stay. Wanted to be his, at least for a little longer. He'd take it. "My parents are going to wonder where I am. What am I supposed to say? 'Sorry to bail on family vacay, I'm busy getting dicked down'?"

Slipping out of his seat of the booth, he shushed her when she protested as he slid in beside her, pressing his thigh against hers and draping his arm around her shoulders.

"That fucking mouth," he drawled on a chuckle, then silenced her with his mouth on hers. "You're going to be a handful."

"Good thing you have two hands," she snapped dryly, but he recognized the breathlessness in her voice. The fight had gone out of her sometime in the last twelve hours. She fought valiantly to maintain it, but he knew it was rapidly disintegrating.

"What's your favorite color?" he asked, and nearly chuckled at the confusion that crossed her beautiful face.

"Excuse me?" she asked, her eyebrows drawing close together in a V.

Tapping her on the tip of the nose, he quipped, "Come on now, I know you know English. What is your favorite color?"

"What does that matter?" Leaning away from him slightly, she shook her head.

He shrugged. "I can guess if you'd like. See how close I am."

She laughed and rolled her eyes, tossing her braid over her shoulder as she reached for her coffee. Bringing it to her lips, she took a long drink, then turned those stunning sapphire eyes on him again. Defiance, a taunt, hung in the air. "Go right ahead, big guy."

Taking a drink of his own coffee, he studied her. "Blue." Her face went blank and he grinned. "Am I correct?"

Her eyes narrowed on him. "That wasn't even a fair question, half the world's population's favorite color is blue. That's just a lucky guess. You won't get that lucky twice."

"Try me," he murmured, sitting back in the booth next to her, his thigh still pressed close against the length of hers under the table. The waitress arrived then with their plates of food, and they each said a quiet thank you before she turned back to him. "You choose the question."

Stabbing her fork into the decadent, strawberry cream cheese stuffed French toast, she stuck a bite into her mouth and moaned, the sound going straight to Kasey's dick, making it thicken in his sweatpants. Not great timing.

"What's my favorite movie?"

Slathering his omelet with the sausage gravy, he used his fork to cut a bite before sticking it into his mouth. "That's a very broad question. Narrow it down a bit. Are we talking favorite overall, favorite comfort movie, or what?"

Chewing on a bite of her food, she swallowed, then turned to him. "Favorite comfort movie."

"*Princess Bride.*"

Her gasp made him grin. She didn't even have to say the words; he knew he was right. "But your guilty pleasure movies are *The Fast and the Furious* series."

"Have you been spying on me?" she snapped, setting down her fork and staring at him. "This isn't funny, Kasey. That's creepy as fuck."

"You're much easier to read than you think," he said simply. "Your phone case has blue tiger lilies on it, and the tag on your suitcase is some other kind of blue flowers. That one *was* just a lucky guess. I didn't take you for a pink kind of girl. *The Fast and the Furious* series is a no brainer with your affinity for cars. I'll bet you and Tristan have had marathons watching those movies just the two of you." Picking up his coffee, he took another drink. "*The Princess Bride* was a little tougher, but you made several references to it in your maid of honor speech yesterday; so that was really just a wild guess."

"That's still creepy," Shaun muttered, turning back to her food.

"I'm just observant," he chuckled. "I was the odd man out, the middle child, so I spent a lot of time watching other people as a kid. Just something that followed me into adulthood, I suppose."

"Is that how you knew?" she whispered, looking at him with narrowed eyes. "You could see it?"

His heart thudded in his chest. He knew what she was referring to. "It was more… what I *didn't* see."

Her fingers tightened around the fork in her hand and she stabbed another bite of French toast, her motions stilted and angry.

"What happened, Shaun?" he asked quietly.

She shook her head, then turned to fix him with that intense sapphire gaze. "I'm not rehashing my failed engagement with you, Kase. If I decide to stay, and that's a big if mind you, there's no digging into pasts, no long, heartfelt talks. I don't want to get to know you, and quite honestly, I don't want you to know anymore about me than you already do. This can be a break from constantly making each other's lives hell, but at the end of it, nothing changes. This is just to scratch the itch of whatever this is. Understand?"

His lips twitched with the need to smile at her fervent

declaration, knowing full well that this wasn't going to be finished at the end of this holiday break.

Her eyes narrowed, witness to the teasing glint in his own, and she waved the tines of her fork in his direction. "I mean it, Kasey. We get this out of our system, and we go our separate ways. I can't deny that we have chemistry, and clearly we are attracted to each other. But at the end of the day, I can't stand you and you can't stand me."

"Bet I can change your mind, darlin'," he drawled, reaching out and running his finger down the edge of her jaw and down the side of her neck.

"Kasey…" she muttered through clenched teeth, though her head did tilt into his touch, her eyes softening as desire took over. Damn woman would try to fight to the bitter end.

"Get that whipped cream to go," he murmured, sliding his mouth over hers languidly. "If this weekend is all I get, I'm going to ruin you, darlin'."

TWENTY-FIVE

"Do you not know how to answer a cell phone?" her mother demanded the second she stepped inside the front door of the rental lodge. Her face flamed a hundred shades of red when her aunts turned to look at her with knowing eyes.

"I'm sorry, I was safe," she mumbled, dropping her eyes to the floor. "I was… with Kasey."

"Roxy let me know," Serenity said gently, though her blue eyes were still narrowed. "Still, you could have let me know yourself so I wasn't worried last night when you couldn't be found after the reception ended. For all I knew you'd been kidnapped or murdered."

Summer laughed out loud, shaking her head. "You're being intentionally overdramatic." Turning to Shaun, Summer murmured in a hushed tone, "She watched you hightail it out the door after Kasey, and when neither of you returned, we put two and two together. We knew where you were."

Shaun grimaced, letting out a sigh. "Awesome." Raising her eyes to her mother's, she said with more bravado than she felt, "I actually just came to get my bag."

"What? Why? Are you trying to go home early? Did he hurt you?" her mother asked, looking her up and down once, as if checking for injury.

"No! Ugh, no, Mom. I'm fine," Shaun muttered on a whisper, her face flaming again. *Oh my god this is worse than I thought.* "I'm—I'm going to—"

"She's going to go with Kasey is what she's trying to say," Sadie laughed as she walked up, leaning over the marble island in the kitchen, winking. "They're not finished yet. Nice walk of shame outfit, by the way."

"*Ohmygod,*" Shaun groaned, covering her face with her hands. "Can we *not*?!"

The three older women laughed, and Summer squeezed Shaun's shoulder gently. "There is nothing wrong with having a healthy and active… life."

"I'm going to die," Shaun breathed from behind her hands, shaking her head. "Okay! You all get it—"

"Well, yes, we do, but we're talking about *you* getting it right now—" Sadie chortled, making Shaun groan in agony at the embarrassment that had taken up residence in her body.

"Ahht!" she snapped, covering her ears with her hands. "I don't want to know *anything about anything!*" When the women laughed again, she lowered her hands from her ears and straightened her back. "Can we be done? This is torture."

"Are you being safe?"

"Oh, yes, good question. Do you need condoms? What size? I'm sure Micah has—"

"I mean, I guess, I'm not *opposed* to grandbabies right away, but—"

"Ohmygod you guys, stop!" Shaun laughed on a shout, looking from her mother to her two aunts. "You all need hobbies! I'm leaving!"

Taking the stairs two at a time, she raced for the room she'd been designated and flopped down onto the center of the bed, face down, groaning audibly into the pillow. Bunch of biddies.

Standing and moving into the bathroom, she showered quickly, washing the gallon of hairspray out of her curls from the day before and scrubbing the red lip stain off her lips finally. She shaved her legs, then climbed out, towel drying as fast as she could.

She dressed in a pair of skintight black jeans and a black long-sleeved shirt that clung to her curves. Pulling on a cream-colored vest that was lined in fleece, she zipped it to just below her breasts, then combed through her curls, adding a liberal amount of cream to tame them before letting her hair fall around her shoulders and down her back to air dry. She put on minimal makeup, just blush and mascara, then packed her toiletries and stuffed a couple changes of clothes into the travel backpack that doubled as a purse, including Kasey's clothes she'd worn that morning. Hanging her dress and placing it in the garment bag, she placed the black high heels in their box and left them on the bed for later.

She was just exiting the room when Roxy walked out of the room across the hall with her suitcase behind her and her garment bag over her arm. When she spotted Shaun, the redhead winked at her.

"Are you leaving?" Shaun asked as they made their way down the hallway.

"Yeah, I'm headed out. I don't like the cold," she grumbled, but smiled. "You?"

"I'm uhh—going to the main lodge," she stammered, blushing again. What the fuck was wrong with her?

Roxy elbowed her in the side and waggled her dark red eyebrows at her, making Shaun laugh. "Get it, sis. Just do me a favor?"

"Uhh, sure?"

"Don't break his heart, please."

Shaun scoffed, shaking her head. "That's not what this is. Hearts aren't involved. This is just… getting it out of our systems."

"Okay."

"Why does it sound like you're skeptical?" Shaun asked, eyeing the redhead warily.

Roxy shrugged, pulling on their jackets as they made it to

the front door. "I just see more there than 'just getting it out of your system' is all."

"I can't stand Kasey," Shaun muttered, pulling on her boots. "And he can't stand me. The only time we're not arguing is when we're—well, you know. Nothing else has changed."

"Mmhmm," Roxy hummed in agreement, but again, Shaun sensed a note of skepticism in the other woman's tone.

"This is just a nice vacation with the added bonus of really great sex with no strings attached," Shaun continued, zipping her coat. "Scratching an itch. That's all."

Roxy nodded, then winked. "Okay."

"I'm serious!" Shaun exclaimed, her heart starting to race with anxiety as they made their way outside, where a taxi was waiting for Roxy to take her to the airport, just as another shuttle arrived for Shaun to take her back to the main lodge.

"Whatever you say," Roxy drawled in that heavy Texas twang. Closing the door after loading her suitcase and garment bag into the backseat, she walked around the back of the car and opened the rear driver's side door. "Have fun scratchin' that itch, doll."

Roxy climbed into the backseat and closed the door and the taxi rolled away. The shuttle door opened, and still she stood in the middle of the snowy driveway as panic began to claw at her chest.

This wasn't scratching an itch. This wasn't no-strings-attached, vacation sex.

Waving the shuttle off, she watched the door slide shut, and then heard the hiss of the brakes being released as it rolled away. Clutching at the neckline of her shirt, she sucked in lungful after lungful of air, then let her head fall back until she stared up into the bluest of skies above. It was a stunning beginning to the new year. The temperature was still bitingly cold, but the sun was shining, the sky was impossibly blue, and the clouds in the sky were big and fluffy and brilliantly white.

Darting back inside, she hurried up the stairs and into the room she'd just left minutes before. Slamming her suitcase on the bed, she threw her things inside, not even taking the time to fold or caring that everything would be wrinkled before she got home. Pulling out her phone, she pulled up the number for a taxi company. Moments later she hung up. She had ten minutes.

She stuffed the garment bag with her dress inside and barely got the zipper closed around it and the high heels she shoved in unceremoniously before leaving the room again, dragging her suitcase behind her.

"What on earth, where are you going? I thought you were heading to the main lodge," her mother said with alarm when Shaun dragged her suitcase down the stairs.

"Zoey called," she lied, swallowing hard. Her mother's blue eyes lit up with joy and she clapped her hands. Guilt for lying to her mother assailed her, but she needed to go, and she needed to go *now*.

"Baby time?" Seren asked excitedly, and it was all Shaun could do to nod her head yes. "Oh, this is just so exciting! Go, go! We'll be home in a week! Be careful and let me know when you land!"

Nodding, she hugged her mom hard, squeezing tight for an extended moment. "I'll see you guys when you get home. Have fun."

A horn honked outside, and she pulled away from her mother and headed toward the door. She spotted her father out of the corner of her eye and turned to wave, blowing him a kiss as she exited. Nearly tripping down the wide stone steps, she rushed toward the cab, hauling the suitcase into the trunk before climbing into the backseat.

Resting her head against the headrest behind her, she squeezed her eyes shut and tried not to think about the man that would be waiting for her, or his reaction when he realized she wasn't returning.

TWENTY-SIX

"Let me get your bag," Chase said as he turned the Jeep Rubicon into Shaun's driveway in front of the duplex apartment she rented. Her neighbor's car was gone, fresh tire marks cutting through the deep snow. An older set had cut through her side, and footprints led to her door. "I'll make sure you get inside safely. Zoey and I were here yesterday to check on Steve, but I'd rather be safe than sorry."

Shaun smiled gently over at him as she climbed down out of the Rubicon. He had been more than willing to come pick her up from the airport a half an hour away, and she was grateful that he hadn't asked why she'd come home a week early, like Zoey would have. "Thank you, Deputy Manning. I appreciate it."

Zoey's husband was a deputy at the local sheriff's department and took the safety of those he cared about very seriously. Tall, dark, and handsome with a sweet personality and a protective streak to boot, he'd been perfect for her timid and shy best friend.

He lugged her suitcase through the snow like it weighed

nothing. She unlocked the front door and he stepped inside, making a quick check of all the rooms, which didn't take long because her apartment wasn't very large, and then he was back with a smile. "Everything looks good."

"Thank you, Chase," she said and kicked the snow off her boots by the door. "And thank you for the ride."

"Zoey would have had my hide if you'd taken an uber all the way from Pellston," he laughed, stopping at the door.

"It's not that far," Shaun said with a roll of her eyes.

"All the more reason for you to not take an uber," Chase said drolly and she sighed, and then his cobalt blue gaze met hers and it was gentle, though a little sad. "Strangers still make her nervous. She just wants to make sure you're safe."

Shaun nodded. "I know."

"The doctor told us today that if she doesn't go into labor by tomorrow they'll induce, so I guess it's a good thing you came home early," he chuckled. "She really wanted you here."

She swallowed hard and forced a smile. "I just had a feeling."

"I should get back home," he said and smiled again. "I'll keep you posted."

"Thank you, Chase."

He winked at her and then was out the door, closing it behind him.

Steve, her tortie cat, wound herself between her legs,

meowing in hello. Shaun bent down and picked her up, cradling her against her chest. Steve purred, rubbing her little face into Shaun's hands for aggressive pets, making her chuckle.

"I missed you, too," she murmured, walking down the hall to the bedroom. Setting Steve down at the foot of the bed, she flopped into the middle of the mattress, burying her face in the pillows.

She'd done everything in her power to forget the last several days. The brooding, heavy lidded stares from those storm cloud eyes, the way his fingers had felt against every inch of her body, or the rush of electricity when his mouth would crush against hers… she wouldn't even let herself think of the way it had felt to have him buried so deep inside her—

No, ma'am. Rolling into a sitting position, she shook herself. *Nope. Don't even go there. Don't think about that.* Whatever this was, it was over. Done. Finite. They'd gotten it over with, and now they could both move on. And it would be a *long* time before she would have to see Kasey again.

Standing, she walked into the bathroom and turned on the shower, letting the water heat up until the small bathroom was filled with steam. Stripping, she dropped her clothes to the floor and then stepped into the shower, reveling in the scorching spray of water as it did wonders to relieve the tension that had tightened her shoulders into knots.

She felt a million times better by the time she stepped out

of the shower. Passing the towel over her body to dry, she then wrapped it around her hair and walked naked back into the bedroom. She skipped underwear and chose a tightly fitted pair of yoga shorts, the inseams high on the inside of her thighs. Pulling a loose, long-sleeved shirt over her head, her breasts swayed unrestrained beneath it.

Pulling the towel from around her hair, she combed through it and then used her fingers to apply a curl cream, then left it to air dry.

The flight she'd managed to get on from Colorado the evening before had gotten her to Detroit, but she'd had a ten-hour layover between that flight and the flight to get her to the small Pellston airport in northern Michigan. Yawning broadly, she walked into the kitchen. Steve jumped up onto the counter, meowing excitedly as Shaun scooped dry food into her bowl.

Despite the fact that it was barely noon, she was exhausted, having not slept since she'd woken in Kasey's arms the morning before. Falling into bed, she pulled the comforter up around her chin and fell into a deep, dreamless sleep mere minutes later.

TWENTY-SEVEN

Jolted awake, Shaun sat upright in bed, her hair a tousled mess around her head. Pushing the rioting curls away from her face, she blinked several times to clear the sleep from her eyes, listening for whatever it was that had woken her so abruptly.

A hard, impatient knock sounded again, and she jumped out of the bed, nearly tripping on the sheet in her haste. Grabbing her phone, she saw several missed calls from Chase and her heart jumped into her throat. Racing down the hall, she skidded to a stop at the door, unlatching the lock and pulling it open frantically.

"Is it time— Kasey!" she stuttered, stunned when she came face to face with him on her doorstep. "What are you doing here?"

"I told you I'd follow you if you ran," he murmured darkly, stepping over the threshold until he stood directly in front of her. Gripping her hips in his hands roughly, she was hauled up against him and her mouth parted in a silent gasp when she felt him pressed up against her. "I can't stay away. You've made it impossible for me to stay away, Shaun."

"No, this was supposed to be done—*over*—in Colorado—"

"No, *we were supposed to have the weekend,*" he countered roughly.

"—yeah well, we didn't. Whatever that was, it's over now—"

"Is that really what you want?" he interrupted, dropping his voice. "Be honest, because if you really wanted that to be over, you wouldn't be pressing that greedy pussy against my cock right now."

She spluttered in a derisive laugh. "*God!* You are such an arrogant son of a bitch—"

"And you lie like a goddamn rug, darlin'," he interrupted on a snarl, talking over her. She clicked her teeth shut, grinding them together until her jaw ached. "You lie to yourself; you try to lie to me… But I'm not listening to those lies anymore. You can't hide the way you feel, the way I make you feel when I'm buried so deep—"

Shoving her hands into his shoulders as hard as she could, she pushed him away, but barely. His hands never relinquished their bruising hold on her hips, their middles pressed tight together. Heaving breaths expanded her chest, her heart hammering a heavy cadence beneath her breasts as anger twisted through her.

"Fuck you," she whispered a heartbeat before she launched

herself into his arms, his mouth crashing down onto hers ferociously. Picking her up beneath her ass, he stepped inside and kicked the door closed with a resounding slam.

He made it half a dozen steps into the living room before setting her down none too gently and immediately tearing his jacket off his arms, dropping it to the floor, then reaching for the stretchy material of the tight fitted yoga shorts that had ridden high on her thighs. He dropped to his knees and ripped them straight down the middle, eliciting a shocked gasp from her as he shredded them with his fingers. She wasn't wearing panties, and the next heartbeat he'd caught her around the knees with both hands and yanked her down to the floor with him, pushing her down onto her back and following with his own body.

Manacling her wrists, he hauled them over her head and pinned them to the floor, at the same time grinding into her, between her already spread thighs, groaning audibly against the skin of her neck. With his other hand, he released the button and lowered the zipper of his jeans, tugging his boxer briefs down until his cock sprang free. Shaun moaned when he rubbed his length up and down her cleft, teasing, before he sank two fingers into her, testing her readiness.

"Why do you do this to me?" he growled fiercely, lining himself up against her, just the head of his shaft pressing into her. She cried out in frustration, gyrating her hips upward, trying to take more of him. Slamming into her hard and oh-so deep, she let her head fall back against the floor as he pounded into her over and over. "Why do you fight me, Shaun? Why do you fight this? *Why did you run from me?*"

Circling his hips, she groaned in ecstasy when he hit just the right spot inside her, her clit rubbing against him as he ground into her.

Gripping the hem of her sweatshirt, he yanked it up until he uncovered one breast, dipping his head to take the pierced nipple into his mouth, biting and sucking, until she writhed beneath him, cries of intense pleasure escaping her throat. Flutters began to tighten her inner muscles around him, and she gasped out breathlessly, "Oh my god, Kase. I'm going to come—"

Slamming his hips into hers, he stilled completely, stopping her from going over that edge and she groaned, yanking on her hands, but still he kept them pinned above her head. "Not yet."

"Ohmygod Ohmy*god*," she panted, grinding against him in a desperate circle. "Please. *Oooh* fuck."

"Are you going to run from me again?" he panted raggedly, his voice low and demanding, and it skittered over every nerve ending in her body, lighting it up like a Christmas tree.

"N-no," Shaun sobbed, pressing into him. "Please!"

"Are you going to be a good girl and take this dick

however I want to give it to you?" he snarled into the heat of her neck. She nodded frantically, inhaling the intoxicating scent of him. Clamping down on him where he was pressed so deep, she felt his cock jump and he groaned into her ear. His hand found her breast half hidden beneath the sweatshirt and palmed it fully, then his fingers pinched her nipple sharply, and again she tightened around him with a gasp. "You're so naughty. You want this so bad, don't you darlin'?"

"Yes," she sobbed, nodding. "Yes, Kasey."

"I told you I'd follow you," he whispered roughly into the skin of her neck as he started to move again, hard, brutal thrusts that sent him as deep as he could possibly go. "I can't stay away, Shaun. I can't."

Wrapping her legs around his hips, she lifted to meet each thrust, and when his mouth found her nipple again, she detonated like a bomb. Her back arched, her legs shook, stars burst behind her tightly clenched eyelids, and the cry that was torn from her throat was half sob. In some part of her brain, she registered his answering growl of approval as she closed around him again and again, even as he continued to piston his hips, driving into her until he came with a rough shout.

Her wrists were released, and she pulled them from above her head, wrapping her arms around Kasey's waist, splaying her hands wide on the back of his shirt. Her breathing was ragged as she pressed her face into the crook of his neck, her lips moving against the pulse that fluttered wildly, his own breathing none too steady.

Aftershocks fluttered through both of them, and still they lay locked together on the floor as their breathing returned to normal.

Her phone, which had clattered to the floor earlier, started ringing, the buzzing from the vibration muted from the carpet. Stretching her hand out, she grasped it and swiped to answer, bringing it to her ear and doing her best to not sound out of breath as she asked, "Go time?"

"Go time," Chase's voice came across the line, a mix of fear and excitement in his tone. "She still has a way to go, so I'll let you know when it's closer."

"I'll see you guys soon," she said, then let out a heavy sigh when she hung up the phone, letting it fall back to the carpet near her head. Kasey had raised up onto his elbows above her, his gray-blue gaze steady on her face as she turned back to look at him. His fingers were combing through the mess of curls surrounding her head, and she couldn't stop the blush that stained her cheeks, because he was still buried inside her. Wiggling slightly beneath him, she stammered, "Well, this is awkward. Kasey, I need to get up."

"Why did you run, Shaun?"

Groaning, she squeezed her eyes shut. "Kasey. Please let's not do this right now."

"I don't think there's a better time to do this, darlin'," he murmured, and she hated how much she liked the feel of his chest rumbling against hers as he spoke, or the husky, intimate way his words touched her. "I want to know what I did to make you run away."

"Nothing!" she exclaimed, throwing her arms wide and letting them fall to the carpet on either side of them. "Nothing, Kasey. You did nothing. I came home because Zoey was close to going into labor—"

"I told you to stop lying to me," he growled, pinning her head between his hands and forcing her to look at him. Glaring up at him, her lips tightened into a hard line. "You ran. Plain and simple. Don't try and spin it any other way."

Pressing his hips between her legs, she gasped as she felt him fill her again.

"I didn't know if you'd gotten into a wreck on the side of that damn mountain. I didn't know if you'd been kidnapped by some creep. I had to walk up to that vacation rental and ask your parents where you'd disappeared to, because when I'd sent you off after breakfast, it was with the understanding that you were coming back to me." Braced on his elbows on either side of her, he moved his hips, sliding in and out of her slowly, leisurely. Biting her lip, her eyelids fluttered closed for a heartbeat before he pressed his mouth to hers. Kissing her until she was breathless, he finally released her lips and whispered huskily, "To *this*, Shaun."

TWENTY-EIGHT

Her face was clasped between his hands, his fingers spearing up into her curls as they lay spread out around her head in a riotous halo. It had been obvious as soon as she'd opened the door that she had just woken up, her face was clean of all make-up… and she was the most beautiful thing he'd ever seen, spread out beneath him, taking everything he was giving her.

He'd wanted to throttle her when Serenity had told him she'd high-tailed it back to Michigan, hours prior. At the time, he'd thought he was giving her the time that she needed to gather her things, give an explanation of where she was going… Little did he know he was giving her ample time to *run*.

Trepidation had risen in his chest when Levi had walked into the great room, impaling him with that intense blue stare he shared with his middle daughter. But the elder gentleman had just nodded his head, to which Kasey had taken as grudging acceptance.

It was better than a black eye, he'd reminded himself, remembering the shiner Levi had given to Freeman when the man had found out his best friend had intentions with his oldest daughter.

He'd packed his bag and had been on the next flight to Michigan. He was only hours behind her. His anger had fueled him.

Now, as he watched her beneath him, that anger faded, replaced with such intense longing it burned in his chest, making it tight. Her lips, full and plump and well kissed, were parted slightly, her head inching back, the thin column of her throat arching, those soft, breathy moans falling from her lips driving him damn near crazy. His dick got harder, somehow, and he clenched his jaw against the intense pleasure spearing through him.

"You're mine," he breathed raggedly, tilting her face forward again. "Shaun."

She shook her head, keeping her eyes closed. Her fingers moved against his ribs, curling into fists in the fabric of his shirt. Her hips moved with his, maintaining the tempo he set; slow, deep, unhurried.

"Shaun," he growled through clenched teeth. "Look at me."

Again, she shook her head where it was clasped between his palms. "No," she panted.

"Then say it."

"No," cried, arching her back as he drove in, harder than

before.

"You stubborn woman," he groaned. "You can either look at me while I fuck you, or you can say the words we both know are true. Your choice, darlin'."

After what felt like a lifetime, those deep sapphire blue eyes of hers opened and met his, and he was gone. Even if she refused to say the words, he knew it was true. She knew it was true. He just had to make her see it, too.

"That's a good girl," he murmured low, his voice cracking as he let go of his restraint. Slamming into her again and again, he knew when she was close, could feel the little tremors that gripped him where he was pressed so deeply, felt it in the way her legs trembled where they were wrapped around his hips, the way her mouth parted on a silent 'o'. "Yes, Shaun. Give it to me."

And then she was coming apart in his arms, again, and it was the most amazing thing he'd ever witnessed, the way she came with her entire being. His own release was converging at the base of his spine, drawing tight with every spasm that choked the life out of his cock.

"Kase!" she cried, her eyes wide as she stared up at him. "Please!"

His movements stuttered as he started to come, and he slammed in one more time as rope after rope of cum jetted deep. He wanted to kiss her, wanted to feel her mouth against his as they came together, but he stayed where he was so he could watch her face, be witness to the kaleidoscope of emotions that passed over her. She felt it, whatever this was, just as he did. He was surer of it now than ever before.

That's why she'd refused to say it. Not because it wasn't true… but because it was.

TWENTY-NINE

Thoughts tumbled around her head like a loose rock in a dryer, bouncing and clanging so loudly she couldn't concentrate. *What the hell had just happened?*

Kasey had helped her to her feet and she'd nearly died as evidence of what they'd just done started sliding down the inside of her thighs. He'd grinned at her as she darted past him to the bathroom. Turning on the shower, she'd climbed in, not even waiting for the water to heat up, shrieking silently as the cold spray hit her square in the back. Her own personal penance for her actions.

Grabbing a claw clip from the shower rod she kept it stashed on, she gathered her curls and pinned them to the top of her head, having just washed them several hours before. She scrubbed her body as the water slowly warmed, and just about the time that it was comfortable, she turned it off and climbed out.

Wrapping the towel around her body, she exited, crossing to the bedroom quickly, only to stop when she found Kasey reclining on her pillows, his phone in hand, scrolling aimlessly.

The movement in the doorway must have caught his attention because he raised his eyes from the screen of his phone to hers and then that grin was back, his eyes mischievous.

"Now that's a sight I could get used to," he murmured huskily.

"Yeah, well don't," she snapped, striding into the bedroom and over to the dresser. Snatching open the drawer, she grabbed a pair of boy short underwear and managed to step into them and pull them up her legs and into place without giving him a show. Next, she took a black sports bra out and shoved her arms into it, pulling it over her head. That was trickier, getting the tight material into place with the towel still tucked around her upper body, but she managed, though it was a struggle.

The towel dropped to the floor around her feet and she sighed in aggravation, but didn't bother grabbing it back up. She picked out a long-sleeved, olive-green shirt and tugged it over her head, then shoved her feet into the first pair of jeans she could find, tugging them up over her hips and fastening them. Turning, she braced her hands on her hips and glared at him, where he still lay in the center of her bed, one knee raised, that foot flat on the bed.

"Why are you here, Kasey?" she demanded.

He impaled her with that gray-blue stare long enough to make her squirm. Crossing her arms over her middle, she cocked one hip out defensively.

"You ran."

She rolled her eyes and he growled from where he was, the sound skittering over her nerves and making her shiver. "And?"

He rolled to a sitting position, throwing his legs over the side of the bed, then stood. "And? I told you I'd follow, Shaun."

"Do you understand how creepy that is?" she demanded, though her heart had started hammering in her chest as he took slow, measured steps toward her. "Kind of stalkerish, don't you think?"

"If I thought you didn't want this as much as I do, sure," he murmured, shoving his hands in his pockets in that classic Kasey move. "But you do, don't you, darlin'? You just don't want to admit it."

Chewing on the inside of her cheek, she raised her eyes to somewhere over his shoulder to avoid looking him in the eyes.

"Why is it so impossible for you to admit that you're enjoying this? I am. I would like the chance to explore this further." He stepped into her line of sight, and she brought her gaze back to his. "So can we just enjoy this? See what happens?"

Everything in her was screaming no. This was dangerous, and the reason she had run from him in Colorado in the first place. She didn't do casual hookups… but she wasn't sure she was ready to let anyone in yet, either. Especially Kasey.

"I honestly can't think about any of this right now," Shaun finally said, shaking her head. "I really need to get to the hospital."

"I can drive you," he said, motioning toward the door. She swung her eyes up to his.

"No, that's not necessary, really," she mumbled. "You don't want to sit in a hospital waiting room for who knows how long."

"I can keep you company while you wait, too," he said quietly, shrugging. "I don't mind."

"Kasey—"

He took her shoulders in his hands, pulling her toward him and kissing her soundly, effectively shutting her up. "Do you have to argue about everything?"

"It would seem so," she grumbled, rolling her eyes up at him.

"Get your shoes on, grab your purse, do whatever you need to do to get ready, and we will head over there so you can be with your friend," he said gently, turning her and giving her a soft shove out the bedroom door. "No more arguing."

Glaring at him over her shoulder, she disappeared back into the bathroom, rifling through the few cosmetics that were in the drawer, the rest still packed in her suitcase that she hadn't taken the time to unpack. A touch of concealer under her eyes to combat the lack of quality sleep, a swipe of blush for color, and a quick flick of mascara on her lashes was enough to make her feel a little better. Her hair was a hot mess, having fallen asleep with it still wet earlier, but she twisted it into a knot at the top of her head and re-secured it with the claw clip. Tendrils framed her face, but there was no taming those.

Walking into the kitchen, she saw Steve standing on the counter, shamelessly purring and rubbing against Kasey, who was giving her all the attention she could possibly want.

"Steve, get your furry ass off the counter," she snapped. "You bad girl."

"You named your female cat *Steve*?" Kasey asked, and his eyebrows rose in surprise.

"She was a rescue. I found her out by the trash bins last year when she was like three weeks old, and apparently, I wasn't very good at telling the difference between a male and female kitten. I thought *she* was a *he*. I tried renaming her El but Steve had already stuck," Shaun muttered, shoving her feet into her boots and then straightening, hands on her hips.

His answering grin annoyed the shit out of her.

"El? Like, Eleven?" he asked innocently. She rolled her eyes and shrugged. "*Stranger Things* fan, I take it?"

"Yeah, so? I went through a *Pirates of the Caribbean* phase when I was fourteen, too. Named our dog Rum so I could yell through the house 'Why's the Rum gone?'."

Kasey's burst of laughter made her lips twitch with the need to smile, but she fought it back as she pulled on her winter coat. "There's no way that's a true story."

"Swear to God," she said and crossed her finger over her heart in an X as they exited her apartment. "Ask Free. I'm sure he remembers. Jodi was *obsessed* with Orlando Bloom. She wanted to name the dog *Will Turner*. I won."

Kasey held his hand out toward her and she stared at it, then raised her eyes to his in confusion. "Keys, Shaun."

"You're not driving my truck," Shaun laughed, shaking her head.

"Really? You don't trust me to drive?" he asked, stepping between her and the car door. "I drive for a living."

"Yeah, on perfectly conditioned pavement making only left banks," she muttered dryly, and fully enjoyed the annoyance that flashed across his stupidly handsome face. "You don't know the first thing about driving on Michigan winter roads, Kasey."

"Shaun..."

"Look, I have been driving myself since I was sixteen. I don't need you or anyone else to chauffeur me around. I'm not some passenger princess, Kase," she snapped, throwing her arms wide. "If that's what you're looking for, then you might as well hit the road, because that's not the kind of woman I am."

"You're not the kind of woman that likes to be taken care of?" he asked, crossing his arms over his chest.

Her heart thudded in her chest. She took a long time to answer before saying quietly, "No. I'm not. I don't need to be taken care of, or have some man do what they think is best for me because they think they know better."

His dark blonde brows rose just the slightest in surprise, and she dropped her gaze to the snow-covered ground before reaching around him for the door handle. He stepped aside, and she climbed into the driver's seat. She started the truck and then swallowed hard when he walked around the hood to open the passenger side door before climbing up into the seat. Neither one of them said anything as they fastened their seatbelts, and then Shaun backed the truck out of the driveway.

The short ride to the local hospital was quiet, which Shaun was grateful for. Her mind was still a mess; a lot had happened in a very short amount of time and her brain was still trying to play catch up.

The absolute kaleidoscope of emotions that Kasey elicited from her were on their own confusing as hell. Up until three days ago, she'd been convinced she hated him with everything in her.

Two days ago, she'd had a grudging acceptance that maybe he wasn't all *that* terrible.

Thirty-six hours ago, she'd been drunk on tequila and high on a multitude of world altering orgasms.

The last eighteen hours had been an exhausting rollercoaster. She liked the witty, snarky banter between them. She liked the way those gray-blue eyes watched her, made her feel like the most beautiful woman in the world, even just for a few moments. She liked his sense of humor when he wasn't being a total dick. She liked his smile, that dimple that showed up in the center of one cheek, the quiet way he seemed to watch everyone and everything all at once, missing nothing. She liked the way his kisses made the world disappear, or the way she'd never felt more alive than when she was with him. No matter what they were doing. Arguing. Teasing. Fucking. She liked all of it.

She liked… well, him. She liked *him*.

FML.

Shaun peeked at him out of the corner of her eye as she drove, both hands on the wheel to keep them to herself. She hated to admit it, but she'd known all along that if she left without a word, he would follow her. He had told her he would. If she were to be honest with herself, for once, she had *wanted* him to follow her. What woman didn't like being pursued, wooed?

But that was where things got complicated. Where her mind started balking like a damn spooked horse. The last thing she needed, the last thing she wanted, was another man expecting things from her, speaking over her, making decisions for her without giving a thought or consideration to what she wanted. Kasey didn't ask for anything. He gave and he took, without remorse or apology.

She didn't want a man that wouldn't let her have her own voice, her own opinions, her own choices, just because he thought he knew better.

No matter how much she wanted Kasey, whatever this was between them would never work. If she let him in, he would push and push until she finally caved, giving in to whatever his requests and demands would be of her. And she would hate herself in the end.

No, it was better to end this now, rip the band-aid off and say 'sayonara' than to let any man have that kind of control of her. Even if the orgasms were top notch, chef's kiss, crème de le creme… nope. No man was worth that. Hell to the naw.

So when she finally pulled into the parking lot of the hospital and climbed out of the truck, she squared her shoulders and rounded the hood, stopping as he stepped close to her. "Kasey—"

"Nope," he muttered, laying a finger vertically along her lips to shush her, and she glared up at him. "Whatever bullshit excuse that's about to come out of that pretty mouth of yours can wait. I realize that you're stuck up in that head of yours for God only knows what reason—though I do think I'm starting to see the big picture here, darlin', and we'll talk about that later. Don't let that douche canoe and whatever dumb shit he did ruin what could be a very enjoyable weekend. That's all I'm asking for; just the weekend, Shaun. If by the end of the weekend you still feel the same way, that will be it."

He removed his finger from her lips and cupped either side of her head in his hands, leaning in to press his mouth to hers, and she melted when his tongue swept between her lips. Damn the man could kiss.

Whispering directly against her lips, he breathed, "If you say the words, I'll walk away, and you can go back to hating me if that's what you'd like. If that's what makes it easier for you to pretend there isn't something here."

THIRTY

He was playing dirty, and he knew it.

Kasey watched Shaun as she paced around the small waiting room. She'd sat beside him for a time, leg bouncing with nervous energy, before she'd stood and started making laps around the room.

He had met Chase, Zoey's husband, when he'd popped in to give Shaun an update, and they'd shaken hands briefly. The expression on the other man's face was unreadable as they'd introduced themselves. He got the distinct impression that the impossibly tall and broad-shouldered man with the piercing blue eyes knew much more about him than the simple "This is Free's cousin, Kasey" had let on.

"You don't sit still very well, do you?" he asked from where he was seated in one of the uncomfortable vinyl chairs.

"I'm just anxious," she said quietly. "She had a rough delivery with her first. At her last checkup the doctor was saying the baby may be over ten pounds."

"Is that big?" he asked.

Shaun stopped in her pacing and turned to look at him,

hands on her hips. "That's like pushing a small thanksgiving turkey out of your hoo-ha, Kasey. Yes, that's a big baby."

He couldn't stop the laugh that escaped him. "You're a lot to handle, you know that?"

Dropping her eyes to the floor, she resumed her pacing and nodded just the slightest. "So I've been told."

He stood, crossing to her to take her shoulders in his hands, forcing her to stop in her march around the room. "Hey," he said gently, until she looked up at him. The thinly disguised sadness that clouded those sapphire eyes gutted him. "I didn't mean it as an insult."

She shrugged, flitting her eyes to a point over his shoulder to avoid looking at him directly. He tipped her chin up with his fingers until she looked at him again. He pressed a quick, chaste kiss to her mouth.

"Get out of your head, darlin'," he murmured gently. "If you'll let me, I'll show you what an idiot he was to ever let you go."

She sighed heavily, dropping her shoulders. "Kasey—"

The door opened then and Chase stepped through, his shoulders relaxed, and a wide grin plastered on his face as he announced, "We have a healthy baby boy! Zoey did…she was incredible. What a rockstar."

Shaun clapped her hands and made the cutest bounce of excitement he'd ever seen, something totally out of character for her, and he enjoyed seeing this different side of her. She wasn't nearly as prickly as he'd always assumed, a fact that had dawned on him throughout the weekend as he watched her with her family. The tough exterior he'd grown accustomed to, that he had always thought was just part of who she was… he'd started to realize it was more of a mask than anything. She was a smart ass, funny to boot, but there was a softness to her that he'd never witnessed before, and he liked that he was finally allowed to see it.

Shaun stepped forward and hugged Chase hard, congratulating him, and then Kasey reached his hand out and shook the proud new dad's hand.

"Zoey sent me out to get you," Chase said then, glancing at Shaun, and Kasey nodded with a grin.

"I'll be here when you're done getting your baby fix," he chuckled, returning to his seat.

Shaun's eyes met his for a heartbeat before she followed Chase out of the door, letting it click behind them.

His phone vibrated in his pocket, and he pulled it out, swiping open the email from Charlie. Scanning it briefly, excitement swept through him. He was ready for the season to start. Training would begin in two weeks, and he'd never been more ready to get back behind the wheel. The rush of adrenaline, roaring around the track at two hundred miles an hour surrounded by dozens of other machines and drivers gunning for that top spot… It was his happy place.

The door opened and he glanced up, nodding a silent hello to the older gentleman that entered. His jeans were tattered at the hems around work boots, a flannel shirt buttoned down his chest, which was soft and slightly round. Sandy brown hair with sprinkles of gray that was kept a touch too long fell over a wrinkled brow and kind brown eyes met his as he chose a seat across the room.

"I'm here to see my daughter and new grandson," the older man said softly, a smile crinkling the corners of his brown eyes, and Kasey grinned.

"I take it you're Zoey's dad?" he asked, sitting straighter in his seat.

"I sure am," the man said, nodding. "Thom Chandler. How do you know my Zoey?"

"I'm just an acquaintance," he said and nodded toward the door. "I'm actually just here keeping Shauntelle Kendall some company. She's back seeing Zoey and the baby now, Chase just came to fetch her."

Sandy brown brows raised slightly and he nodded, making Kasey wonder briefly if Thom had ill feelings toward Shaun since she and his son had split. His hackles went up instinctively.

"Those girls have been best friends since the first day of kindergarten," Thom said then, smiling gently, his tone soft, and Kasey forced his protectiveness to take a back seat. "Shaun has always been more like family."

"She's special, that's for sure," Kasey agreed.

Kasey's gaze was drawn to the door when it opened again, and his entire body tensed, his jaw clenching so tightly it ached, as Tommy Chandler stepped through the door.

The click of the door shutting echoed like a bomb in the room, or perhaps it was just inside Kasey's head. Tommy stopped where he was, brown eyes the same shade as his father's but far less soft, meeting Kasey's from across the room.

But it wasn't anger, or hatred, or rage, or even jealousy that appeared in the other man's eyes like he expected. They were surprisingly empty, shuttered, and Kasey immediately recognized the brokenness inside Tommy. He could only imagine what losing a woman like Shaun could do to a man. He knew he sure as hell didn't want to find out.

Tommy continued forward, taking a seat next to his father, directly across from Kasey, but their eyes never met again.

"This is my son, Tommy, Zoey's brother," Thom said then, making introductions that were wholly unnecessary, but the man clearly had no idea that the two of them already knew each other. That Kasey had lusted after and actively pursued his son's fiancé… or that he had been buried balls deep in her mere hours before.

Just because Thom was oblivious to the situation, didn't mean that Tommy didn't understand the implication of why Kasey was there, or that it was clear that he was there with Shaun. Kasey shifted in his seat.

Kasey cleared his throat to speak, but it was Tommy that responded, his tone dull. "Yeah, we've met."

Well, this is awkward.

The door opened again, and he stood, that instinctual protectiveness flaring in him as she stepped through the door, her eyes meeting his with a smile. But then her eyes shifted toward the other two in the room, and he watched, aching inside, as her face fell, her eyes going wide and shuttering almost immediately, the joy and carefreeness from moments ago disappearing instantly.

Kasey refused to take his eyes off of her face, his heart hammering in his chest at the pain he could sense radiating off of her, even if she was trying her damndest to hide it. Out of his peripheral vision, he knew Thom had stood, taking steps toward her to embrace her in a gentle hug.

"Hi, Shaun honey," the older man said softly. Pulling away, he asked, "How's our girl?"

Kasey watched as Shaun swallowed hard, glancing over Thom's shoulder at Tommy briefly, before raising her eyes back to his and said, "She's good. Tired. Baby boy is doing great. Did you let Chase know you're here?"

"I called him and left a voicemail," Thom said, patting her arm in a kind, fatherly gesture. Kasey remained where he was, standing several feet away, watching everything. "I figured he was busy. He'll come get us when they're ready for us."

"Does Zoey know you're here?" she asked then, her voice breaking slightly as she spoke directly to Tommy, who had remained sitting when his father had stood to greet Shaun. "I didn't know you were even home."

Kasey glanced at Tommy, saw his head shake in a silent no. "I wasn't sure if she wanted me here. Dad told me I didn't have a choice. I'm only here for a day or two."

"She'll be happy to see you," Shaun said quietly, but Tommy just shrugged, returning his gaze to the floor between dirty work boots. "So will Chase."

Thom squeezed Shaun's arm where his hand still rested, and she brought her eyes to his again. His lips had pulled into a sad line and he just shook his head slightly, and Shaun nodded. Those dark sapphire eyes finally came back to his, and Kasey read the plea in them.

"Well, we should probably go," Shaun said then, reaching out a hand and accepting the jacket that Kasey held out for her. "Let you guys have some time with Zoey and the baby. Chase said she's requesting a Northman pizza as a push present."

"He better not forget the banana peppers," Tommy said then from where he sat, raising his head to look at her, a half-smile pulling one corner of his mouth up. Shaun's grudging chuckle made jealousy crash through him.

"She was mad at you for a week," Shaun said with a small smile, and that jealousy inside Kasey turned into a rage as he watched a flicker of life return to the other man's eyes.

But then Shaun moved her eyes away from Tommy's and those sapphire eyes met his again, and in that moment, he didn't blame Tommy for clinging to that feeling after being denied it for nearly a year. It was like taking a hit of the best drug possible, the strongest high.

This woman had the capability to become an addiction he had no chance in hell of kicking.

THIRTY-ONE

It was after eleven by the time they pulled back into the driveway in front of her apartment. She shut the truck off but didn't climb out, instead resting her forehead against the steering wheel in front of her for a long time, the darkness shrouding her. She knew Kasey was watching her from where he sat in the passenger seat, but she was grateful that for once he remained quiet, letting her have this moment in the silence.

It had been almost eleven months since she'd seen Tommy. Eleven months since she'd thrown her engagement ring back at him, ending a two-year relationship, and any future they would have had together. As angry as she still was at him for what he'd done, how he'd manipulated the lives of the people he swore to love, she hated the emptiness she'd seen in him. He looked… awful. Tired. The red, glassiness in his eyes, the dark circles under them, the way his body seemed to be shrinking, shriveling. She knew he was still drinking heavily, but was this something heavier?

I did this to him, she thought miserably.

"You're not to blame, Shaun."

Raising her forehead from where it had been resting on the steering wheel, she whipped around to glare at Kasey. *Had she said that outloud?*

Shifting in his seat to angle his body more toward hers to look at her better through the darkness of the truck, he reached out a hand toward her, twisting one curl around his finger.

"Excuse me?" she asked, her tone acerbic.

His lips pulled into a tight line before he exhaled through his nose. "Whatever Tommy is struggling with, it's not your fault, Shaun. His actions and whatever the consequences are, they are his own. He is a broken man—"

"And I did that," she snapped, turning her head to stare out the windshield.

"Stop," Kasey snapped back, the heat in his voice enough to make her look at him again. "I can only imagine what losing a woman like you did to him—" She opened her mouth to protest, but he shushed her, continuing roughly, "—but that's on him; not you. Whatever mistakes he made to lose you are his own, and he has to learn to live with that. Blaming yourself for how he's living his life will do you absolutely no good."

"Zoey told me he's still drinking. That he refused rehab a few months ago."

"And that is in no way your fault," Kasey insisted, cupping the side of her neck in his palm. The heat of his hand against her skin was like an inferno in the rapidly cooling cab of the truck without the heat to battle against the January cold. His fingers stroked the back of her neck, and she leaned into his touch, closing her eyes. "What did he do, Shaun?"

She shook her head, letting her chin drop down. "Putting it into words now makes it sound so stupid, Kasey. It makes me sound ungrateful and petty."

"Your feelings about what happened are not invalidated now because of how your brain is telling you to feel about it through your misplaced guilt," he said gently, and tears sprang to her eyes. Blinking rapidly to whisk them away before they could fall, she turned to look out the windshield again. "What happened? Please, darlin'. Talk to me."

Taking a deep breath, she let it out slowly, squeezing her eyes shut. "I don't know if you know the whole story, about what happened to Zoey two years ago. She was drugged and raped by a college kid in one of her classes, and she had her daughter Verity because of it. She struggled with severe PTSD afterward, and then their mom died right before Verity was born. Thom, their dad who you just met, checked out emotionally from them after her death, and taking care of Zoey and Verity fell to Tommy, who was also grieving. He started drinking more often, drinking more heavily. He just… changed. And I know that grief can change people, and I wanted to be there for him and for Zoey and Verity. I love them all so much."

When she paused, he nodded for her to continue, so she took another breath in and said, "That's when Chase moved home. He and Tommy were best friends for as long as I can remember. He moved home for a job at the local sheriff's department, and needed a place to stay, so Tommy and Zoey offered him their spare bedroom. Well, Zoey had one of her panic attacks one night, and apparently Tommy concocted this scheme, this deal with Chase. He wanted Zoey safe, taken care of, and Chase was the ideal candidate."

"Candidate for what?" Kasey asked gently.

"To marry his sister. To take care of her, and Verity."

She felt more than saw the shock as it processed through Kasey. His hand stilled in its strumming along the back of her neck, and she nodded.

"Yeah. Well, what we didn't know was that Chase and Zoey had already started falling for each other, and the next thing we know we're planning a whirlwind wedding. It wasn't until after the wedding, at the reception, that Zoey found out about the deal her brother had made with her new husband. She didn't know if Chase had married her because Tommy had asked him to, or if he'd done it because he wanted to, because he loved her."

"But they just had a baby, so things are better now?" he asked.

"Yes, things are better now. They're honestly perfect for

each other. Chase says that even if Tommy hadn't asked him to marry her, they would have ended up there anyway. But, she felt incredibly betrayed by the two of them. Everything up until then had been shoved on her without her consent; she was understandably upset by the two of them choosing something for her without her fully in on the decision." She glanced over at him then, looking him in the eye through the dark as she said, "I was furious with Tommy. He knew how betrayed she would feel, and he did it anyway, because he felt it was his job to do whatever necessary to protect her. He told me he would do the same for me if he felt it was needed." Kasey's hand tightened around the back of her neck, and she saw his jaw clench. "I told him he wouldn't have the chance. I refused to marry someone I couldn't trust, and it was painfully obvious that I couldn't trust him anymore. So, I gave him the ring back and broke off our engagement. It killed me and destroyed him."

"Are you still in love with him?" he asked through the darkness.

Dropping her gaze to her lap, she said quietly, "No. I realized that we can't be what the other one needs. He needs someone that needs him to protect her, someone that wants and needs him to take care of her. I'm not a damsel in distress and I don't need anyone to take care of me; that's just how I am. And I don't want or need anyone that's going to make decisions for me because they think they know better than I do. I don't need saving."

"Is this a newer revelation?" he asked.

She shook her head. "No, I've always been more independent. It drove my parents crazy as a teenager, I'm sure. I love my family, and my parents are wonderful, but I moved out into my own apartment as soon as I turned eighteen, right after graduation. I just knew that I wanted my own space, my freedom to be my own person. My dad's name is big in the area, but I didn't want to ride on his coattails. I applied to trade schools and have several certificates in different areas, and I busted my ass to make it all happen. I live in a small apartment, just me and my cat, and I love it. Tommy asked me probably a hundred times to move in with him, or to let him move in here. I like my freedom too much, I think. I didn't want to share my space with anyone, even my fiancé."

"Do you like your freedom too much, or did you just know somewhere that it wasn't going to last?"

"I didn't self-sabotage my relationship with Tommy, Kasey," she snapped, attempting to pull away from his hand, but his fingers tightened just the slightest, and she stayed put.

"That wasn't my question, and you know it," he growled. "Stop getting prickly."

"I'm not prickly," she retorted sharply, and gasped when his fingers tightened again, making her belly flutter. *Oh.*

"I told you the first time we met that I could tell there was no chemistry between you two. Not the right kind, anyway. I think somewhere inside that pretty head of yours you knew he wasn't right for you. You were forcing it," he murmured low, his voice husky.

"I loved him," she countered quietly.

He was quiet for a long moment, before whispering, "I don't doubt that you did, Shaun. But did you love him the way Jodi loves Free? The way your mom loves your dad? Or did you love him because he's your best friend's brother, and because it was easy to pretend that was what you wanted, because it was comfortable?"

"I swear you and Roxy are the same person," she grumbled, turning her eyes down to her lap. "She asked the same thing. I thought you put her up to it."

He laughed lightly and resumed strumming the back of her neck, making her shiver. "Roxy has a way of seeing past people's bullshit. I think it's the red hair: it's like a superpower. But don't change the subject."

She huffed out a heavy sigh and shrugged her shoulders. It was getting steadily colder in the cab of the truck, the windshield slowly beginning to frost over as they sat. She watched as the diamond crystals formed one by one, creeping almost unnoticed up the glass. "If you'd asked me six or eight months ago, I would have adamantly said yes, I did love him that way. Now… I'm not so sure."

"Why's that?" he asked, leaning closer.

She swallowed hard. "I don't know."

"Yes, you do."

"Because you give me the best orgasms I've ever had in my entire life?" she quipped dryly, and the glint in his eyes in the darkness made her clench her thighs together.

"Is that all?" he asked, dragging his thumb over her jaw, down and under her chin until he could grip the point of her chin between his thumb and index finger.

"Yes," she whispered, her breathing ragged in the quiet.

Kasey was silent for a long time, their eyes searching the others, his fingers tight on her chin. He looked like he wanted to say something more, his gaze intense with something she didn't want to name.

Finally, after what felt like a small eternity, he nodded slowly, his eyes dropping to her mouth, and he murmured, "It's not stupid or petty, by the way. What he did was wrong, even if his intentions came from the right place, and he got what was coming to him because of it." His thumb swept over her lower lip, making her tremble, and then he whispered, "Now, I want to go inside, and I want to hear my name come off these lips while I'm between those pretty thighs, darlin'."

Good lord. How was she supposed to say no to that?

THIRTY-TWO

Raising her arms to remove the claw clip from her hair, Shaun paused and watched in the mirror as Kasey stepped out of the shower behind her, gloriously naked, steam billowing out around him. He grabbed the towel on the hook next to the shower and with both hands, ran it first over his face, his head, then down his chest, each arm, his legs… between them.

Her arms were suspended over her head as she stared unabashedly at the beauty that was naked Kasey. His legs were long, and his thighs bunched with lean muscle as he moved, the tendons in his arms and shoulders working as he ran the towel over his wet skin. Catching her gaze in the mirror, he grinned, then winked.

Turning, her hair tumbling around her shoulders, Shaun dropped her arms and set the hair clip on the sink. Still staring, he started to grow hard at her attention. Kasey tossed the towel away, then his hand dropped to his cock, palming it before running his hand from tip to root and back again.

"Don't be shy, darlin'."

She shook her head, her gaze raising to meet his eyes, lids

heavy with arousal as he continued to stroke himself. Her breaths were coming in short, rapid puffs. *Dammit why did he always have such an effect on her?* It had been a week of nonstop sexathon, more orgasms than she could count… and still the sight of him made her knees weak.

He took two steps toward her, bringing them within arm's reach. "Do you want to touch me, Shaun?"

She nodded, dropping her eyes back to where his hand fisted himself, stroking slowly, over and over again. She wanted to touch… but not with her hands.

"I'm all yours, darlin'," he murmured low, his voice gravelly.

Sinking to her knees, she watched as his eyes widened in surprise when she moved his hand away, taking him in her own. She ran her hand along his hard length several times, enjoying the way his mouth dropped open and his eyes fluttered closed, and then she leaned forward and took him in her mouth, swirling her tongue over the rounded head. He groaned above her, his fingers sliding up through her hair on either side of her head, pulling it away from her face and gathering it into his fists. She took him to the back of her throat and the noise that came out of him was part sigh, part garbled moan, his hips thrusting forward just slightly.

"Fuck," he breathed raggedly as she sucked him down, bobbing her head even as his fingers tightened in her hair.

"That fucking mouth, Shaun. Oh, god, yes. Take all of me."

Her other hand slid up his thigh, reveling in the way the muscles beneath her fingertips bunched and tensed as he fought to control the urge to thrust harder, faster. He let go of her hair with one hand, and his fingers strummed along the underside of her jaw as she moved, his touch feather light.

Swirling her tongue around the crown, she heard his sharp intake of breath just before his fingers slid back into her hair, his hands bracketing her head and holding tight as he began to piston his hips.

She took everything he gave. Glancing up his body, she reveled in the way his chest heaved with panting breaths, his throat arched, head thrown back in ecstasy.

His fingers were tight on her head as he fucked her mouth with abandon, his hips thrusting on their own as he held her still. She was so wet, achingly turned on as he lost control. Clenching her legs tight, she moaned around his length buried in her mouth and he hissed from above her. She felt his hips begin to stutter, his balls drawing up tight in her hand and he groaned raggedly, "Shaun, I'm going to–"

Taking him as deep as she could, she hummed around his length in approval and he shouted incoherently as he fisted her hair tight enough to sting, pulling her off of him just as he came, his cock jumping as rope after rope of cum painted her chest and throat.

Her knees ached from kneeling on the hard floor, but she remained where she was as he shuddered before her, and his fingers loosened in her hair to stroke it tenderly. She breathed raggedly, eyes on his face. He opened his eyes, far bluer than gray at the moment, and then he was bending at the waist as his hands cupped her jaw. His mouth landed on hers in a heated, scorching kiss, his tongue spearing into her mouth much like his cock had just done, and they kissed until they were both breathless.

"You are fucking perfect," he whispered against her mouth, his voice shaky. Kissing each corner of her mouth, then fully on the lips again, his thumbs stroked her cheeks. "I'm going to have dreams about that mouth, darlin'."

One of his hands dropped, running his finger through the mess he'd made of her chest, where it had trailed down between her breasts in the thin strapped tank top she wore. Picking up the discarded towel, he cleaned the mess he'd made, then dropped his mouth to the meaty part of her neck where it met with her shoulder, taking a love bite that made her gasp.

"You are going to be the death of me," he chuckled wickedly, then straightened. Offering her his hand, she stood on wobbly legs. Reaching between her thighs, he strummed his fingers along the edge of her panties before moving them aside to slide two fingers in deep. Shaun moaned, tipping her head back when he found that secret spot only he seemed to know how to find. His answering groan rumbled against her chest where she'd pressed herself. His other arm banded around her waist, holding her to him. "You're so fucking wet, darlin'. Did you like that?"

She nodded mutely, her mouth falling open as he manipulated that spot deep inside. She was already so close; watching him come undone at her hands–and mouth–had been like her own personal aphrodisiac.

"I'd like to repay the favor, but I think if I just..." he whispered huskily against her temple, at the same time crooking his fingers inside over and over again, and she let out a sharp cry. Her legs shook violently, and she clutched at him, the arm wrapped around her waist the only thing keeping her on her feet. "There it is... That's my girl. That's it, Shaun. Come on my fingers, darlin'. Let me feel you come."

She shattered, exploding around his fingers as wave after wave of pleasure rocked through her. It was as if his touch was some form of magic. She'd never experienced anything like how Kasey made her feel. It was intoxicating, how hard he could make her fall apart.

Or how hard he could make her fall... for him. *No. There's no way I'm falling for Kasey... It's just the orgasms, Shaun. Pull yourself together.*

"I hate how good you are at this," she panted brokenly as she sagged against him, her arms wrapping around his neck even as she continued to tremble with aftershocks. He wrapped both arms around her waist, securing her against him, and she pressed her cheek against his chest, listening to the cadence of his heart where it beat beneath her ear. His mouth pressed against her forehead, trailing kisses along her hairline.

He chuckled and she pressed closer against him to listen to the sound of it rumble in his chest.

"Good thing you already planned on taking a shower," he laughed, pushing her away. "You're a little… sticky."

"I was *trying* to put it somewhere else–"

He kissed her before she could finish the sentence.

THIRTY-THREE

"I am perfectly capable of going to the store by myself, Kasey," Shaun argued, standing in front of the door, arms crossed over her chest.

Dangling her truck keys in front of her face, he waggled his eyebrows. "Yes, I am aware. But I'd like to go. There are a few things I need, anyway."

Swiping in the air for the keys, he barely pulled them out of reach before she could grab them. She growled in frustration, and he grinned down at her. *Damn she was cute when she was riled.*

"Nice try. You're stuck with me." Pointing toward the door, he smirked. "Let's go, darlin'."

"You're not driving," she muttered sourly as they exited her apartment, walking toward her truck.

"For once, can you please just not argue?" he asked, pushing her up against the side of the truck and curving his body over hers. "I'm not trying to protect you, or save you, or turn you into a passenger princess or whatever you called it. I am a driver, Shaun. Driving is what I do. I enjoy it. It's like…breathing for me. A necessity. Even if it's just driving to the store and back."

She glared up at him and he tilted his head to one side, one eyebrow rising, waiting for her response. Finally, she rolled her eyes and muttered, "Fine."

"Good girl," he whispered before kissing her soundly.

Releasing her, he stepped back enough to open the passenger door for her to climb into, and then rounded the hood of the truck to climb in behind the wheel. "You might have to point me in the direction we're going. I'm still unfamiliar with the area."

Crossing her arms over her chest, she smirked over at him. "If you'd have let me drive, you wouldn't need directions." He sent a pointed glare over the console at her.

She guided him through the snow-covered streets of Petoskey, along the frozen bay that lined the highway, and then into the parking lot of a local grocer. She didn't wait for him to come open her door, climbing out before he could. They walked side by side into the market and she stopped for a grocery cart.

"Wanna race?" he asked, pointing to the carts with cars attached to them, the kind that little kids rode in to keep the basket of the shopping cart open for other things. She rolled her eyes, but the laugh she couldn't stifle made his chest warm.

Stopping first in the produce, he watched as Shaun picked

through until she found what she needed.

Kasey was content to follow, watching her as she moved from one item to the next. She had pulled on a pair of cock-teasingly tight black leggings that hit high on her waist, and her feet were covered in thick winter boots. A loose, cropped sweater in a seafoam green color covered her chest and stomach, but as she reached for a produce bag over her head, the cropped hem of the sweater rode up, baring a couple inches of her midriff, at which Kasey couldn't tear his eyes away. Her long, spiral curls had been left down after her shower, and they'd dried in riotous ringlets down around her shoulders and back. She'd pulled on a simple, brown leather jacket, but hadn't zipped it, so it hung open as she moved.

The sun had been especially bright as it reflected off the white snow, and she'd pulled a pair of Aviator sunglasses from the center console of the truck, sliding them on her nose. Now, inside the store, she'd pushed them up to the top of her head.

When she caught him staring, she gave him a lopsided grin and shook her head. He stepped forward, stalling her hand as she spun the plastic bag that held two giant zucchinis. She gazed up at him with those damn insanely blue eyes of hers, and in that moment, he knew he would never get enough of this woman.

He'd gone and fallen head over heels for Shauntelle Kendall.

"You are so beautiful."

She rolled her eyes and set the zucchini in the cart, then glanced back up at him. "You already got me into bed, Kasey. You don't have to say stuff like that."

His eyebrows pulled together in a frown, and he opened his mouth, but then she glanced over his shoulder and her eyes widened, and the smile he knew she reserved for those she wasn't particularly fond of pulled at her lips.

Turning, he saw a middle-aged woman approach them, a wide smile on her face. She stood nearly the same height as Shaun, plus sized, with ashy blonde hair and blue eyes.

"Well, my gosh, hi Shaun!" the woman said as she stopped beside their grocery cart with her own. "I don't think I've seen you since you and Dustin broke up!"

Kasey's brows pulled together again, jealousy rampaging through him at the thought of some other guy with Shaun.

"That was what, way back in high school?" the woman continued, and he watched as Shaun nodded, then the woman's gaze turned to him. "I'm Karen. And who is this handsome thing?"

He opened his mouth to answer, but Shaun beat him to it. "This is uhh, my friend, Kasey."

"Oh, just friend?" Karen asked, her blue eyes bouncing from Shaun to him and back. When Shaun nodded stiffly, Karen said gently, "Well, that's okay. My Dustin always had such wonderful things to say about you, just that you were… well you know you were a lot to handle when you were younger! So strong-willed and of course, you could be pretty wild back then! But you'll find someone that can handle you. Dustin always liked that you were so… so free spirited, he just had a hard time keeping up with you! I'm sure your parents are glad you've mellowed out a little, too!"

Kasey's mouth had hardened into a tight line at the sheer gall of this woman, but it was the almost invisible hurt that had clouded Shaun's eyes that cut him to the quick and made him adjust the two of them so that he stood between the two women. Extending his hand, he murmured low, his voice tight, "It was so nice to meet you, Kathy."

"Oh, my name is Karen," the woman said, shaking his hand in return.

"My apologies," he muttered, then turned back to Shaun, who had dropped her gaze to the list in her hand. "Shall we?"

She nodded as Karen walked away, leaving the two of them alone near the Brussel sprouts.

"So, I'm thinking about roasted chicken and veggies–"

"Please tell me you don't believe a word that woman said."

Pinning him with a stare, she laughed, though it didn't reach her eyes, and it gutted him. "Who, Karen? Not at all."

"Then why are you mangling that grocery list in your hand?" he asked softly, pointing at the crumpled piece of paper in one fist. She glanced down at it and released the death grip she had on the paper. Taking it from her, he grasped her chin in his fingers and forced her eyes up to his. "Tell me you don't put stock into one single word that she said."

She shrugged, her eyes searching his. "She's not wrong, Kasey. I know I'm a lot to handle. You've said it yourself. Tommy didn't like how wild I am, either."

He was shaking his head before she finished talking. "I want you to listen to me, Shaun, and listen good. Tommy wanted to water you down, make you easier to swallow. Because yes, you are a lot. You are so fiercely your own person, and I pray to whatever God there is that you never fucking change. I told you once that I couldn't wait to let out all that fire that I see inside you. I want you to burn me up, darlin'. Can you be absolutely maddening sometimes? One thousand percent yes. Would I change one single thing about that wild heart of yours? Absolutely not. If they thought you were too much, that's their problem, and bears no reflection on you. Do you hear me?"

She nodded, though he knew by that stubborn tick in her jaw that she was going to dig her heels in and wouldn't believe a word he'd just said. He sighed heavily in frustration, his mouth tightening into a hard line. Shaun was so fiercely steadfast in remaining true to herself, it was refreshing. Maddening at times, yes, but so vastly different than how

Savannah had been during their relationship.

Savannah had attempted to mold herself into being the perfect girlfriend in order to secure an engagement ring, it wasn't until it was nearly too late that Kasey had realized she had no true or genuine thoughts or feelings for him. It had all been contrived to get what she wanted, and she nearly had. Shaun's fiery nature and total lack of a filter were intoxicating. She never pulled her punches and there was no beating around the bush; she just cut the damn thing down out of her way. She didn't hesitate to let her feelings be known and was adorably independent. He had a feeling she would fight like hell for the things she wanted, too, the things she loved…

Christ, this fucking feeling. There was so much more he could say, so much more that he *wanted* to say… but she wasn't ready to hear it. And he wasn't ready to lay his heart out on the line like that, at least not yet. Not when he knew if that's not what she wanted, she wouldn't hesitate to let it be known. And he wasn't entirely a masochist.

"Can we please finish our shopping so I can get you back home and naked?" he asked roughly, kissing her quickly. She pursed her lips when he released her, and he muttered, "Because every time you have to reach for something up high that sweater rides up, and I can't walk around a family market with a hard on."

THIRTY-FOUR

Laying against the pillows at the head of Shaun's bed, he grinned down at her, where she was propped up on an elbow at the foot of the bed, their bodies parallel to each other. His feet were at her head, hers tucked under the pillow at his elbow, the sheet draped over them in the middle.

"I didn't even know that was possible," she laughed from the foot of the bed. He winked at her, the light of the bedside lamp next to the bed illuminating her in a golden glow. Her hair was a wild mess around her head. Ten minutes ago, she'd been riding his face while her mouth had been doing delightfully dirty things to him at the same time. *That* was going to be a highlight of his fantasies for a long while.

"You have a lot to learn, darlin'."

She lowered her blue eyes to the sheet, picking at it with her fingernail. "You certainly know a lot more than I do. I'm sure you stay… busy… while you're traveling."

Plucking her feet out from under the edge of the pillow, he hauled them both onto his chest, rubbing her calves with his thumbs. "Are you jealous, Shaun?"

"Pfft, no," she mumbled, tossing her hair back away from her face and fixing him with a stare. Then she shrugged, the sheet slipping off one breast, leaving that pierced nipple bare for his gaze. "I just wonder how you got so good at all this."

Massaging the arches of one of her feet, he smiled down at her when she moaned, her eyes drifting shut.

"So, you are jealous."

"No. I'm curious," she amended, shifting on her elbow.

"Curious about what?" he asked, pressing his thumb into the arch of her foot again.

"Well, you know about Tommy. I'm just wondering if there is some other woman out there waiting for K.C. Corcoran to return to the circuit and continue breaking her heart with an obnoxious amount of orgasms."

He sighed, massaging each of her toes in turn. "I won't lie to you, Shaun. I have fully enjoyed being a celebrity and some of the… baser perks of it. I like women. I like sex. A lot."

Shaun nodded, lowering her gaze again. "Who is Savannah, Kasey?"

"Ahhh," he murmured, smiling gently. "Did you cyber stalk me?"

She rolled her eyes and huffed in annoyance. "Ugh, just never mind. I don't know why I asked. Morbid curiosity."

She made to roll away, but he held fast. "Hey, you started this, Miss Feisty-Pants." When she stopped trying to move away, he said softly, "Savannah was my fiancé. A long time ago. I thought I knew who she was, and I was wrong. I felt betrayed and hurt. I've tried my damndest not to let anyone in since then."

Until you, he thought, staring at the woman who had irrevocably stolen his heart. It didn't belong to him anymore. It was hers. Quite possibly always had been.

She nodded, as if his answer made perfect sense, unaware of the tumult of emotions wreaking havoc internally, and then she was moving. Crawling up his body, she slid beneath the covers next to him, turning her back and pressing it against his front.

He grunted as her ass settled against his lap, his cock stirring as she wiggled just slightly. "Shaun… You know what's going to happen if you wiggle your ass against my dick like that."

She peered at him over her shoulder and one corner of her mouth tilted up in a sly smile. "I'm counting on it."

He chuckled, wrapping his arm around her and sliding his hand between her thighs, lifting the top one until he could position his once again rock-hard erection at her entrance before sliding in as deep as he could go. Her head fell back against his shoulder and his dick got even harder at the sound of her moan escaping her mouth. "You like this, don't you, darlin'?"

She nodded, her fingers gripping the sheet in front of her as she rocked backwards against him. "Yes, Kasey."

"You can't get enough," he whispered roughly, his hand spanning across the front of her throat.

"No, I can't," she cried as he picked up speed, his hips slapping hard against the softness of her backside. He was already so close, so he reached around her, and his fingers found her clit, circling and pinching lightly. "Oh god, Kasey."

"Come on, darlin'," he grunted, slamming his hips against hers. She was there, shimmering, right there on the brink. He could feel it. "Give it to me, Shaun. I need to feel it."

She had just started spasming around him when he came with a guttural, low groan. Burying his face in the back of her neck, he bit down on the meaty part of her shoulder as she came around him, at the same time he emptied everything inside her.

Sliding his hand up her body, over the curve of her hip, the dip of her waist, and back down, he pressed his palm against the lower part of her abdomen. Holding her as firmly against him as possible while he was still buried so deep inside, he whispered raggedly against the curve of her shoulder, "I can't get enough, either."

THIRTY-FIVE

"You know, the weekend ended like, two weeks ago."

"And yet you haven't thrown my ass out in the snow," Kasey countered from where he sat at her tiny dining table in the kitchen, his fingers wrapped around a cup of coffee, a white mug with a picture of *Rosie the Riveter* on it, below the words *Girl Boss* emblazoned in red letters. He lifted it to his lips, taking a sip of the strong black coffee he'd poured into it.

Standing with her back against the kitchen counter, she narrowed her gaze on him, but couldn't completely stop the tug at one corner of her mouth as it tipped up. She had on one of his Henley shirts and nothing else, the shirt hitting high on her thighs, leaving the rest of her long legs bare for his perusal. Her hair had been finger tousled fifteen minutes prior when she woke up to Kasey sliding between her legs from behind, his hand buried in her hair to hold her still as his mouth did deliciously wicked things to the side of her throat and the meaty part of her shoulder. His other hand had disappeared between her thighs, his fingers finding her clit. It hadn't taken long for him to hurtle her over that precipice, slamming into her from behind while she convulsed around him and in his arms as she came.

"I have to go back to work today, I really shouldn't take any more time off. I stayed home an extra week," she said, lifting her cup of coffee to her lips. This one was a cobalt blue glass mug with yellow-gold stars and a crescent moon on it. She'd stolen it from her dad ages ago. Shifting from one foot to the other, she swallowed hard, then asked, "Will uhh, will you be here when I get back?"

Kasey's gray-blue eyes found hers and a slow grin spread across his face. Standing, he crossed toward her, a pair of gray sweatpants slung indecently low around his hips. His upper body was still bare, the broad expanse of his back, shoulders, and arms on display for her. His feet were bare, his hair a tousled mess on the top of his head, like he'd shoved his fingers haphazardly through it mere seconds before. Only she knew it had in fact been *her* fingers that had made that mess.

Stepping in front of her, he plucked the cup of coffee out of her hands, despite her protest and attempt to grab it back, and set it on the counter next to them, before settling his large hands on her hips. Leaning close, he let the full length of their bodies press against each other, and whispered huskily, "Do you want me to be here when you get back, darlin'?"

Rolling her eyes, she tightened her lips to keep from smiling. "I don't care."

Lowering his mouth to her throat, she tipped her head back to grant him better access, humming in pleasure as his mouth did wonderful things to her. Speaking directly against the skin over her collarbone, he murmured, "I think you've liked having me here."

"I've liked the orgasms," she whispered raggedly, shifting her body along his as she felt him growing hard between them.

"I think you like sharing your space with me. Sharing your bed. Sleeping with you in that bed every night," he countered. "Sharing meals, watching movies."

"We haven't watched a single movie," Shaun exclaimed, her hands finding purchase on his back and gripping hard even as she moved against him. She *had* liked it. All of it. A lot more than she expected. This wasn't supposed to happen. It wasn't supposed to be like this. But she liked it too much to stop it. She liked *him* too much to stop it.

"Only because we're too busy necking before the opening credits," Kasey chuckled, his tongue sliding over the hollow at the base of her throat.

"Necking? What are we, teenagers in the eighties? Oh fuck," she gasped out as his hand slid beneath the hem of the shirt she wore to slip between her legs. "Kasey, I have to get ready for work."

"Then I guess you better be quick," he whispered, capturing her mouth with his in a fiery, heated kiss that left her totally breathless. When he finally released her lips, he dropped to his knees in front of her, lifting one of her legs behind the knee to drape it over his shoulder. "You have sixty seconds."

His fingers speared into her, curling in and hitting that sweet spot deep inside, at the same time that his lips found her clit, his tongue lashing, suckling, circling. Her fingers fisted into his hair, the leg she stood on trembling while the one draped over his shoulder shook. A high, keening cry escaping her as he tore the first orgasm out of her, her inner muscles clenching around his fingers. She felt more than heard his guttural hum of approval, his free hand squeezing the handful of her ass that he was holding onto.

It only took forty-five seconds for the first one. The second one avalanched over the first before it ever stopped. The man had a magic mouth and dear sweet Barbara Streisand, he knew how to use it.

She was still shaking, her breathing still ragged, when he let her leg drop back to the floor, rising to his feet. Using the pad of his thumb, he wiped his mouth, and she blushed all the way down to her toes as he grinned wolfishly down at her.

Reaching for the waistband of his sweats, she made a soft whine of disappointment when he caught her wrists, keeping her from touching what she was desperate to find. "If I let you touch me now, you won't make it to work, darlin'. I already want to keep you tied up to the bed all day and not let you leave."

"Okay," she whispered, nodding, rising onto her tiptoes to reach for his mouth with her own. "I'm down."

"Shaun," he warned on a growl, clamping his hands down more firmly around her wrists. "Don't tempt me."

"But what about you?" she asked. "That doesn't seem fair to you."

"Mmmm but I can't have you late to work on my account. This way, you can think about this all day long, making the anticipation sweeter."

"I'm not a delayed gratification kinda gal, Kasey," she grumbled petulantly, pouting.

"Most of your generation isn't," he chuckled, swatting her sharply on the ass, making her gasp.

"Hey!" Glaring at him, she shoved him back with her heels in his shoulders. "You're not that much older than I am, you jerk."

"Darlin', eight years is enough to put me into a different generational bracket," he laughed. "Go get ready for work."

"Buzzkill," she muttered, but stepped past him toward the hallway, at the same time gripping the hem of his Henley that she still wore. Lifting it up and over her head, she let it drop to the kitchen floor as she sauntered away, making sure to give her hips an extra sway as she did so.

She hadn't made it five steps down the hall when she heard

the thunder of his footsteps behind her and then his arms banded around her, flattening her against his chest as he lifted her off her feet. She squeaked in surprise and laughed out loud as he carried her into the bathroom. Setting her back on her feet, he pushed on her upper back until she bent at the waist.

"Grab hold of the sink," he growled low, and she did as he instructed. A sharp, stinging slap to her ass made her gasp and she bit her lip, her entire body clenching with anticipation when she felt his hands grab hold of her hips roughly, and then the head of his cock pressed against her already wet entrance. "You naughty little brat. Is this what you wanted?"

She nodded mutely, unable to produce any sound as he slammed inside hard, nearly lifting her off her feet as he entered her from behind.

Another stinging, biting slap cracked across the opposite ass cheek and Shaun was almost certain she was going to melt into a puddle. *Holy shit.* "Hold on, darlin'. This is going to be fast."

Gripping the edge of the sink with tightly clenched fingers, she held on as he fucked her senseless. It was fast, hard, and oh-so-good. Just as she started to clench around him with another mind-altering orgasm, he ran his fingers up the column of her spine, flattening his palm along her back, before letting his fingers curl around the back of her neck, his thumb pressing in on one side, his fingers on the other.

"You've ruined me," he ground out hoarsely, continuing to hammer into her from behind. Shattering into a million pieces, she came hard around him at his passion filled words, a cry ripping from her lips. His hips stuttered in that telltale way when she knew he was about to come, and he slammed in as deep as he could go just as she felt the first spasms and the heat that filled her.

"Holy shit," she panted, her arms giving out, and she rested with her torso hanging over the sink as her legs shook. His fingers strummed along the ridge of her spine, but still they remained as they were, his body pressed deep inside hers. Aftershocks pulsed through them both, and Shaun moaned, pressing her bottom against his hips, circling again as she felt another spasm. She was delivered another slap to the ass, though this one lacked the bite from before. "Ohmygod. I don't know if I should be concerned with how much I like that."

His quiet chuckle from behind her made her smile. Rubbing his palm over her bottom, he soothed the stinging flesh before gripping a handful and squeezing lightly. "You won't hear any complaints from me, darlin'."

He stepped back, pulling from her body, and Shaun dropped her forehead to the sink countertop with a groan, before pushing herself up to straighten. She turned to face Kasey as he turned on the shower taps, adjusting them and then pulling the shower curtain closed. He turned toward her, and one side of his mouth tilted up, his eyes dancing with mischief the way she liked.

Clasping her face between both hands, he kissed her soundly, thoroughly, before releasing her. "Shower, and I will bring your coffee to you."

She did as she was told, stepping into the shower and letting the hot spray wash over her. She heard him reenter and the soft clink of the glass coffee cup on the sink top. She showered hastily, then stepped out and dried off, wrapping the towel around her as she padded to the bedroom. She wrapped the towel around her hair and pulled on a pair of boy short underwear and wrestled a tight-fitting sports bra over her damp skin. Grunting, she panted as she fought with the tight material.

"You okay in there?" she heard Kasey call from down the hall.

"Yup, I'm fine," she panted raggedly. "Fuck this is tight."

Finally wrestling it into place, she unwrapped her hair and pulled a brush through the wet strands, then fastened it into a quick braid over one shoulder. A pair of oil-stained jeans and two layers of long-sleeved shirts were next. She grabbed her camel colored Carhartt vest off the hook on the back of her closet door and a thick pair of wool socks from the drawer before heading back down the hallway, where she found Kasey lounging comfortably on the couch, Steve the cat curled up into a ball in his lap, purring contentedly.

She sat on the edge of the couch near his hip, pulling the socks on her feet and then putting her work boots on, lacing them. She stood and turned to face him, leaning down to press a kiss to his mouth.

"You rest and enjoy your day, princess. Let Momma take care of you," she murmured coyly, and winked.

His gray-blue eyes darkened, and he growled ominously. She laughed, dancing out of his reach when he swiped an arm out to try and grab her around the backs of the knees to haul her close again.

"Bye!" she called, still laughing, as she pulled the vest on as she headed out the door.

THIRTY-SIX

"Heyo!"

"Look who decided to grace us with her presence!"

"Did you get enough pampering in Colorado? Ready to get dirt under those nails again?"

"About time you decided to do some work!"

"Shut the hell up you guys! She brought donuts!"

Shaun smiled as she walked into the garage, a large, Johan's Bakery signature pink baker's box held between her hands. "Hi, guys. Did you miss me?"

"Hell no, it was nice and quiet without your ass here!"

Brent elbowed Nick in the ribs and hissed, "You shut the hell up, I want donuts! Did you bring any Bear Claws? How about any custard Long Johns?"

Setting the large box on the worktable in the employee break room, she opened it with a flourish, and the six guys crowded around to take a peek at what she'd brought.

"Have I mentioned you're my favorite?" Jake said reverently as he snagged a chocolate frosted cinnamon roll.

"Yeah, you're not so bad," Matt said with a grin as he took

a donut in each hand then headed off to take a seat in a chair.

"We did actually miss you, I swear," Brent muttered around a behemoth bite of a Bear Claw.

Ben, her boss, sidled up and bumped his shoulder into hers in hello. He stood several inches taller than her, his body long and lean. With his short blonde hair and China blue eyes, he was a strikingly handsome guy. "How was the wedding? Did you get hammered?"

"Jodi and Free are, I'm sure, enjoying the last days of their honeymoon as we speak. The wedding was wonderful, exactly what she wanted. Thank you for letting me have the time off to go," she said with a smile, lifting her coffee to her lips. "And for the extra time."

"Shaun, you've got so many back hours logged, you could take the next three months off and never miss a full paycheck," he laughed, crossing his arms over his chest and standing with his feet spread wide. "I think it was good for you to take a little time off. You look different."

She gulped her coffee, burning her throat as she swung her eyes up to his. "Different? How?"

He shrugged wide shoulders, arms still crossed across his chest, and winked. "Just different."

Nate strolled into the breakroom then, his dark eyes spearing into Shaun's for a heartbeat before they shifted away. His shoulders were tense, the way he moved rigid. He never glanced at her again as the group of them finished their donut breakfast and then headed out to the bays to start working.

Shaun was elbows deep in an oil change when she saw Nate's boots appear to her left. Sighing heavily, she finished what she was doing and slid out from under the vehicle, standing and dusting her hands off. Glancing at him, she gave him a strained smile and asked, "Is there something you need?"

"So, you get home almost two weeks ago and you didn't bother to come back to work on time?"

Taken back by the heat in his tone and the anger in his eyes, she stepped back. "Excuse me?"

"We could have used you here all week," he stated flatly, placing his hands on his hips.

Shaking her head, her brows drew into a deep V as she muttered, "I'm sorry, what? I had pre-approved PTO that I used, Nate. That Ben and Rod both approved. I came home early because my best friend had her baby, and what do you care if I took off extra time? I don't recall having to ask your permission to take time off for my sister's wedding. A wedding that you were trying to convince me to take you as a date to, might I remind you. I don't date coworkers, and even if I did, I'm not interested in you."

"We could have had a good time, Shaun. You don't know what you're missing. All you have to do is let me slide between those thighs and I know I can change your mind," he murmured in an effort to sound seductive, at the same time sliding slightly closer to her. She recoiled as he reached out his hand as if to touch her.

"Keep your fucking hands to yourself or I'll cut them off," she warned, taking a step back away from him. "Fuck around and find out, I dare you. I could have you fired for sexual harassment, you dumbass."

"Go ahead and try," he laughed darkly. Then his voice dropped again, that effort to be charming returning. The man was giving her whiplash with the abrupt changes in demeanor, and he murmured, "Come on, sweetheart. Give me a chance. I'll show you what you've been missing, I promise. I'll be the best you've ever had."

"Not a fucking chance in hell," she said through clenched teeth.

His cynical laugh grated on her nerves, and he twisted his head around to the side, working his jaw in clear annoyance before swinging his head back around to her. "That's right, you were too busy spreading your legs for that rich asshole, weren't you? Guess money buys whores like you."

Fury lashed through her, and she snapped, "You're a pig, Nate. Again, I don't recall having to ask your permission for anything regarding my life, so fuck off."

"Is there a problem here?"

Shaun whipped her head around and was impaled by

furious storm cloud eyes beneath dark blonde brows that were pulled low over them in a deep V. His body language was deceptively calm, only Shaun could see the thunder in his eyes. A brown paper sack was clutched in one hand, his knuckles white.

Kasey moved those eyes to Nate, who was stupid enough not to move away from Shaun, instead raising his chin haughtily.

"The lady told you to back off, asshole." Kasey's voice was low, ominous, and tingled along every nerve inside her, making her shiver. She'd never seen him so angry. "I suggest you do as she said."

"Fuck you, this is between me and her," Nate snapped, his stupidity making more of a show. A muscle jumped in Kasey's jaw.

"There is *nothing* between you and her, and this conversation is over," Kasey snarled, taking several steps closer. He set the paper sack on a work bench beside him, then leaning down into Nate's face, he snarled through gritted teeth, "And you'll apologize to her for the name calling. She doesn't owe you shit, and if she wants me and not you, that's our business, not yours. So, you and your little tic-tac dick, that I'm sure is the reason you're such a delightful asshole, can get the fuck away from her right now."

Mortification swallowed her whole when Brent and Nick

stepped through one of the garage doors from a different bay, staring at the three of them. Ben appeared next, stopping in the middle of the doorway, arms crossed over his chest.

Nate backed away from her, a sneer marring his face. "Mother fucker," he muttered under his breath as he walked away, shoving past the three men in the doorway.

"Is there an issue?" Ben asked, his blonde brows rising, his gaze following Nate as he stalked away.

"Yes."

"*No*," Shaun grated out over Kasey's affirmative. "Everything is fine."

"Shaun," Kasey growled in warning, but she sliced her eyes to his and glared at him fiercely. "Sexual harassment in the workplace isn't 'fine'."

"Kasey!" she exclaimed, letting her hands slap against her jean-clad thighs in frustration. "*Can I talk to you outside, please*?"

Without waiting for his response, she shoved him hard in the chest, pushing him backward out of the large bay door that had been left open until they were both outside. She kept shoving until they'd rounded the corner of the building, hidden from the others. The mid-January cold was biting, but she barely felt it, the fury rolling through her making her hot.

Pointing his finger at the building, he snarled, "How often does that happen, Shaun?"

"It's *nothing*, Kasey," she ground out, taking a deep, steadying breath to combat the embarrassment and rage rolling through her. "I work in a mechanic shop, with a bunch of men, who all have very dirty minds and no filters on their mouths. I say just as raunchy, depraved things as they do some days."

"*That* was not workshop banter, Shaun!" Kasey shouted, waving his arm wide. "Trust me, I'm around mechanics day in and day out, too, darlin'. If anybody on my team treated a woman like that, they'd be fired so fast their head would spin."

"When I'm here, I'm not a woman. I'm one of the guys," Shaun argued, her hands shaking with fury.

"I'd argue that, and clearly that asshole doesn't understand the word no," he countered. Stepping closer to her, making her lift her chin to raise her eyes to his, which were a dangerous shade of slate, and he snarled, "I'll ask again: How often does that happen, Shaun?"

"I don't need a knight in shining armor to rescue me, Kasey," Shaun deflected, fear tingling down her spine when his eyes darkened dangerously.

Grabbing hold of her upper arms, he pushed her backward until her back came to rest against the faded red metal siding of the building, his body slanting over hers. Her head tilted up, way up, to stare at him. His jaw was tight, a muscle jumping with what she could tell was barely contained anger.

"I'm no knight in shining armor, darlin'," he whispered darkly, his voice a low growl. "And I'm not here to rescue you. I'm here to ruin you, just like you've ruined me. But I won't stand by and let some other man touch what's mine."

"I'm not yours," she whispered, more out of habit than out of denial at this point.

"Keep telling yourself that, darlin'," he growled before dropping his mouth to hers fiercely, and her eyes closed as she met his kiss just as fervently. When his mouth released hers, she sighed, her eyes fluttering open.

"You're a bully."

"One thousand percent," he whispered against her mouth, smirking. "And you love it."

"I'm at work, Kasey," she whined, pushing against his chest halfheartedly. "You can't just show up here and—"

"And what? Stop some douche from harassing you, bring you lunch, or kiss you senseless?"

"Well, no…" she mumbled, narrowing her eyes up at him. "Don't be cute. I'm mad at you."

"Nothing new," he muttered, winking, and she rolled her eyes. "Are you going to tell me that you're going to turn your nose up at a giant bowl of lemon chicken soup and some of the best smelling, freshly baked bread I've ever found?"

Her eyebrows went up. "You found *Roast n Toast*, didn't you?"

"I googled coffee shops in the area and found that they had the best ratings. Really cool little place. Love the coffee cups on the wall outside," he said and shrugged, leading her back around the building and through the garage bay door.

Shaun laughed, nodding. "It's my favorite place for lunch. I actually think Jodi has a picture of me trying to 'drink' from one of those cups, absolutely blitzed on my twenty-first birthday."

Kasey laughed, and five grown men rushed to look like they were working as the two of them came into view. Brad, a big bear of a man with a thick, dark beard threaded with silver, sidled over, sticking his hand out to Kasey.

"You're K.C.," he said reverently, his deep voice rumbling, and Shaun rolled her eyes. "Love watching you race, man. Absolute dynamite on the track."

Kasey grinned and said, "Thanks, the team works very hard to make sure my job is real easy."

Brad stepped back and his hazel eyes bounced from Kasey's face to Shaun's and back. Gesturing between the two of them, he asked, "Uhh, so how did you meet our Shaun? You uhh, treating her right? We would have some words if you're not."

Groaning inwardly, she pinched the bridge of her nose between her finger and thumb. "Oh my god."

Kasey chuckled, draping his arm over her shoulders, and

tugged her close even as she protested weakly, her face flaming. Jake, Ben, and Nick had all walked closer, listening in on the conversation. "I met Shaun last year at my cousin's wedding, but in respect for her relationship at the time, I didn't pursue anything further. At least not until last weekend. The Colorado Rockies can be such a romantic place, can't they?"

"*Oh my gawd,*" she groaned again, elbowing him in the side of the ribs. He grunted but didn't move his arm from around her shoulders. "You are the absolute worst human being."

"Alright guys, if we're all taking breaks, punch out for lunch," Ben called over, though his tone was light. When Shaun glanced over at him, he winked. "I don't pay you for social hour."

THIRTY-SEVEN

"So then, Ben pulls me into the office and tells me that he sent Nate home for the remainder of the day, and that he is on a weeklong suspension, with a formal write up," Shaun said, rounding the corner of the couch to sink into it. Raising his arm, she settled into the crook of his body, leaning with her back angled against his side and chest. Steaming bowl of chili piled high with diced white onions, a dollop of sour cream, and a handful of cheddar cheese balanced in her hands, she wiggled back, lifting her legs to tuck them beneath her crisscross. Her hair was damp from the shower she'd taken after she'd gotten home, and she'd only pulled on one of his shirts afterward, the hem riding up as she sat cross legged. She turned her head to look back at him. "I know I shouldn't, but I feel bad for him getting in trouble."

His own empty chili bowl sat on the coffee table next to them. Picking up his beer, he took a drink before responding.

"You have this very misplaced sense of guilt," he murmured, sweeping her curls away from the side of her neck as she took a bite. "First Tommy, now this asshole. You shouldn't feel bad at all. His own actions got him into hot water. He could have been a decent human being and taken the first no as an answer."

Craning her neck around to fix him with a dubious stare, he let his mouth tilt up in a half grin as she muttered dryly, "*You* didn't take the first *hundred* no's as an answer."

Leaning forward, he pressed a quick kiss to her mouth. "No, I didn't. If I'd thought any part of you actually meant it, I would have left you alone, darlin'. But I knew the first time I laid my eyes on you; we would end up just like this. I just had to convince you, first."

He felt her body stiffen where she was pressed against him and knew before she opened her mouth that the protest was coming and braced for it. She set her chili in her lap and half turned to face him.

"Kasey—"

"Don't, please. Just… Don't."

Her dark, raven's wing brows drew close over those deep sapphire blue eyes as she stared at him. "Don't what?"

"You're getting ready to run again. Don't," he murmured, his voice low, raw.

"This is my house, I have nowhere else to run to," she said, her tone sharp and defensive. She shook her head then, rolling her eyes. "I'm not running."

"Physically, no," he said gently, running his fingers down

her arm where his still lay across her shoulders. "You're either going to push me away or pull away yourself. Don't, please. Let us have this."

"You've been here over two weeks already, Kasey," she stammered on a sardonic laugh. Exhaling roughly, she turned her head back forward, her hair falling over her shoulder again. "You asked me to give you the weekend, the week, which we had, plus some. What more do you want?"

"Exactly that. I want more."

"More what?" she asked defensively, uncrossing her legs and swinging them over the edge of the couch. The shirt rode up higher, giving him a glimpse of her ass in the cheeky thong she had on. Setting her chili on the table in front of them, she twisted so that she was facing him more fully. Goddamn she was beautiful when she got riled. "More time? More blow jobs? More what, Kasey?"

"Oh, for fuck's sake— Why is it so impossible for you to just accept that maybe I like spending time with you?" he asked, sitting up straighter on the couch himself. "*I like you, Shaun.* A fucking hell of a lot. No, *more* than a hell of a lot, and I like whatever *this* is that we're doing right now. At least I did until thirty seconds ago."

Rolling her eyes and blowing out an exasperated breath, she stood, picking up her chili bowl and heading to the small kitchen. He followed.

She set the bowl down on the counter with a loud thunk, the spoon clattering out onto the counter noisily. Rounding on him, she placed her hands on her hips and glared up at him, the movement causing the shirt to ride up higher on her bare thighs. He could just make out the splash of red that were her panties at the junction of her legs.

Scrubbing his hand down his face, he sighed heavily. "You do realize you're angry at me because I said I like you, right? Do you understand how ass-backward that is?"

"I made myself very clear that I wasn't looking for something more at the beginning of this, Kasey," she snapped, and he squeezed his eyes shut for a long heartbeat before opening them. "I don't want a relationship. I don't want anyone to have that much of me again, I explained that. This is just scratching that itch. Nothing more."

"So just hate sex, then?" he asked darkly, taking a step toward her, until she had to tilt her head back to continue to glare at him. "So, you're just in this for all the orgasms, is that right?"

"I thought I've been very transparent on that front," she said stiffly, her voice breaking slightly. Damn stubborn woman. He couldn't even be offended by her words, because they were nothing but lies, and he knew it. Knew it by the stubborn tick in her jaw, the tight way her lips pulled together, the nervous swallow that flexed her throat.

Leaning forward to place his hands on the edge of the counter on either side of her hips, he towered over her, bringing his face close to hers. The fabric of his shirt fluttered over the base of her throat where it lay against her skin, testament to the erratic beat of her heart. "You're a fucking liar, Shaun. And I'm getting real tired of it."

She continued to glare up at him, and he could see the war raging in those sapphire eyes of hers. *She* didn't even believe the words coming out of her mouth.

Lowering his head, he swept his mouth over the corner of hers in the briefest of caresses. Breathing against the soft skin of her cheek, he whispered, "God dammit, you are the most stubborn, pain-in-the-ass woman I have ever fucking met. I have to leave for training in two days, Shaun, or I can pack my bags right now and be out the door. Your choice."

Pulling his hands away from the counter where he'd been leaning, he took a step back, her will still battling against his. She remained silent, and finally he nodded. He'd call her bluff.

"Okay. You win this one, darlin'. I'll see myself out," he said quietly, and watched as her chin tilted up higher in defiance. Fucking woman.

It didn't take long to pack his bag, and when he returned to the kitchen, she was still exactly where she had been. Her arms crossed tight over her chest, one bare foot pressed against the top of the other. Her body was stiff where she stood, and the pain that lanced through him was piercing. Damn woman had wiggled her way into his heart, which currently felt like it was splintering into pieces inside his chest.

Stepping in front of her, he took her face between both of his hands, forcing her to tilt her head up to look at him. Tears shimmered in her eyes, making them glisten, and his heart broke a little more.

"You know that this is real, Shaun. You fucking know it, and you're going to let me walk away from you because of your damned stubborn pride, because you're too chicken shit to let yourself be vulnerable again. *I'm not Tommy,* Shaun." One of those tears slid down her cheek and it gutted him. "I want *you*. All of you; unabashedly, no filter, no watered-down bullshit. God dammit, darlin', you knew it, just like I did, that very first night. *I am yours, and you are mine.* I'll be back when you're ready to admit it to me, and to yourself."

He kissed her then, voraciously, hungrily, imprinting himself so deeply into her heart and soul she wouldn't have a choice but to admit she felt the same way he did. Because God dammit, he knew she did. He knew it in every fiber of his being; their souls were meant for each other.

He just needed her to see it.

He felt her hands at his sides, her fingers gripped the fabric of his jacket as she kissed him back. Tears slid over his thumbs where they cupped her cheeks, twisting his stomach into knots with the knowledge that she was hurting as much as he was. But she was too stubborn to admit he was right.

He released her then, and without a look back, strode out the door and into the night before she could see the way his own heart was breaking.

THIRTY-EIGHT

Shaun stared at the door after he closed it behind him for a long time.

She almost expected him to come back.

But he didn't.

The car he'd been renting from the airport had disappeared out of her driveway, the taillights fading as he drove away.

His half empty beer still sat on the end table next to the couch, the football game they'd turned on still playing on the TV in the background.

Her apartment suddenly felt too large and much too empty without him there taking up her space, driving her up the wall with his smart mouth and sarcastic wit.

Finally able to force herself to move, she walked down the hall to the bedroom, immediately hating how empty it was without his clothes hanging off the back of the chair, his cologne and deodorant no longer sitting on the top of her dresser next to her perfume. His side of the bed was still rumpled from where he'd slept next to her the night before.

She was unable to stem the flow of tears as they slid down her cheeks. Swiping at them angrily, she returned to the living room, picking up the half empty beer bottle and his empty chili bowl, taking them to the sink. Dumping the beer down the drain with angry, jerky movements, she slammed it down on the counter once it was empty.

Damn you, Kasey Corcoran! her mind screamed. *Why couldn't you have just left me alone? I was* fine, *before you came along!*

Steve jumped up onto the counter, sitting on the corner and meowed pitifully at her, as if blaming her for Kasey's absence.

"It's better this way, Steve. We would never have worked, and this was just for fun anyway," she snapped at the cat, who was eyeing her with judgmental green eyes.

If this was just supposed to be for fun, then why does it hurt so much?

She had no good answer for the question, choosing to ignore it instead of digging into it any further. Self-reflection wasn't one of her strong suits.

Her phone vibrated where it was still sitting on the coffee table next to her forgotten chili, and she walked over to it, swiping the message from Jodi open.

Okay, we're home. Now SPILL! I want all the details! I know he's been at your place for two weeks,
Roxy told me!

Letting her head fall back against her shoulders, she sighed up at the ceiling before looking back at the phone, typing a quick message. She hated how much the words hurt as she sent the text.

There's nothing to tell.
He left. The end.

The three dots popped up then disappeared several times before Jodi's next message came through. Shaun couldn't help the sad smile that tugged at one corner of her lips.

I'll bring tequila and ice cream.
Be there in twenty minutes.

Shaun set the phone down on the coffee table, scraping her mostly uneaten chili into the garbage under the sink. Then she forced herself down the hall to the bedroom again, pulling on a pair of fleece pajama pants and an oversized hoodie over Kasey's shirt that she still wore.

Jodi came in fifteen minutes later, grocery bag in one hand and a pizza box in the other, overnight bag slung over her shoulder.

"No, I don't want a hug, and I don't know that I

particularly want to talk about it yet," Shaun said as Jodi stepped into the kitchen, depositing the bags and the pizza onto the counter. "I do, however, want to know how your honeymoon went."

Jodi waved one hand and made a pfft sound, taking the contents out of the grocery bag one at a time. "Yeah, well I've been waiting over two weeks to hear about this, and you promised."

"Jodi," Shaun whined, crossing her arms over her stomach and squeezing her eyes shut. "He literally just left like, an hour ago."

"So you guys had a fight?" her sister asked, turning toward her with the bottle of tequila in one hand and the ice cream in the other. She held them both up and raised her eyebrows.

Shaun sighed heavily and pointed toward the tequila. It had been a day. She deserved some tequila.

"We're always fighting," Shaun muttered and turned to grab two shot glasses from the cupboard, along with two margarita glasses as Jodi placed the tequila and a bottle of margarita mix on the counter. Shaun cracked the seal on the tequila and poured out two shots of the golden liquor, while Jodi found a cutting board and a knife, slicing up the lime she'd pulled out of the bag as well. Shaun slid the saltshaker closer to them both as Jodi put the ice cream container in the freezer for later. "This was never going to work, Jodi. This wasn't meant to last. We're too different."

"Or too much the same," Jodi countered, raising her dark brows.

They both picked up their shot glasses and limes. They clinked their shots together and licked the salt off the back of their hands, then tossed the tequila back. Jodi cringed and put the lime in her mouth, sucking as she danced a little. Shaun poured another shot into her glass, taking that one in rapid succession to the first before putting the lime between her lips.

"Can I tell you what I think?" Jodi asked.

"I'd rather you not, but I feel like that's not going to stop you," Shaun muttered dryly, rolling her eyes.

"You're right, it's not," her sister said simply, and Shaun sighed, once again crossing her arms over her stomach. "I think you're so scared of letting anyone in again after Tommy that you'll find any way to self-sabotage. That you're so worried about not feeling like you're your own person, or like yourself, with someone else. But Shaun, honey, when you find the right person… you don't have to worry about any of that. It just happens. I know we've never really talked about what happened with Tommy—"

"And I don't really want to now," Shaun grumbled, making Jodi glare at her.

"—but we're going to. Starting with why you were trying to hide from him the night he proposed."

Shaun cringed, burying her face in her hands. *Oh god. I did hide. Behind a tree.*

"You told me that night that you liked Tommy. Not that you loved him," Jodi said softly. "I think you knew long before you ended things that it wasn't right. I just always felt that you needed someone that could handle you."

Shaun lowered her hands from her face to glare at her sister. "You make me sound like I'm a petulant brat."

"I mean, yeah, sometimes," Jodi teased with a laugh. "But that's not what I mean and you know it, so don't go getting all bent out of shape until you hear me out." Shaun blew out an annoyed breath but nodded, and Jodi continued. "You are fire, Shaun. So wild and untamed and so authentically who you are… I hated seeing that part of you being smothered while you were with Tommy. Like he was trying his best to be able to handle you, but his way was to try to control you, to water down what makes you truly you."

Shaun swallowed hard, reaching for the bottle of tequila and pouring another shot. The first two had already started to make her feel fuzzy. Kasey's words came back to her as she tilted the shot glass back. *I want you. All of you. Unabashedly, no filter, no watered-down bullshit.*

"With Kasey… I don't know, Shaun. It just seemed like you were still able to be *you*, unapologetically and without any pretenses or trying to fit into a mold that you just weren't made for," Jodi whispered fervently. "Yes, you guys fight, a lot. But that's who you are; you're not built to be small or quiet or fragile. He lets you be as fiery and as wild as you want or need to be, and he revels in it. The way he looks at you… It's the way Dad looks at Mom. Like you're the most incredible thing he's ever seen. Don't you feel that?" she asked, pressing her hand over her heart. Shaun tossed the tequila back, exhaling as it burned going down. "You do, don't you? That's why this hurts so bad."

"I don't want to feel like I have to change, or in ten years realize that I have changed, just to be with someone," she said quietly. Admitting it out loud was painful.

"I don't think that you would have to worry about that with Kasey," Jodi murmured. "I think he loves you just like you are."

Shaun whipped her head toward her sister, her eyes wide. "Don't say that."

"What, that he loves you?" Jodi asked, her eyebrows shooting up in surprise. "Isn't it obvious?"

"No," she whispered, turning her head to stare at the floor. "We hate each other. We just have really great sex, but nothing else has changed, Jodi." *Girl, your pants are going to catch on fire one of these days. The man admitted to liking you, you idiot.*

"Yeah, okay," Jodi scoffed, leaning forward to grab the pizza box. Flipping the lid open, she grabbed a slice laden with ham, bacon, and pineapple before taking a bite of it. Chewing, she swallowed, then muttered sourly, "That man is crazy about you, and if you try to tell me you're not crazy about him, I'll hit you with this slice of pizza."

Instead of lying, Shaun took a slice of pizza from the box and brought it to her mouth. Jodi eyed her warily, but then nodded triumphantly.

"That's what I thought," she murmured slyly, winking.

Shaun flipped her off with her free hand as she took another bite of pizza.

THIRTY-NINE

February dawned cold and gloomy; the sun hidden by layers of thick gray clouds. Shaun hadn't heard from Kasey and hadn't reached out to him in the week and a half since he'd left. She knew he was busy in pre-season training, the first race of the season scheduled for the following weekend.

She ached to text him, to call, anything. She missed his voice, missed that snarky, sarcastic sense of humor, missed the comfortable companionship she'd grown far too accustomed to in the short time he'd been there. She missed his smile and that dimple in his cheek, those gray-blue eyes that always looked at her with such heat. Missed his body pressed against hers in her bed, missed reaching for him in the middle of the night just to feel him close.

The damn man had gone and made her fall in love with him and she was *pissed* about it.

Sitting on the couch, not really watching what she'd put on the tv, she jerked her head around when she heard the crunch of gravel on the driveway, and then the slam of a car door closing. Jumping to her feet, she rushed down the hall, checking her reflection frantically, just as a knock sounded on the door.

Rushing back down to the door, she paused for a heartbeat before pulling it open.

Disappointment washed over her before the shock really kicked in. "Hi… I wasn't expecting you."

Tommy nodded, lowering his brown eyes from hers to a spot somewhere near her chin. "I know, I'm sorry. Can I come in? Or do you still have company?"

"Uhh," she murmured, "No, I don't have company. Come on in."

Stepping back away from the door, she let her ex-fiancé in, and he waited for her to lead him into the kitchen that he had once frequented.

"I can make some coffee?" she asked, and he nodded. Moving to the counter, she prepped a large pot of coffee quickly, setting it to percolate, before turning back toward him. "Please, have a seat."

He sank into one of the dining chairs, and after the coffee had brewed enough to pour out two cups, she brought them with her and sat opposite him, sliding one of the cups toward him.

"You look good," she said softly, though she knew it was a lie.

He huffed out a wry laugh and glanced at her. "I look like shit, and you know it."

"Well, yeah," she mumbled, laughing quietly too. Then, "Why are you here, Tommy? Why now?"

Rolling his shoulders, he took a sip of the coffee before setting it down on the table, then raised his brown eyes to hers fully. "I'm checking myself into a rehab center downstate in a couple days."

"Oh." Shock made her eyebrows shoot up.

He nodded, shoving his fingers through his hair that was too long. "I uh–I fucked up, Shaun. I fucked… everything up. I lost my best friend, I destroyed the relationship that I had with my sister and my niece and now my nephew… I lost you." He lowered his gaze down to the coffee cup between his hands. "I realize now that we were never going to work. Even before I fucked everything up. I was never going to be enough for you. Even though I wanted to be. I tried."

Emotion clogged her throat, making her nose sting with tears. Even though she didn't love him anymore, she still cared about him, and seeing him in so much pain, so broken, it killed her.

"I realize that the way I handled everything was wrong. I was suffering through a lot of grief, depression, anxiety… And I didn't handle it. I just tried to drink it away. Tried to control everything else that I could." She swallowed hard. "I tried to control the people that I loved the most, and I hurt them. I have to do this for me, for Zoey. I know I won't ever get the chance to make things right with you, and that's okay. Because you deserve that big kind of happy, too. You know that, right?"

She nodded as a tear slid down her cheek. Goddamn crazy emotions! She never cried, and now she couldn't seem to stop!

He stood then, as did she, and when he held his arms out to her, she went into them willingly, hugging him tightly around the middle. They swayed that way for a long time, just in silence.

"I hope you find that big happy, Shaun," he murmured above her head, his hands rubbing up and down her back, and she hiccupped on a sad whimper. She inhaled, and sadness hit her all over again at the strange, unfamiliar scent. *She missed Kasey*. "Don't let that pride of yours get in the way, okay?"

She laughed sadly. *Too late*. "Okay."

When they finally pulled apart, she felt like something had lifted; that closure that neither of them had been granted finally shifted into place. She walked him to the door, and she opened it, stopping just inside as he turned back toward her.

"I'm proud of you," she said softly, reaching her hand out to him one more time. He reached out and squeezed her fingers gently. "Take care of you."

He released her hand and nodded, then said, "You, too." She watched him as he jogged down the steps to his truck. He climbed in and then waved before driving away.

Sighing heavily and squeezing her eyes shut against another wave of tears, she closed the door.

FORTY

When Shaun woke the next morning, still with no text or call from Kasey, she threw herself into work; going in early and staying late every day, helping the other guys with their jobs when she'd completed all of hers.

All except Nate, who had returned to work at the beginning of the week. He'd kept his distance for most of the first week, but had since resumed his usual behavior of standing too close, watching her from afar, and the occasional unwelcome sexual advance.

Waking early, Shaun lay in bed for a moment trying to figure out what had woken her so abruptly, when she bolted out of bed, racing to the bathroom. She'd barely made it before throwing up wretchedly multiple times. Standing, she rinsed her mouth and then walked slowly out to the kitchen, starting the coffee to percolate, but the smell of the coffee as it brewed made her nauseous again, and moments later she threw up in the kitchen sink.

Calling in sick wasn't an option. If she stayed at home, it left far too much time to think about how much she missed

Kasey, or the conversation she'd had with Tommy several days prior. So, still a little green around the gills, she lugged herself to the shop, several cans of warm ginger ale and a sleeve of crackers sitting on her work bench, close at hand.

"Oy, you don't look too good," Brent muttered, giving her a wide berth as she walked through the shop. "Brown bag flu?"

She shook her head. "No. Not sure. Maybe it was something I ate last night."

"Why don't you go home," Ben said from the doorway, arms crossed over his chest, as usual.

"I'm fine," she muttered sourly. He grumbled something and then walked away, leaving her to her work.

Several hours later, she stood from where she'd been hunkered down next to the Ford Escape she'd been working on, and she reeled slightly, a wave of dizziness washing over her as stars danced in her vision. Reaching out, she grabbed hold of the side of the vehicle, closing her eyes tightly. She took a deep breath in, hoping it would help steady her, releasing it slowly, but it did nothing to combat the vertigo. Nausea rolled through her again, her mouth watering with the urge to vomit.

"Shaun? Hey, are you alright?" she heard from her left, and she nodded, hoping it would be enough to send Nate on his way. "Hey, you don't look too good. Let me help you."

She shrugged his hands off her shoulders, but still he moved forward, bracketing her in against the side of the car.

Shoving against him with as much strength as she could muster, she tried to dislodge him. "Come on, Shaun. You know you want this."

His breath was hot as it hit her in the face, his mouth getting closer and closer to her own. Nausea rolled through her at the thought of his mouth connecting with hers, and she shoved against him again. He finally stumbled back, and she twisted away from him sharply.

Oh god, I'm going to throw up.

She squeezed her eyes shut as another debilitating wave of dizziness flashed over her. Swallowing the saliva that had pooled in her mouth, she shook her head and opened her eyes just in time to see him advance on her again, those creepy black eyes intent on her face. She shook her head, willing her throat to open enough to call out for help, but she knew if she opened her mouth, she was going to vomit everywhere. Instead, she took an instinctual, unsteady step backward, her only means of escape.

"Oh, fuck!" she heard, just as her heel connected with something heavy just behind her, and she tripped, falling backward.

It felt as if she was falling for a long time, suspended in the air for way longer than she should have. When she finally landed, she only had a half a second to register the pain that exploded in her side before her head connected with the concrete ground and everything went black.

FORTY-ONE

"I'm fine, honestly," Shaun argued through clenched teeth as the paramedics lifted her on the gurney that she'd been placed on.

"Yeah, you said that earlier, and then we found you knocked out on the concrete floor for nearly five minutes, Shaun," Ben snapped to her right, near her feet. He was standing with his legs braced wide, arms crossed over his chest angrily. "You're going to get checked out whether you like it or not. You fell over that tire jack and cracked your skull on the damn floor. Stomach bug or not. Company policy."

Her head ached abominably, admittedly, and she'd gotten nauseated by the sight of the blood that had pooled on the floor beneath her head, throwing up wretchedly over the side of the gurney. But it was the constant, burning pain in her left side that she was trying to conceal. Breathing carefully, because even breathing hurt, she nodded. Vomiting made it almost unbearable.

Nate had been nowhere to be found when she'd come to. According to the other guys, he'd left in a hurry, before any of them had found her on the ground. After telling Ben and the paramedics what had happened, Ben was furious. Nate was fired, whenever he showed his face again. Ben also wanted her to press charges, but she'd insisted on waiting until her head cleared a little before making that decision.

"She probably has a concussion and I suspect broken ribs, but we need to do X-Rays and an MRI," the paramedic said to Ben as they hoisted her up and into the back of the ambulance that had been called. How embarrassing.

"I called your parents, they're meeting you at the hospital," Ben called into the ambulance and she groaned, then immediately regretted it, the sound and motion hurting everything inside her.

By the time they reached the hospital and transferred her into the ER, her parents, and Jodi and Free had convened upon the ER staff.

"Can you have them wait out in the waiting room, please?" Shaun asked, her eyelids heavy, her sight still fuzzy.

"If that's what you want," the triage nurse said gently. "They're just worried about you."

"I know. I just… my head hurts," she admitted weakly. The nurse nodded and placed a new, heated blanket around her legs, then set the overhead light to low. She'd had blood drawn and an IV started in the back of her right hand. "Thank you."

"We can give you something for that headache, and for

the pain in your ribs. Is there any chance of pregnancy?" she asked, wiggling the mouse on the rolling triage cart with a laptop perched on it.

"No," she said. "I'm not pregnant."

"We'll run a blood test just to be sure," the nurse said and typed away on the computer. "Just so we know what we can give you for pain."

Settling down into the warmth of the blanket, she just nodded. "Am I allowed to sleep?"

"We'd prefer if you stayed awake, but if you do fall asleep it won't hurt," the nurse murmured, glancing at her from where she stood at the cart. "I'll be back as soon as I know what we can give you for pain management, and then we'll get you taken down for X-Rays and that MRI. Doctor will probably want to do some sutures on that laceration on the back of your head, too."

Fifteen minutes later, a man in a white lab coat knocked on the door, then entered with a kind smile. "Hello, I'm Dr. Hudson. I hear we had a bit of a fall earlier?"

Nodding, she shifted on the uncomfortable hospital bed and winced as the pain in her ribs stole her breath.

"Well, we're going to probably skip those X-Rays today. Fairly safe to say we've got some broken ribs, but I'm just not comfortable doing those this early," he said as he washed his hands across the room.

Frowning, she asked, "What do you mean, this early?"

Dr. Hudson dried his hands on a paper towel, using his foot to lift the lid of the little garbage can by the door and turned to her, smiling. "This early in the pregnancy. It's just good practice to wait until a little further along before doing any kind of X-Rays that close to the abdomen."

Shaun felt like her head was about to explode. "I'm sorry, what?"

"You're pregnant, Miss Kendall. Approximately three weeks. Still very early," he said kindly, patting her knee. "So we can give you some Tylenol, but nothing stronger, unfortunately. You'll probably be pretty uncomfortable for a little while. I wish there was something stronger that we could give you. I'll be back after your MRI, and I'll send the nurse in with that Tylenol."

She nodded dumbly, her hands dropping to her stomach that was buried beneath the blanket and the thin hospital gown they'd made her change into upon arrival. Tears burned her eyes and she blinked rapidly, but they spilled over her lids and down her cheeks.

The nurse returned a few minutes later and Shaun tried to stem the tears to no avail. "Here you go," she heard, and raised her eyes just as a box of tissues was placed in her lap. "Are you sure I can't bring someone in for you? Is the baby's father here?"

"N-no," Shaun mumbled through her tears, shredding a

tissue between her fingers. "I don't want them to see me like this. And he's not here."

The nurse nodded, her kindness making Shaun cry all the harder. She was left alone after the dose of Tylenol. It was an hour before she would be done with the MRI and she received six stitches to close the cut on the back of her head.

Wheeled out to the waiting room in a wheelchair, she grimaced when she saw her mother's tear-streaked face and felt a flush of guilt that she hadn't at least let her come back with her. Seren's usually unflappable poise was clearly rattled; and more tears welled in Shaun's eyes that she was unable to stop. Her father took over pushing the wheelchair, moving her gently out the double sliding doors and out into the cold, dark parking lot. A fresh layer of snow had dusted the pavement and the vehicles in the parking lot, the tall light poles highlighting the snow as it drifted down.

Jodi and Serenity helped her out of the wheelchair as carefully as they could, but even so, the pain in her ribs was excruciating. She climbed into the backseat of her mother's SUV, which was thankfully already turned on and warm on the inside. Levi closed the door and then assisted her mother into the passenger seat, ever the gentleman, before rounding the hood of the car and climbing in behind the wheel. Jodi and Free waved from the parking spot next to them in Free's truck, and off they went.

"Why don't you come to the house, that way we can take care of you for a few days?" Serenity said from the front seat. Shaun closed her eyes against the blindingly bright headlights of the vehicles that passed them, but closing her eyes made her dizzy, so she just bowed her head and stared into the darkness at her feet. "I hate the idea of you being home alone."

"I'll be fine, Mom, but thank you," she whispered. She wanted to go home, to be alone, to cry where no one could see her. She didn't want to tell anyone, not yet. "I just want to go to sleep."

"You really shouldn't be alone, sweetheart," Levi rumbled, his voice low. "Let Mom fuss over you."

"If I come over, can I just sleep, please?" she asked. She knew a losing battle when she saw one.

"Of course," her mother said gently. "I'll just run upstairs and get your old room ready when we get home."

By the time they pulled into the driveway in front of the sprawling ranch house, Shaun's head was pounding again, and every single movement made her want to throw up from the pain. Levi and Seren helped her up the wide front steps and into the house. Levi stayed with her while Seren rushed up the stairs and turned down the bedding in Shaun's old room, then the two of them made their way, very slowly, up the staircase and into her room, which had thankfully been repainted into a pretty shade of olive green from the garish blood red she'd insisted on as a teenager.

"You left Jodi's room the same color it was," Shaun pointed out as her mother helped her climb into the bed carefully.

"Jodi's room didn't make me think a clown had gone on a serial murdering spree in it," her mother countered dryly, winking.

A quiet knock sounded on the still open door, and she looked over to see Levi in the doorway with a tall glass of ice water and two ice packs. He ambled inside, setting the glass of water on the bedside table and lowered his tall frame to the edge of her bed. He found her knee under the comforter that Seren had tucked up around her waist and squeezed it gently.

"One for your ribs, one for your head," he said gruffly. His dark, silver streaked hair looked rumpled, like he'd shoved his fingers through it a dozen times, and his dark blue eyes that were so much like her own were crinkled at the corners in worry. "How many ribs are broken?"

"Uhh," she stammered, unsure how to respond. If she admitted that the doctor had not done X-Rays, they would demand to know why. "Two, I think they said."

"You poor thing," Seren whispered, fussing over her again, the crease between her brows deepening. "I swear, those garages are so dangerous."

"I just tripped, Mom," she said defensively. "I stood up

too fast and got dizzy for a second—"

"Dizzy?" her mother asked, halting in her fluffing of the pillows behind Shaun's back. "Why were you dizzy?"

"I just stood up too fast—"

"Did you eat today? Have too much coffee on an empty stomach?" Seren asked, sitting on the opposite side of the bed as Levi.

"Yeah, probably just too much coffee and no lunch," Shaun mumbled, dropping her gaze to her tightly clasped fingers that were resting on her belly. Oh god.

Nausea rolled through her again at the thought, but she closed her eyes, taking several long, deep breaths.

"We'll let you rest," Levi rumbled gently, patting her clasped hands. "Call us if you need anything."

"Okay," she whispered, letting her head rest back on the pillow that Seren had propped up behind her, as it was too painful to lay flat. "Good night. Thank you."

"Good night, sweetheart," Levi said, clasping Seren's hand in his own and dragging her toward the door. "Love you."

"Love you, too," she murmured as he shut off the light, closing the door behind them as they took their leave.

Finally, blessedly alone in the darkness, Shaun let the tears track down her cheeks in a relentless flow, soaking her hair and the pillow beneath her head.

FORTY-TWO

She could only handle two nights at her parent's house with her mother hovering over her almost constantly. By the third day she was going crazy and informed her mother that she would be returning home, despite Seren's arguments about how it was better for her to stay with them.

"Mom, I need to go home. Steve probably misses me. And I miss my bed," she said, the first part being a truth, the second part being a half-truth. Her bed hadn't felt the same since Kasey left. Seren finally relented, agreeing to let Levi drive her home.

An hour later she was home and in bed after a very long, very hot shower. Her ribs ached more than they had the first day. Seren and Levi had set her up with several reusable ice packs, putting them in the freezer so they would be ready when she needed a fresh one. Climbing into the softest, most comfortable pajamas she could find that didn't hurt to put on, she had just climbed into bed when her phone started buzzing.

Groaning, she stared at it, where it glowed several feet out of reach on the nightstand. "Sorry, whoever it is. I'm not moving."

The call ended, the buzzing going silent, but almost immediately it began buzzing again. She remained where she was, finally comfortable, and glared at it as it started to buzz a third time.

"I'm not getting up! Stop calling me!" she whined at the phone as it stopped ringing for the third time. Holding her breath, she growled in frustration when it started ringing again. "Ugh, fine!"

Inching closer to the edge of the bed, she grabbed it, fumbling it. As she saw the name on the screen, she panicked, but the damage was done, she'd already answered it by accident by sliding her finger across the screen as she'd fumbled it. "Fuck," she hissed silently, then took a deep breath and brought it to her ear. "I'm not in the mood to talk. Goodbye, Kasey."

She hung up as his voice cut through, and she closed her eyes, letting the phone drop to the bed beside her.

"God dammit," she snarled as it began ringing again, swiping it to send to voicemail. He called back immediately, and she answered it, snarling into the phone, "Stop calling me, Kase! I don't want to talk to you right now!"

She hung up then turned her phone all the way off, tossing it across the bed and wincing with the movement as it sent nausea rolling through her all over again. Settling into the pillows again, she placed the ice pack on her side and closed her eyes. She'd cried most of her tears the first night, waking up the following morning with an even worse headache than she'd gone to sleep with and eyes that felt like sandpaper.

She had just started to drift off to sleep when she heard a car door close with a slam, then a loud, unrelenting banging on her door. She didn't even have the energy to get up, just covered her head with the pillow and prayed whoever it was would get the hint and go away soon.

The knocking ended, then the car door closed again, and a moment later she heard the engine turn over as whoever it was left, and she was finally able to drift off to sleep.

It couldn't have been twenty minutes later that she woke up to the sound of her door opening, then angry, heavy footfalls down the hallway. Groggily, she blinked rapidly just as he appeared in the doorway, his body tense and his eyes a terrifying mix of gray and blue. His blonde brows were pulled low over them, but when he caught sight of her laying in the bed, his entire body seemed to sigh as his shoulders released all the tension in them, his gaze softening.

"Why aren't you answering your phone?" he snapped, though there was little heat in his words. He strode over to the bed, swiping the Texas Longhorn ball cap off his head and tossing it to the foot of her bed. He then sat on the edge of the bed facing her, and he smoothed his hand over her curls, down her shoulder. "Do you have any idea how worried I've been?"

She shook her head dumbly, staring up at him from where she still lay on her right side. The ice pack had slid off her left side, and he picked it up, returning it to its place on her ribcage. She winced slightly at the light pressure, and his brows drew into a deep V again.

"Jesus, Shaun," he whispered, running his hand over her gently again, his eyes roving over every inch of her. "Free texted me, told me you'd been hurt at work. That bastard put his hands on you, I'll fucking kill him—"

Squeezing her eyes shut, she took a deep breath in at the annoyance that flashed through her. Meddling brother-in-law. "Of course he told you."

"Well, I'm glad someone did," he snapped. "Since obviously you had no intention of telling me yourself."

"I had nothing to say to you," she hissed through clenched teeth as she struggled to a sitting position. Gingerly, she moved her legs to the opposite side of the bed and stood.

"Sit down," he said gruffly and then his hands were on her shoulders. She shrugged away, baring her teeth as the motion caused another flash of pain to lance through her side. "Sit down, Shaun. Don't make me say it again."

"You don't get to come in here and boss me around," she snapped, backing up a step, her eyes fierce. "I've had enough of people telling me what to do the last three days."

Kasey scrubbed one hand down his face, over the scruff that was dusting his upper lip, chin, and cheeks. *He needs a shave*, she thought absently. "I'm sorry. I've just been worried sick. You wouldn't answer my texts or calls."

"I didn't have anything to say," she said again, crossing her arms over her stomach. *He didn't know, did he?* There was no way he could know. No one knew yet.

Kasey's face went taut as he stared down at her. "So, you just weren't going to tell me? About any of it? You didn't think I would want to know?"

Shaun raised one shoulder in an indifferent shrug, her face pulling with the pain of the movement. "Nothing has changed."

Liar. Everything has changed. He deserves to know.

Oh god, she thought miserably, then turned and raced toward the door, barely making it to the toilet before vomiting violently. Agony shot through her side and head as she vomited, the action making her ribs ache abominably. Sweat broke out along her entire body in swells as the pain undulated over her.

She moaned when she realized Kasey had followed, and that he was kneeling next to her. He smoothed her hair away from the side of her face, then rubbed her back as she continued to dry heave.

"Is it normal to vomit this long after a concussion?" he

asked, still rubbing along the curve of her back.

The doctors had said that it was normal to have nausea for up to two weeks following a concussion… but to expect the morning sickness could last much longer.

Oh my god, I'm pregnant, she thought again and moaned miserably. She panted, squeezing her eyes shut against another wave of nausea that enveloped her, sweat making her feel clammy and cold. Embarrassment made her nose sting with unshed tears as he continued to rub her back soothingly.

When she had finally spent herself, she flushed the toilet and then rested her cheek along her arm as it rested on the seat of the toilet. She shivered in the aftermath and protested only mildly when Kasey scooped her into his arms as gently as possible, carrying her back to the bed, where he deposited her carefully. He disappeared for a moment, returning to sit on the edge of the bed beside her with a cool, damp cloth that he used to dab at her forehead and temples, wiping away the sweat there. Tears blurred her eyes, and she squeezed them shut again. Why was he being so sweet to her when she was only ever awful to him? She didn't deserve this, or him.

His thumb swept away the first tear that escaped as it rolled down her cheek. "Are you in pain?"

Shaun shrugged, not wanting him to know just how badly she was hurting. Physically, emotionally, mentally. It all hurt.

"What can I do to help you?" he asked, still rubbing his

thumb over her cheek. She stared up at him, then her lower lip began to wobble. His eyebrows pulled together in a worried V, those wonderful storm cloud eyes troubled. He leaned down and pressed a kiss to her forehead, which just made her cry harder. "I've been worried out of my mind, darlin'. Let me help you, please."

"I think you helped enough," she accused weakly. When confusion clouded his eyes, she caught a sob, her lip trembling more as she whispered, "You knocked me up."

His face went completely blank, his gaze bouncing from one of her eyes to the other. Color drained from his face, but then he asked, "Is— fuck. Is everything okay? With the baby? Is the baby okay?"

She nodded, just barely, tears leaking unchecked down her face. "You're not mad?"

Surprise made him lean back. "Mad? No, darlin', of course I'm not mad. Is that why you didn't answer the phone? Because you didn't want to tell me?" She lowered her gaze guiltily, and then he murmured, his voice harder than before, "You were going to tell me, right?"

She shrugged, twisting her fingers in her lap. "I already said, this changes nothing."

Kasey stood, pacing several feet away, scrubbing his hand down his face before turning to fix her with a chilling stare. "*This changes nothing*? You don't think the fact that you're carrying my baby changes anything?"

"No," she snapped. "I don't see how it changes anything."

Making a quarter turn away from her so she was staring at him in profile, he tilted his head up to stare at the ceiling before turning again to stare at her. "You're coming on the road with me, so I can take care of you. We'll get married."

Shaun's eyes widened and she sat upright in bed, gasping sharply in pain. "Like hell we are."

"Jesus Christ, Shaun— do you have to argue about everything?" he asked in exasperation as he stepped closer to the bed, reaching a hand out to her.

"I'm not arguing. I'm *telling* you I'm not marrying you, Kasey. This isn't the 1950's. Women can and do raise babies all by themselves."

Kasey pointed to her stomach and snarled, "If you think I'm walking away from you and this baby you're out of your damn mind. And if you think I'm going to leave you here alone while you recover from a concussion and broken ribs after being assaulted by some creep *again*, you're straight up delusional. You're mine, Shaun."

"Stop saying that!" she shouted, thumping her fists on the mattress next to her. "I'm not yours! Goddammit, Kasey! I don't need you to swoop in and be some knight in shining armor, caped hero! I don't need you to save me!"

"You're carrying my baby, Shaun," he answered darkly.

"And I keep telling you that this changes nothing!" she shouted. Her head was pounding.

"Why not? Huh? *Why goddammit*? I love you, Shaun! I fucking love you so much I'm going crazy with it! Why can't this change *everything*? Why can't I be your Superman? *Why can't you let me in?*" he shouted, holding her hands tight. Tears still tracked down her cheeks.

"You don't get to come in here and just *tell* me we're getting married," she argued, though her heart was racing at what he'd just admitted. "That's not how that works. I'm not marrying you, Kasey."

"But you would have married Tommy?" he asked dully, staring at her.

Shaun rolled her eyes, and she heard him growl in annoyance. "That's neither here nor there at this point, and you know why I ended things with Tommy; because I couldn't trust him not to try to manhandle my life. Which means you know why there is no way in hell that I'm going to marry you after *demanding* it. Don't act like this is a surprise."

"I have never been anything but honest with you, Shaun!" he exclaimed heatedly and finally let her hands go. She pulled them into her lap as he continued, "Not once have I ever lied to you, or tried to deceive you, or lead you on in the slightest. From the moment we fucking met, I was brutally honest about my intentions, how I felt about you. I've told you over and over again I want you to be you, no matter what. You wanna fight with me every goddamn day? Fine. I'll go toe-to-toe with you, darlin, and enjoy every second of it. I want all of that fire you keep inside, Shaun. So don't you dare try to tell me you can't trust me. You don't get to shove all that bullshit Tommy did onto me. I didn't lie to you. He did."

Leaning forward to cup the side of her face in his hand, she was powerless to turn away as he whispered, "I told you from the first time we danced together what it would be like with us, if you would just let it happen, and I fucking meant it. You knew it then, just like you've known it all along, just like I have. *You belong to me.* So does that baby. And even though you say it over and over again, that you're not mine, I refuse to accept that. I love you, and I think if you would just get out of your own fucking way, you'd see that you love me, too! Otherwise, what the fuck have we been doing for the last month, Shaun? For the last *year*?"

Fear clogged her throat, made her heart hammer inside her chest. It was all too much. It was terrifying. Yes, she loved him, but letting him in was too great of a risk. He would want too much of her.

"You were a distraction, Kasey," she whispered, aiming for the jugular. Anything to get him to go away, to leave her alone to wallow in her own anxiety and self-loathing. She swallowed around the lump in her throat, nearly choking on the outrageous lie.

She watched as his head tipped back like he'd been hit on the chin, and she *almost* took it back. *She didn't mean it.* She just couldn't let down the walls enough to let him in, just like he'd accused her of. He'd already burrowed into her body and heart and soul more than she'd wanted him to. More than any other man ever had. And that was terrifying.

But then his face hardened, and his jaw tightened like steel, his eyes meeting hers again. "You're a real heartless bitch, you know that, Shaun?"

Kasey's words cut her like a knife, eerily close to the words that Tommy had thrown at her once upon a time, and pain ricocheted through her for the briefest moment before she steeled her facial expression.

She deserved it, this anger, this loathing she could sense emanating off of him in waves. She hurt the people she loved. It seemed to be all she knew how to do.

So, she hitched her chin up, willing the tears not to fall and her lip not to tremble.

He swiped up his hat that he'd tossed onto the foot of the bed and clamped it on his head, each of his movements jerky and filled with rage, and so much hurt. He turned and stepped toward the door, but before he walked through it, he stopped and looked back at her, his expression frigid.

"This conversation isn't over," he murmured with a

freezing calmness that made her shiver, those storm cloud eyes deadly.

"Go to hell," she whispered, her voice breaking. *Dammit!* "Get out of my house."

He slapped the door jamb with his palm and scoffed bitterly, "Thanks for the loving send off, darlin'."

FORTY-THREE

Jodi arrived an hour later, not to Shaun's surprise.

Lowering her small frame onto the bed next to Shaun, she tucked a stray strand of hair behind Shaun's ear. She knew her face was tear-streaked and blotchy, her nose running, box of tissues sitting on the comforter next to her. One look into Jodi's eyes and she started crying all over again, sobs wracking her already battered and bruised body.

When she had finally cried herself out, she swiped her hands over her face pathetically, then stacked her hands beneath her cheek as she lay facing her sister, who had let her cry without interruption.

"Why didn't you tell me?" she asked softly, rubbing her hand over Shaun's shoulder and down her arm. Of course Kasey would have told Freeman already, who couldn't keep a single damn secret from his new wife. Meddlers, all of them.

Shaun shrugged, swallowing hard. "I don't know. I was struggling with the news; I didn't want anyone to know. I don't want Mom and Dad to be disappointed in me." She blinked rapidly to clear the fresh wave of tears that burned her eyes. "I got knocked up by a groomsman in my sister's destination wedding."

"Umm, excuse you, he was the best man," Jodi teased, and Shaun laughed sadly, wincing when pain shot through her. Jodi peered at her despondently, running her fingers over Shaun's hair again. "They're not going to be upset with you. They're more progressive than you might think."

"I hurt people," Shaun whispered miserably, burying her face in her hands. "I hurt the people that I love because I'm too prideful to let myself be vulnerable." Her shoulders shook pitifully as she sniffled, "I said really mean things to him, Jodi."

"You are under a lot of stress," Jodi conceded quietly. "And I'm sure his version of a proposal was less than romantic."

"Oh god," Shaun moaned, covering her face with her hands. "He told you guys that?"

"He knows how he did it was wrong," Jodi murmured. "Once he calmed down, stopped pacing like a damn madman, he was able to see how ambushing you wasn't the proper way to go about it."

"It's not that I never want to get married," she whispered, removing her hands from her face and stacking them under her cheek again. "I just… I don't know. I want to know if it's right. How am I supposed to know if it's right?"

Tommy's words came back to her. *You deserve that big kind of happy, too.* Is that what this was? Because right now, it big *sucked.*

Jodi smiled gently. "You just do, Shaun. I don't know how

to explain it. Do you love him?"

Rolling her head to bury her face in the pillow, she groaned into it. "Yes," she said, her voice sounding muffled through the padding of the pillow. "I still hate him."

She heard her sister laugh, then she said, "Yeah, you'll have that." They were both quiet for a long time before Jodi asked softly, "So what are you going to do about it? Are you going to let him walk away?"

Shaun took a deep breath in, as deep as her battered body would allow, and rolled her head back so she could look at her sister. Tommy's parting advice came to her. *Don't let that pride of yours get in the way, okay?* "What do you think I should do?"

Jodi shrugged, smiling gently. "I think you know. In your heart. Listen to it."

"Bossy," Shaun whispered around a yawn.

"I am the older sister, it is my birthright," Jodi teased gently. "Go to sleep."

Shaun's lips pulled in a small smile. "I love you."

"I love you, too, sissy."

They were quiet for a long time, and Shaun was nearly asleep, when she whispered, "I think I know what I want to do."

"I knew you would. Sleep first, then you can get back to your regularly scheduled badassery in the morning," Jodi murmured, and Shaun nodded.

"Deal."

FORTY-FOUR

"Dammit, K.C., where the fuck is your head at? What the fuck are you doing?!"

Kasey gritted his teeth as he pulled up in front of his team spot on Pit Row for a speed gas fill up. His team moved like a well-oiled machine, and in less than twelve seconds, he was headed back out, rocketing into his first corner as he reentered the race, the first of the season. *The Clash at the Coliseum* was a one hundred and fifty lap race in Los Angeles, California, and the roar of the crowd and the scream of the machines hurtling around the track at over two hundred miles an hour made an intoxicating mix on his senses.

"You've got two laps to make up," Randy, his pit crew boss, shouted over the roar of the engines, the mic set in his helmet speaking to him. "And we've only got twenty-two laps left. Haul. Your. Ass."

Rocketing around each corner, he pushed his car to its limits, gaining inches, then feet on the vehicles in front of him. He flexed his fingers briefly, one at a time, stretching them from the strain of keeping them wrapped around the steering wheel for an extended period of time.

"Move, K.C., move!" Randy bellowed, and Kasey gave the gas another punch. "Six laps left, let's go, kid!"

He would be lucky to place in the top ten today, which was a disappointment to Kasey, but he only had himself to blame. All he'd thought about for two days was Shaun.

Shaun and their baby that she was carrying. His baby.

His baby.

The damn woman was so unbelievably stubborn that she would rather push him away at all costs than to let him in. Even as she was laying in that bed, bruised and in tremendous amounts of pain, violently ill… and he'd let her push him away. He'd walked away when she needed him the most.

Her words still stung. Stung like hell, to be honest. But he knew she hadn't meant it; knew it in the way her throat had closed over the lie she'd told him. Knew it in the way her eyes had betrayed her, beseeching him to see the truth behind her words.

They had a lot of work to do. A lot of communicating to work on. Because he wasn't giving up on her. No, he was just giving her time. Time to accept that she knew just as he did, that she was his. Had always been his. Just like he was hers.

And their baby. Fuck, he was going to be dad!

The joy that had undulated over him at the news had been like a tidal wave. And then that joy was replaced with fear, and worry; was the baby okay? With Shaun's cracked ribs, the concussion… was everything okay? With her? Christ, he needed to know. He needed to know she was okay.

The vehicle behind him nudged him just the slightest on the back end and his hands shook with the effort of keeping his car straight, the entire car shaking violently before coming back to center. "Fuck," he hissed through clenched teeth as he lost several paces as he corrected. "Dammit. Get your head in the fucking race, Kasey."

The whole back end of his car shifted, and he had half a heartbeat to realize what was happening. Training forgotten, he struggled to hold the car steady as it vaulted sideways before being slammed by an oncoming car, the crunch of metal on metal and the scream of metal grinding on pavement, lighting up his peripheral vision with sparks.

Bashed into the concrete barrier between the track and the stands filled with fans, his head bounced off the metal cage inside his helmet, then as quickly as it started, it all stopped as he came to a standstill, crushed between two cars and the concrete barrier as he faced the opposite direction on the track.

"Fuuuuck," Kasey shouted, squeezing his eyes shut. "Fuck."

"K.C., you okay in there, kid?" Randy's voice came over his headset. "Caution Flag is out. We'll get you out of there as quickly as we can."

"Heard," Kasey muttered, opening his eyes to survey the damage. The car next to him was smoking, and ahead, he could see the firetruck and ambulance headed their way. "Sorry, Randy."

"Don't be sorry, kid," his pit boss said. "Hansen lost control and it was all over. Took out half the fucking racers. Fucking rookie."

Minutes later he was being helped out of his car through the window.

The crowd around them cheered as he landed on his feet on the pavement. He reached up and unhooked the toggles of his helmet, then took it off, tossing it back into the open window of his car. He rolled his head around his shoulders to stretch, then waved to the fans as he was walked toward one of the ambulances. He was checked over for a concussion, though that was ruled out quickly, which he was grateful for. His body was stiff from the crash, but he adamantly told the paramedics he was fine, and that he could wait until they'd finished checking the other drivers before assisting him any further.

"Kasey!"

The distant shout of his name didn't bring his head around, so many fans were screaming his name as he and a paramedic walked toward his pit crew that he didn't even care to pay attention.

"*Kasey fucking Corcoran!*"

Snapping his head up, he glanced around, his heart quickening. *There was no way—*

"Ma'am, you can't be back here—" he heard to his left, and he shifted his gaze, scanning the hundreds of faces along Pit Row. "Hey, stop! How did you even get in here?"

"Kasey!"

That was when he saw her, being held back by two security guards on the other side of the tape behind his team's bay, waving her arms over her head to get his attention. Her curly hair was wild around her head, like a testament to just how fucking crazy she was.

"Let her go!" he shouted as he rushed toward them. "I said let her go! She's with me!"

They released her, letting her step past them and she hurried toward him. *God damn she was gorgeous.*

He reached for her at the same time that she launched herself into his arms, her sharp intake of breath the only sign that she was in any kind of pain. He held her to him, lifting her off her feet as he walked them back toward the bay and out of the way of curious fans craning their necks for a view.

"What the hell are you doing here?" he asked heatedly, setting her down and clasping her face between both of his still gloved hands. She reached up and curled her fingers around his where they were cupping her jaw. She stood on tiptoe and kissed him soundly, their lips and tongues meeting fiercely.

Breathless, she pulled away and he pressed his forehead to hers, their lips meeting in brief, sweet kisses. *She was here.*

"I followed you," she whispered against his mouth, and the smile she bestowed upon him was breathtaking. *That fucking smile, the one he'd been waiting what felt like a lifetime for.* "You ran. I followed."

"What changed your mind?" he asked hoarsely, his heart climbing its way into his throat at her words. Emotion clogged his throat and their bodies angled against each other, swaying together.

"You did," she murmured, her blue eyes searching his. "I'm sorry, Kasey. I'm sorry I pushed you away because of my own stubborn pride. You were right. About all of it."

His heart hammered in his chest triple time, and he barely dared to breathe as he stared down into those blue eyes he loved so much. He swallowed hard, his throat working around the emotion clogging his throat, tightening his chest.

Squeezing his fingers where they still clasped her face, she whispered as tears glistened in her eyes, "I love you, Kasey. I fell in love with you the second I saw you at Shane and Cassie's wedding. I'm just a prideful, stubborn mule and couldn't—wouldn't—let myself see what a great thing I had right in front of me. I would rather fight with you every single day, and make love with you every night, than to be with anybody else in this life. I want to have this baby with you."

"What about the other thing?" he asked gruffly, his face lowering toward hers.

"Well," she whispered, that mischievous glint that he loved so much shining in her eyes, "Tommy's proposal was much more romantic—"

"*Woman, I'll turn your ass pink,*" he warned on a growl, though his lips had curved up into a smile as he stared down at her. At the face that he wanted to stare at every day for the rest of his days. She smiled knowingly, biting her lower lip, and his breathing turned ragged as desire crashed through him at the sight. "Will you marry me, Shaun? Marry me, let me be your Superman, your rock, your everything?"

"Just call me Lois," she teased, tears sliding down her cheeks, and he swiped them away with his gloved thumbs. "Yes, Kasey. I'm going to marry you, and we're going to love each other fiercely, and you're going to give me lots of babies."

"Starting now?" he asked, pressing another kiss to her lips. *God how he loved this woman.*

"Starting now," she agreed on a reverent whisper, nodding. "You're my forever, Kasey."

"Glad you finally came around, darlin'," he drawled huskily, teasing, as he dropped his mouth to hers for another heated, soul encompassing kiss. "You're my forever, Shaun, for always."

EPILOGUE

"Ahhh, get over here!" Jodi cheered and stood from her chair, extending her arms out to Shaun for a tight hug. Shaun laughed as she hugged her sister in return, squeezing just as tight. From over her sister's shoulder, she watched as Free stood and shook her husband's hand, and they performed the male version of a hug, that awkward back patting-side hug thing that seemed to be universal to all men. Free slapped Kasey on the back as they switched, Kasey leaning down to hug Jodi tight around the middle, lifting her off the ground while she stepped forward to embrace Free. "Oh my god, tell us everything! How was the honeymoon?"

They all took their seats at the small square table inside their favorite little dive bar. Billiard tables sat off to one side, and Kyle waved at them from behind the bar.

"It was wonderful," Shaun sighed, smiling over at Kasey, who winked. "It was so nice to get out of the cold and just enjoy the sun. If you ever get the chance, definitely go to Cancun. Ugh the *food*! So good!"

Kasey laughed and shook his head. "She lived at the

breakfast buffet every morning. I don't know how you didn't turn into a pineapple."

Shaun shrugged, laughing. "Baby wants pineapple, what can I say?"

Kasey stood, tapping Free on the shoulder. "I'm gonna go grab drinks. Shaun, water? Jodi, what would you like? A beer? Cocktail?"

Shaun almost missed the impossibly quick glance that passed between Jodi and her husband, before Jodi stammered, "Uhh, actually, I kind of have a uhh, a headache and I don't like to drink when I have—"

"You stop it right now!" Shaun exclaimed, twisting in her seat to stare wide eyed at first her sister, then Freeman, then bouncing her eyes back to her sister, who had dropped her gaze to the tabletop in front of her sheepishly. Shaun bounced in her seat before reaching out to grab hold of Kasey's forearm, shaking him with her excitement. "*Stop it right now!*"

Free leaned back in his seat and chuckled, placing his arm across the back of Jodi's chair. "I told you we wouldn't be able to keep it a secret from them."

"If we'd gone out for *breakfast* instead of a *bar*—" Jodi grumbled, giving her husband the stink eye before he clasped her behind the neck and hauled her close for a steamy, open-mouthed kiss that effectively shut her up. Shaun laughed.

"They would have known the second you declined a cup

of coffee," Freeman drawled when he released her mouth. Jodi grinned sheepishly and rolled her eyes.

"Ahhhh!" Shaun crowed, still bouncing with excitement. She had released Kasey's arm, and he took the moment to tug Free out of his seat and whisk him away to the bar, leaving the two women alone. "Ohmygod! This is amazing! When are you due?"

"About four weeks after you," Jodi laughed, smiling. "But I don't want to talk about that, I want to hear about the honeymoon! I feel like the wedding was so quick, we barely got any time to plan or get really excited."

"I did give us longer than Zoey and Chase did," Shaun said with a laugh. "I at least waited two months, and the ceremony was exactly what we needed. Small, just our family and close friends up at Boyne Mountain… It was wonderful to have you and Free return the favor for us. That blue cocktail dress was stunning on you, by the way."

"I wouldn't have missed it," Jodi said and squeezed her hand. "And thank you, Freeman thought the same. It didn't come off all the way before—"

"Eww," Shaun whined, but winked. "And now we get to have babies together. I couldn't imagine doing this with anyone else."

"Our kids are going to be pure hellions," Jodi laughed as Kasey and Free rejoined them at the table, two beers and two tall glasses of ice water in their hands. “Pray for us.”

After a few beers on the guy’s part and several trips to the ladies’ room for Shaun and Jodi, they said their goodbyes. Kasey’s fingers on his left hand were draped loosely over the wheel of Shaun’s truck, black titanium wedding band on his third finger, his other hand riding high on her thigh as she sat in the passenger seat. Now that they were back from their honeymoon, he would be returning to the circuit and she would be traveling with him, at least for a while. He’d warned her that life on the road wasn’t glamorous, but she had insisted that she didn’t want to be away from him for that long. It hadn’t taken much convincing on her part.

“Do you know how badly I wanted to bend you over that pool table earlier?” he asked through the semi darkness, dusk falling rapidly out the windshield in front of them.

Shaun grinned, looking over at him. Her thighs dropped open, allowing him better access to between them and he squeezed the meaty part of her thigh, making her gasp.

“Delayed gratification, Kasey,” she whispered raggedly.

“Delayed gratification my ass,” he muttered as he pulled them into the driveway in front of their apartment. They would have to start looking for a new house, something bigger, more appropriate for their growing family. He climbed out of the truck and rounded the hood, opening her door and hauling her out. She laughed out loud, wrapping her legs around his waist and her arms around his neck as he walked them into their apartment. As usual, they hadn't made it more than a handful of steps inside before he'd set her on her feet, pulling her to the ground with him.

Her black leggings were shimmied off her legs, shoes tossed across the room as he unbuckled his belt and unfastened his jeans enough to lower them, before covering her body with his, positioning his hips between her already parted thighs. And then he was sliding inside, all the way to the hilt, and Shaun tossed her head on the carpeted floor behind her with a moan.

"Ohmygod," she sighed, reaching for him even as he began to move, over her, in her, again and again.

One hand gripped her shirt, pulling it up and he used his teeth to pull the lacy cup of her bra down enough to allow him to clamp his lips around her pierced nipple, lashing and suckling greedily. He panted against the skin of her breasts as he moved, and he groaned, "Do you love being fucked by your husband, darlin'?"

"Oh yes," she moaned, fingers tightening on his ass, urging him deeper, harder. Her body was poised on that precipice, ready to fall, and she knew he knew it, too. "Yes, Kasey."

"I need you to come for me," he growled low. "Now, darlin'."

Flicking his tongue over her nipple again, he then used his teeth around the already sensitive bud, and she was gone. Fireworks exploded inside her, around her, everywhere, singeing her skin and making every muscle tremble with the violence of her release. He hammered into her, prolonging it, and then he slammed in deep and came with a shout of his own.

He rolled them to their sides right there in the middle of the living room and gathered her close against him as they both panted, aftershocks rippling through them. His hands smoothed over her curls, pushing them away from her face so he could trail kisses over her forehead, her cheek, her mouth, the underside of her jaw.

He pressed another kiss to her temple and then leaned back to look down at her. "You didn't tell them the news."

Shaun shrugged, pressing her cheek to his chest and trailing her fingers along his back slowly. "I didn't want to ruin Jodi's surprise."

Kasey pressed his palm to her stomach and kissed her. "I still can't believe you're giving me twins, darlin'." He chuckled then, and she loved the sound of it as it rumbled beneath her ear. "You really can't do anything small, can you?"

She pinched him on the side and he yelped on another laugh. "What can I say? Go big or go home. Might as well get two out of the deal."

"I love that you're mine, Shaun," he whispered against her temple and she felt his arms tighten around her. She smiled against the fragrant skin of his throat.

"I love being yours," she murmured quietly, reverently. "I'm glad you finally convinced me."

"Me, too, darlin'. Me, too," he whispered. "I love you and that wild heart. Don't ever change."

She pressed a kiss to his throat, felt the way his heart beat against her lips, and she whispered, "Never."

ACKNOWLEDGMENTS

First off, WOW!! I cannot believe that we are here at the end of my third novel! What an adventure this has been, and I truly feel so blessed to be doing what I love! Thank you all for your continued love and support throughout this journey!

Mom, you were my first and always my biggest fan, and the best proofreader around. Without your love and support this wouldn't have been possible! You knew when I was fifteen that I would be here one day, even when I doubted it myself. On to book FOUR already with so many others on the way! I love you!

Nick my love, thank you for letting me hide away at my desk for hours—and sometimes days—on end. Thank you for messaging me that my breakfast, lunch, or dinner was waiting for me when I was ready for it, because you knew I wouldn't even think about eating (thank you, Chef). Thank you for your unwavering support, faith, and enthusiasm for this passion of mine. Without you and the love you give me, I wouldn't have started writing again. Without your support, I wouldn't be able to do this full-time. You are my biggest cheerleader, my love.

You are my forever Prince Charming. I love you!

Erin. Sissy. You are the best big sister a girl could ask for. You and that amazing group of ladies in NC have been such a blessing and the best cheerleaders! "Oh, Danielle Baker? Yeah, that's my sister!" I love you, Sissy!

Kara, you have been such a champion in my corner, for your unwavering faith in these stories and in me! And THANK YOU for excitedly and willingly volunteering as tribute to come with me to all our author events! I can't wait to see what kind of trouble we can get into! I'm so glad that you got to be one of the first to see Shaun and Kasey's full story. Thank you for believing in me and in this story!

Haley, KG, Ava, and Melanie; Thank you to these wonderful fellow authors that I have had the pleasure of being on this journey with! Haley, thank you for always being a critical and willing sounding board, and the Tessa to my Jodi! KG, Ava, Melanie, HOLY MOLY, I'm so glad I met you and feel fortunate to be traversing this new journey with you and a million thank you's for taking me under your wings! Thank you, ladies! I can't wait to see you all at future events!

Stasha, you told me almost twenty years ago that you would edit for me when I was ready. I can't believe we finished book three! Thank you for being there through the very rough first draft all those years ago, to the newly polished draft we finished. Thank you for helping me get here and believing in me that I could!

Samantha, Amy, and Melody with Aurora Publicity, thank you sooo much for the absolutely gorgeous discreet cover and beautiful formatting, you took exactly what was in my mind and made it come to life! I look forward to what we can come up with for my future works!

To my **Booktok Baddies**, April and all the wonderful **Smut Sluts**, **The SmutHood**, and Courtney and Dorothy and all the **Michigan Booktok Babes**, THANK YOU for allowing me to be unapologetic in my shameless promotions and all of you that have recommended *Love Unbound* and *Best Kept Secrets* to this absolutely voracious world of spicy romance readers! To my amazing **Street Team**, THANK YOU for loving these crazy characters and their stories as much as I do! I hope you all love Shaun and Kasey's story, too! I love all of you!

E, thank you for being my original sounding board as I built this world of characters and silly little (much tamer) stories twenty years ago, in a spiral notebook as a freshman in high school. Thank you for helping me tell Shaun's story way back when. I hope you love it now as much as I do!

To all the people that are not named but have beta read, listened to me venting or joined in my excitement over each new milestone, and all those that have rooted for me in this scary and enthralling journey, thank you! I wouldn't be here without you!

Lastly, to all my readers, old and new, this has only been possible because of the love and support you've shown me and these characters. I hope you love reading their story as much as I've loved writing it. Shaun and Kasey have been on their way to your hands for a long time, and I'm so glad they're finally here! These two got their start over twenty years ago and they truly have a special place in my heart. I look forward to introducing you to MANY more in the future! Thank you!

MEET THE AUTHOR!

Danielle Baker, romance author of the *Petoskey Stone Series*, including *Love Unbound*, *Best Kept Secrets*, and *A Heart So Wild*, was born and raised in the beautiful city of Petoskey, nestled on the crystalline shores of Lake Michigan. She is married to the love of her life, Nicholas, and they have four children between them. Danielle's love of writing began while she was in high school. She wrote a slew of short stories and had written three novels by the time she graduated. Life got busy and writing was put on hold for many years while she started her family. At the urging of her mother, sister, and husband, Danielle was given the boost she needed to "get back in the saddle" and keep reaching for her lifelong dream of becoming a published author. When Danielle isn't working, writing, or spending time with her family, she can be found with a cup of coffee in one hand and a book in the other.

Coming Spring 2024

from Danielle Baker!

When Hearts Collide

Book 4 in the Petoskey Stone Series

"So, you didn't even get to have hot raunchy groomsmen sex? What's the point of being a bridesmaid if you don't get the one perk of being said bridesmaid?"

Punching into the rubberized dummy in front of her, Roxsanna Roberts huffed out a laugh as she turned to look at her friend, who stood off to the side with her arms crossed, one hip pushed out.

"The only groomsmen there were Kasey—"

"Mmm, I'd tap that."

Roxy glared at her friend and continued, "—who happens to be like my third cousin or something, and the brides two younger brothers, one of them wasn't even over eighteen, so no. No hot raunchy groomsmen sex."

"Laaaame," Natalie groaned, dropping her arms from where they were crossed over her chest. "Pleeease tell me Kasey looked drop dead gorgeous in his tux. And Freeman. Gaawd that man. Bummer he finally got shackled."

Roxy rolled her eyes and turned back to the rubber dummy, raising her fists and correcting her stance before throwing another punch, making the dummy wobble on its stand. "They both looked very handsome. Jodi is awesome, though," Roxy huffed on an exhale after another solid hit. "And I think Kasey's about to be tied down, too. Sorry for your luck, sis."

"That's alright, I've been trying to get Travis' attention, but the man is like a machine. All he does is train and be all broody and silent," Natalie muttered, leaning against the wall.

"Are you actually going to work out, or are you just going to stand here and bug me while I do?" Roxy snapped, turning to face her again. "Why do you pay for the membership if you don't do anything while you're here?"

"Umm, I get in plenty of cardio elsewhere, thank you very much," Natalie snapped back, though she was grinning. "I'm here for the views."

Following her friend's brown eyes, Roxy turned her head and found what had captured the other woman's attention; former MMA fighter, Travis 'The Reaper' Hayes, known best for his deadly left hook in the cage.

Standing on the other side of the rec center, Travis paid them no attention as he wrapped his hands with red sports tape. Standing in profile, they watched as he wrapped first his right hand, then his left, crossing the roll of tape in an X formation across each hand to protect the knuckles. Light, golden brown hair with streaks of silver throughout hung down past his insanely broad and heavily tattooed shoulders, obscuring his face as he concentrated on his task. A thick but well-maintained beard covered his upper lip, cheeks, and chin. Roxy admired the way his muscles moved across wide shoulders, down massive arms that were nearly as big as her thighs, across an outrageously well-defined chest and abdomen… Also all heavily tattooed. In fact, nearly every visible inch of skin on his body was covered in tattoos, something Roxy had always found undeniably sexy, and the air of danger around the man was intoxicating.

And that was exactly why Roxy had only ever spoken to the man in passing.

Because she didn't do dangerous anymore. No ma'am.

Sexy and intimidating and dark and broody were all things that turned into nightmares later. All that sexy intrigue and the thrill of something dangerous that was so fun and exciting in the beginning… But it doesn't stay that way.

That thrill of danger would turn into the reality of danger. That thrill of danger that was oh-so alluring in the beginning would turn into busted lips, black eyes, bruises on wrists. And then of course the cycle of love bombing would start; the special date nights out, a lavish and unexpected gift, or a blood red rose flower arrangement that would show up on the kitchen counter afterward.

As if that was all it took to make it all go away. Sweep it under the rug. At least until the next time. Until enough was enough.

Never again.

No, she would be perfectly fine with a run of the mill, nice, boring, predictable guy… He could wear pleated khakis, eat his turkey sandwich with the crust cut off, and have passively satisfying sex with his socks still on for all she cared. Boring and predictable was A-okay with her. That was *if* she ever decided to date again, which was a *really big* if.

Roxy's attention was brought back to Travis as they watched him bring the roll of sports tape to his mouth and tear it with a set of impeccably straight white teeth. *He must have a killer orthodontist*, Roxy thought hazily, then shook her head and glanced at Natalie when she heard a small moan come from her friend, rolling her eyes to the ceiling.

"You're droolin', doll," Roxy whispered, shoving her friend in the shoulder as she turned back toward the dummy once more.

"I just wanna give him a go," Natalie whispered wistfully as she continued to stare at the man across the room. "You know with moves like that he's got to be great in the sack. Shit, I'll join his class. I don't care. I just want to get closer."

"His kickboxing class?" Roxy asked on a rough laugh. "You'd break a nail in the first five minutes and never go back."

"I'd push through just to spend more time with all that," Natalie murmured, waving her hands in his general direction, pantomiming running them along his body, at the same time that he turned his head toward the two of them. The squeak of abject horror from her friend at being caught ogling him was enough to make Roxy's entire night.

Roxy laughed out loud, though she admittedly felt a flush

of heat rise to her cheeks when his eyes rose to meet hers before he turned away as if he hadn't noticed a thing. Almost like they weren't worth being noticed in the first place. Jerk.

Bending to pick up her water bottle from the floor, Roxy took a drink before taking a step in the direction of the wide bench that housed several other people's bags, as well as her own. Natalie grabbed her arm, hissing, "Where are you going?"

"I actually did my workout, Nat," Roxy drawled dryly, giving her friend a withering look. "So I'm going home."

"Don't leave me heeere," Natalie whined, trailing after her. Roxy pulled a hooded sweatshirt on over her sports bra and loose fitted tank top. She removed her sneakers, placing them in her bag sitting on the bench, before sliding her feet into checkered Vans slip-ons that had seen better days.

"I'm not leaving you. I'm going home."

"Party pooper," Natalie grumbled, but Roxy merely rolled her eyes and hoisted her bag onto her shoulder. "Well, have a good night, you old maid."

"You're older than I am," Roxy reminded her with a wink, making her friend gasp in feigned outrage.

"You take that back."

Roxy laughed, blowing her friend a kiss. "Can't do that. It's the honest truth."

"You're only younger than me by a year!" Roxy heard Natalie hiss to her retreating back, making her laugh harder as she walked out into the early evening air, the sun setting on the horizon. It was a mild evening for January in Melody Hills, Texas, just chilly enough to warrant bundling up in an extra layer.

Roxy shivered, recalling the bitter cold and far too much snow she'd just returned from in the Colorado Rocky Mountains for her best friend Freeman Thorp's wedding the weekend prior. Ugh. So much snow and cold that just seeped into her bones.

Making the short drive from the rec center to the small ranch style cabin she'd taken over the rental lease on when Freeman had moved back to northern Michigan, she pulled into the driveway and stared at the small house for a long time.

She still remembered the night she'd shown up on the doorstep, asking Freeman if it was okay if she stayed there for a few days after she left her boyfriend at the time, Neal Johnson, after he'd put his hands on her one time too many. Free had opened his home to her without a second of hesitation. He'd helped her get a restraining order on him when he began to show up at her work, harassing her for leaving him, accusing her of choosing Free over him, convinced she'd been sleeping with Freeman the entire time.

She couldn't blame him for the assumption; her relationship with Freeman Thorp was unconventional at best. They'd met years ago and had become 'best-friends-with-benefits' or so Kasey had dubbed them ages ago, at least until she'd met Neal. Sex with the rugged and sexy Freeman was always just sex, something to scratch the itch. And when she'd met Neal, that aspect of their relationship had stopped immediately. They'd seamlessly transitioned to simply best friends, something not many people understood. Neal being one of them.

This home was also where Neal had followed her to late one night, knowing she was there alone with Free away in Michigan, and had beaten the hell out of her after she left him. Blind with rage and jealousy that she'd chosen to go to Free's home to escape him, he'd unleashed all his fury on her. She still carried the scar on her lip and her vision was blurry in her left eye from the force he'd used that night.

Neal had fled the area, presumably leaving Texas altogether. The police had not located him, a fact that bothered Freeman and his new wife to no end. They had already started hounding her to consider moving to northern Michigan, to be closer to a bigger and better safety net.

But Roxy didn't mind living alone because he'd never come back. She hadn't seen or heard from Neal Johnson in almost a year and a half. Each day got a little easier, those gray clouds of doom shifting further and further into the distance.

Picking up her duffel bag from the passenger seat, Roxy climbed out of her little Rav4 and walked inside, flipping on lights as she went, dusk darkening the small home as the sun set beyond the horizon.

Crossing to the refrigerator, she pulled out a bottle of chilled white wine, turning to the cupboard and picking up a wine glass, before spinning on her heel to place them both on the counter behind her.

The bottle of wine slid from her hand and fell to the smooth brick floor, shattering and spilling wine in every direction, but Roxy didn't care. She barely noticed.

Because there, sitting in the very center of the island countertop in her kitchen, was a bouquet of blood red roses.

Milton Keynes UK
Ingram Content Group UK Ltd.
UKHW040145091123
432191UK00004B/56

9 798988 045625